The
Accidental
Virgin

Also by Valerie Frankel

SMART VS. PRETTY

The Accidental Virgin

Valerie Frankel

AVON BOOKS
An Imprint of HarperCollinsPublishers

HarperCollins books may be purchased for educational, business, or sales promotional use. For information please write: Special Markets Department, HarperCollins Publishers Inc., 10 East 53rd Street, New York, NY 10022.

FIRST EDITION

Designed by Rhea Braunstein

Library of Congress Cataloging-in-Publication Data

Frankel, Valerie.
    The accidental virgin / by Valerie Frankel.—1st ed.
    p. cm.
ISBN 0-06-093841-2
1. Separation (Psychology)—Fiction. 2. Dating (Social customs)—Fiction. I. Title.

PS3556.R3358 A64 2003
813'.54—dc21   2002068721

02 03 04 05 06   RRD   10 9 8 7 6 5 4 3 2 1

Dedicated to
Stephen Quint:
Dry spell breaker;
Magic spell binder.

Chapter One

Monday morning

*S*tacy Temple, 32, redheaded and pink of cheek, the very picture of health, if not happiness, lifted the pointed chin of her heart-shaped face and said, "Suicide on a roll."

She'd been waiting on line at the deli for over ten minutes, and had managed to apply full makeup and read up to page six of the *New York Post* before placing her order.

"Butter, too?" asked the man in the apron behind the chrome counter.

"No, thanks," she said, turning the page of her paper.

"Oh, go ahead," said the deli man. "Two fried eggs with bacon and cheese on a roll? Why not add some butter to lube up your digestion?"

Stacy had been coming to this hole-in-the-wall greasy spoon, crammed between two fifty-story silver towers on Park Avenue, for her weekday breakfasts for over a year. Never once had her conversation with the grill man varied from the usual pattern: her pleasantly issued request, his grunt of acknowledgment, her barely audible appreciation, his forking over the food.

Thrown by the shift from their usual exchange, Stacy looked at the man who prepared her morning meal. He was 24, 25 maybe, with wiry black hair. Greek? Italian? Mediterranean ancestry, but no trace of an accent. His round face rested solidly on a thick bull neck. He showed her his smile now, a wide one that spread across his face like the butter he was pushing. Chiclets for teeth. He vibrated with the nervous edge of a pent-up human animal, forced by financial necessity to flip eggs for strangers over a hot grill in New York City July, seeking a bit of kindness on a Monday morning, a small friendly exchange with a pretty girl to brighten the drudgery of the day.

She smiled back at him. "That's very considerate of you to think of my digestion, but I'll pass. Thanks again."

From beneath a black, bushy eyebrow, the man winked. Then he winked with his other eye. And after that, he puckered his lips and made a "kissy-kissy" sound.

Stacy Temple, redheaded and suddenly redder of cheek, gasped. Someone behind her laughed. She clutched her tote and the *Post* to her chest and exited as quickly as possible in kitten-heeled mules.

"And the worst part about it: Where can I go for breakfast now?" Safely at her desk on a floor near the top of one of those silver Park Avenue towers, Stacy cradled the phone on her shoulder, picked grudgingly at the dry bran muffin she purchased from the building's cafeteria vending machine, and scrolled through her E-mail.

On the phone, the impatient voice of her best friend, Charlie Gabriel, asked, "Are you multitasking me? I hear clicking. And chewing."

"I'm swiveling." Guilty, Stacy turned her chair and attention away from the computer screen. Formerly a segment producer at NPR, she currently served as vice president in charge of merchandising and marketing for thongs.com, the on-line retailer of lacy intimates. Facing her north wall, the one lined with racks of flimsy, strappy things on hangers, bolts of red satin stacked on the industrial gray carpet, Stacy said, "I felt violated."

"Guys must hit on you all the time," ventured Charlie.

"They don't."

"You *are* low frequency," he said. "Every part of your body language communicates, 'Don't look at me. Don't talk to me. Keep two hundred feet back.' Your clothes mix the signals, though." Charlie was high frequency. When they walked into a room together, any room, all eyes turned toward him and stayed there. It wasn't just his physical bearing (tousled blond hair, six-foot six inches of tautness, red lips and otherworldly green eyes) that drew attention. His voice, baritone, bounced, and the words he chose as effortlessly as a fish swims couldn't be discounted.

"Men can tell you're nonsexual," he said. "They can sniff that out. The faintest whiff of indifference to dick will lead a man to completely ignore, with disdain, the most gorgeous woman in the room."

Stacy said, "If I have such indifference to dick—which, by the way, would make a great title for your next documentary—why would the deli man hit on me?"

"Two possible explanations," said Charlie. "His olfactory sense—the means by which men can deduce a woman's sexuality—has been bacon impaired. And, two, he can tell that you are a celibate, and he wanted to rattle you for his personal amusement. It's a power trip. A petty form of sexual harassment."

"Then I'm right to feel violated," said Stacy. "I reject the assumption that the entire world can smell sexual *in*activity. Besides, I am not a celibate who reeks of disuse. It's just been a long dry spell. And stop saying the word *sex* or *sexuality* or *sexual*. It's not even nine o'clock." Stacy checked her watch. "I've got to go. Emergency meeting."

"Miracle advances in thigh highs?" asked Charlie.

"Desperate search for the next big thing. I'll be pushing for a resurgence of the whalebone corselette," she said.

Charlie, a former doctoral candidate in medieval studies (currently a movie reviewer for noir.com and an aspiring documentary filmmaker), asked, "You're selling armored vests?"

"That's a corselet," Stacy corrected. "A corselette is

a rib-crushing encasement of Lycra that fits over a woman's body, cramming her breasts, belly and protruding hips into a compact, tight, saucy package. Think Elizabeth Taylor in *Butterfield 8*. In approximately ninety seconds, I will go into an eight-hour meeting to convince my bosses that this garment of magic and grace would be most appealing to the women of America with silk rosebuds stitched into the cleavage well."

"Then I'll be brief," said Charlie. "Just say yes or no. Are you coming to the screening tonight?"

"No."

"Will I see you for lunch on Thursday?"

"Doubtful."

"That's a no."

"Yes," she said.

"Do you find it ironic that someone who sells crotchless finery for a living never has the occasion to wear it?"

"I'm wearing some right now." Actually, Stacy encased her own tight, saucy body in a knee-length, bias-cut skirt of thin gold leather, a baby-pink T-shirt and, underneath it all, tattered, worn-out white cotton bra and panties. Charlie had a lingerie fetish. He claimed he could spot a La Perla signature bra-strap hook beneath a wool sweater (he found thongs.com merchandise to be on the sleazy side). He also had the most sex of anyone Stacy knew. Charlie had a battalion of lovers, some dating back to his high-school days. It seemed that once a woman had slept with him, she was compelled to return for more whenever she was between boyfriends or husbands (or bored with her boyfriend or husband). Stacy wasn't sure if Charlie's high customer-loyalty rate was due to his erotic mastery or his masterful availability. He was never involved for long. Women seemed to rotate into his schedule for several nights or weeks, and then rotate out, creating a vacuum that could only be filled by another fortnight fling. Cosmic forces at work, women resurfaced only when needed. There was no overlap. Stacy was the only female friend Charlie hadn't slept with. They'd met over a decade ago in college, when she'd kept busy sleeping with all of his friends.

Charlie said, "You might want to reconsider the screening. Jason is going to be there."

"Jason, the handsome hairy man?" she asked. Stacy's other phone line rang. She swiveled back to her desk to check the caller-ID display. It was her boss's extension. The meeting must be starting.

Charlie laughed. "He's hairy?"

Stacy pictured Jason at the blind lunch date Charlie had set up for them a few months ago. It'd been unseasonably hot that spring day and Jason had rolled up his shirtsleeves to just under the elbow. His forearms were covered with dark brown hair to his knuckles. Thick like the jungle floor, his hair. Vines of it burst out of the V of his unbuttoned collar. As they had what anyone would classify as lively conversation (easy flow, broken pleasantly with laughter, the exchange of valuable insight), Stacy traveled the line from Jason's hazel eyes to his tiger mouth, straight to his hirsute hands.

She imagined those hands around her waist, lifting her off her feet (mules dangling) and carrying her into the jungle where less hairy men with shotguns would come to rescue her.

"I have to go," she said to Charlie. "If I'm late, they whip me with underwire bras."

"I wouldn't mind watching that," he said. "I'm sure Jason wouldn't mind, either."

Stacy knew Jason liked her. He'd paid for their lunch, and called her a couple times over the next week. Apparently, as he'd told her in detail at their lunch, he was recently and happily free from an intense relationship with a French ballerina. She'd tortured him (in both the bad and good senses) on and off for several years. After one last "I hate you, I love you, I hate you" fight (which apparently included the hurling of red wine, face slapping, ravenous French kissing and then 3 A.M. sobbing), Jason had decided to say a final adieu. Stacy had a hard time picturing Jason, a quiet, bashful man, pitching angry words and slices of runny Brie at a 100-pound mademoiselle with a bun and a tutu. Then again, who knew where (or why) passion lurked?

"I liked Jason. And I would have called him back," she said to Charlie. "But I was swamped. The job . . ."

"Don't blame the job for the fact that you reek of disuse," he said. "No wonder a wink from the deli guy sends you into a panic. Unwanted sexual attention— *wanted* sexual attention—is beyond your frame of reference."

"You are oversexed," she said. "And my frame is just a little rusty, that's all."

"You're past rusty, Stacy," he said. "You must be rusted shut by now. Two years without sex? How do you do it? And, let me weigh in on this, the deli man may be on to something. I share his concern for your digestion."

"It has NOT been two years," she said defensively. "Brian and I broke up six months ago." Stacy consulted her Palm III. "I can tell you the exact date. Here's the entry. 'Breakup dinner with Brian.' July twenty-third."

Charlie asked, "You had sex with Brian the night you broke up with him?"

"The last hurrah," she said.

"So it's been one week shy of a year," said Charlie.

Had it really been that long? Stacy rechecked the date. She couldn't believe it. In college, she'd studied sex as if it were the ultimate liberal art. In her 20s, a dry *month* had seemed unendurable. And now, in her early 30s, she'd gone nearly 12 months *without even missing it*. How had she changed without even noticing it? Passion had been her life force—with lust in one's heart, there was no room for cholesterol. Disinterest in sex was . . . what? A sign of aging? A slow, downward spiral into withered lifelessness? Stacy felt a chill, a warning, in her flat, limp (cholesterol-clogged?) blood. She'd unwittingly put herself on a path toward self-destruction: lose interest in lust at 32; die—childless and miserable—at 42. Charlie was right. Why on earth would any ordinary woman be that intimidated by a flirtatious deli man? Somewhere in the past year, she'd transformed. She used to be a normal adult female. And she'd become something else. But what?

"You're almost a virgin again," said Charlie.

"Excuse me?"

"I read about it on swerve.com. Born-again virgins. If you go for a year without sex, it's like you've renewed a lapsed membership." Swerve.com was the website for all things "intellectually erotic."

"Is this official?" Stacy asked, horrified.

"I doubt you'll get a certificate in the mail."

Stacy groaned. "My virginity was hard enough to lose the first time." The message light on her phone blinked, angry and red. "This has been a deeply unsettling conversation."

Charlie said, "I'll tell Jason you couldn't make it."

"No," said Stacy. "I'll be there. And don't you dare say anything to Jason about this. Tell him I was too shy to call him back. Or tell him I liked him so much it scared me. No, don't say that. Don't say anything." She'd show up unannounced, flip her hair around, touch his shoulder a few times, and invite him to her place after the show. He'd accept the invitation, they'd proceed to congress, and she'd correct her libidinous oversight tonight.

Stacy Temple was no virgin. And she would never be again. She hung up, grabbed her corselette samples and hurried toward her boss's office.

Chapter Two

Monday night

Stacy was 20 minutes late to the screening. Her haut boss had been in a foul mood (plunging stock price), and her sous-boss had been even worse (plummeting date prospects). United as a team in their condescension, they'd been viciously dismissive of Stacy's whalebone corselettes. She'd limped out of the meeting in a pitiable state, her sateen samples a sad, shiny jumble in her arms. For perhaps the millionth time since signing on as employee number three at thongs.com, Stacy questioned the net worth of her commitment. Surely, the value in cash wasn't what it used to be (the day of the IPO, Stacy's options were worth—on paper—a Victorian mansion in Sag Harbor; now they could barely purchase a studio walk-up in the East Village).

She knew she should put on some makeup. Spritz on some perfume. Do what she could to realign her mood and go to the screening prepared to seduce. But she had to wait. This was a particularly twisted aspect of her job: After a humiliating meeting, one of her bosses would show up in her cubicle and attempt to revive Stacy's loyalty with promises and gifts. Like a battered child with an abusive parent, Stacy reluctantly responded to her boss's peace offerings. She *wanted* to believe the kiss-and-make-up speeches. She *wanted* to drink the Kool-Aid. She'd lap it up, just as long as she felt useful and powerful in the company. She'd been a founding employee. She'd helped create the site, sacrificing her relationship, many friendships, and some ideals along the way. The defining characteristic of a romantic hero(ine) was self-sacrifice. Stacy had made huge sacrifices for this company; ergo, she had to be madly in love with thongs.com. She couldn't possibly leave.

To kill time, she decided to look for the swerve.com article Charlie had mentioned on the phone. A few clicks later, the essay appeared on screen. "Virginity: It Once Was Lost, and now Is Found" was written by Gigi XXX, a regular sex columnist at the site. Her photo appeared alongside the text. She sat on the edge of a bed, barefoot, in a black bra-and-panty set (way too plain and ladylike to be thongs.com products), elbows on knees, head down, a fall of black hair hiding her face except for the red-rimmed pucker of her lips. She had a wowie figure, slim-limbed and busty.

Stacy's eyes moved from the photo to the text. The breathless opening line:

"I love my body. I adore the things it can do for me, and I am committed to do whatever I can to keep my body happy and healthy. Specifically, I will fuck, fuck, and fuck. When that gets old, I'll fuck some more."

Stacy thought, *What of fiber intake?*
The essay continued:

"Not all women share my philosophy of physical and spiritual well-being. It has come to my attention that there is a new sexual movement afoot: celibacy by choice. At least three friends of mine have purposefully decided to stop doing it. I could understand, a couple years ago, when the new trend was for women to stop having sex *with men*. But now this? Celibacy is the new lesbianism? And it doesn't end with simple abstinence. There's a goal: Go a full year without sex, and you become a (theoretical) virgin again. Your sins are washed away clean. Three hundred and sixty-five days of unswept ashes, and it'll be like you didn't screw the entire football team in high school. You're as fresh and innocent as a week-old kitten. For some reason (the football team happens to be one of my most dearly cherished memories), this is appealing to my wayward friends. One (I wouldn't dare print her name and humiliate her) said, 'Sex is a distraction and a nuisance. Without it, I can get my work done, and have energy left over to knit mohair sweaters. I've already done five this week.'

"Another friend said over coffee, 'Okay, I admit,

it seems like an odd way to search for self-awareness. But I want to define myself by other terms. Until now, I've defined myself by sex. Most people do. We are who we're fucking, how we're fucking, when, where, and with what accessories. We never stop to ask, Why? Why does what we're doing for an hour a day with someone else weigh more heavily on our personal success or failure than who we are for the other 23? I am taking a year off to return to a freer mental space. My happiness and fulfillment should not be dependent on the ups and downs of my sex life.'

"I'm glad she didn't say, 'the ins and outs' of her sex life, or I might have gotten excited. This friend, she's a babe. She's got legs that go all the way down to the floor and tits like she's stuck them in a pencil sharpener. My beloved boyfriend has begged me to set up a threesome with her, and lord knows I've tried. But now that she's on this idiotic mission, this dunderheaded pursuit of bullshit, she's a lot less attractive. So it's kind of a relief.

"Sex *is* defining, for good reason. During sex—by sex, I mean the good kind, which may or may not mean the loving kind—you *are* your true self. You become a creature of selfish instinct. You allow your animal nature to shine. Sex strips away artifice (intentionally forgoing sex is artifice), and leaves you naked in every metaphorical way. And if you're looking for self-awareness, there's nothing like one dick in your mouth and another in your pussy to figure out in a hurry exactly what kind of person you are. Connecting (in a deeper sense than insert tab A into slot B—but that, too) with another person (or persons) is the only way to learn and grow. Otherwise, all you'll see, hear and think is what you already know (the same crap that's been fixated on for years), missing out on the fresh insight of someone who might be smarter than you, and denying yourself the chance to share adventures of the body and soul. Attention celibate friends: Call me in a year when you've started fucking again. Until then, enjoy yourself. No one else will."

At the end of the missive, Stacy spotted a red button that read SEND FEEDBACK TO GIGI. She clicked on it and started typing:

"Gigi, my name is Stacy Temple. I'm a vice president at thongs.com, the on-line lingerie store. I would like to talk about possible cross-promotion ideas with you, and with swerve.com. I've just read your revirginity piece, and think you have the wit and wisdom to write some much-needed content for our site."

Stacy had, in the past, tried to convince her bosses that content—some narrative text, perhaps some dirty fiction or even some long captions about the seductive powers of a peekaboo teddy—would improve sales, or at least increase traffic. But she'd been shot down (her

CEO believed that paying for content was an unnecessary expense). So Stacy didn't have much faith that she and Gigi would have a business relationship. But one had to have an ostensible purpose to write such e-mails. Besides which, getting a response from Gigi was more likely if she dangled a potential payday. Underhanded, sneaky—yes, but a girl had to do what a girl had to do.

Stacy typed more:

"Your piece was thought provoking. Being passionate is critical for happiness. Sometimes, though, it can get away from you (well, not *you* clearly; it can get away from some people). I wonder about women who find themselves hovering on the brink of revirginization, but not by design. I suppose you could call these women *accidental* celibates. Their revirginization would be an unhappy accident—and therefore invalid. If one had, say, a demanding job, that doesn't make her a rejecter of adventure. If she's shy, that doesn't mean she's hiding from life. Unintentional revirgins are just distracted by other things, that's all. They're still passionate and potent. They're still vital and relevant. Sex, albeit eye-opening and aerobic, isn't who you are. Accidental revirgins don't deserve your scorn. They're in a special class. They deserve understanding and encouragement."

Time to wrap it up, or I'll sound too defensive, she thought.

"Anyway, just bouncing some ideas off you," typed Stacy. "Please write back and let me know about your availability as a freelancer."

She clicked the SEND NOW button. Her E-mail flying into cyberspace, Stacy felt relieved, but not completely unburdened. Some things in the article had struck her across the brow, in particular, the notion that isolation leads to regurgitation of the same old thoughts rattling around in one's brain, spinning rapidly in circles, getting nowhere fast. An intellectual hamster wheel. Stacy pictured herself on it, sweaty and frustrated. Perhaps Gigi was right: The way to get off the hamster wheel was to get one's rocks off. It seemed convoluted, but there was only one way to find out.

Now inspired to see Jason, Stacy rushed to spread on some lipstick and go. But a voice intoned from outside Stacy's cubicle door: "I know what you're thinking."

Without needing to look, Stacy said, "That you're a pint-sized sadist?"

Janice Strumph, the other of Stacy's two bosses, was impossibly petite. In her late 40s, she had narrow shoulders and hips, a soft belly, a curvy décolletage, and the soulful dark eyes of a sea lion. Her sunny yellow curls, like her boobs, were God-given. She had three freckles on her left cheek that formed an isosceles triangle. Sometimes, when having a heart-to-heart with Janice, Stacy couldn't help connecting the dots.

A divorcée, Janice had been married for seven years

to the father of her three children (two boys and a girl, all in their 20s). He left her the day the youngest son entered kindergarten, announcing that he'd done his service to his children—been a father for the brain-developmentally crucial first five years—and he was now free to move about other women. That was 16 years ago. Janice had never remarried, but not for lack of trying. A point of pride, she'd had a viable date on every Saturday night since her husband left (except for the first six months—which would have been unseemly for a young mother who was not yet divorced). Stacy respected Janice for her perseverance and the belief that, one weekend, she would meet the man to erase a decade and a half of disappointment. Janice once did the calculations: So far, she'd been on 786 Saturday night dates, estimating that 40 percent of the relationships ended there, 40 percent stretched across a month (four dates), and 20 percent were good for over a month (five or more). Janice hadn't attempted to calculate how many men she'd put on her pearls for or how many times she'd had to retell her life story (a stat that might be too depressing, even for Janice). Stacy had little faith in the magic of Saturday night. But Janice was devout. Nearly every Monday morning, she would bolster her faith by declaring that if she couldn't secure a decent date by the weekend, she'd put away her dating shoes forever. Had yet to happen.

"I have a limo waiting for you downstairs," said Janice in her small-person voice as she leaned against

Stacy's office doorway. "You can have it for the whole night, anywhere you want to go, with anyone, clean out the bar, use the phone, play the VCR."

Stacy said, "You were merciless in there."

"Whalebone corselettes, suggested retail price, one fifty? It's incredible that you'd even present it."

"The lower the stock price, the lower our aspirations."

"When you put it like that, our sales philosophy sounds like a compromise," said Janice. "Think quantity. The more items ordered, the more money we make."

Like all mail-order companies, Internet or otherwise, the profits were in shipping and handling charges. When a customer placed an order for 10 items, thongs.com routinely shipped half right away, and then sent the remaining items in three business days, making it possible to double the handling charges on a single order (all the while telling the customer she was getting a discount on shipping). The income of their client base was, on average, $46,000 a year; the median amount spent on a thongs.com order was $58; the inflated S&H charge brought in an additional $8 profit per order. Janice liked to call it "superhighway robbery."

Overwhelmingly, customers made multiple orders of low-priced items (five thongs plus a few bras, for example). High-priced garments were one-shot orders, limiting S&H charges and stretching the customer's lingerie budget. But Stacy stubbornly clung to the notion of aspirational (life-changing) underthings. The product profit margins were higher, and if a woman fell in love with a corselette, she'd come back to the site for all her panty needs (repeat business was the lifeblood of any retail operation). Janice's business plan—quantity over quality—might work for McDonald's, but thongs.com was selling intimacy, not chicken nuggets. Stacy had never presented the notion that Janice's dating life—a reflection of her retail philosophy—could explain why she had never remarried.

Stacy said, "For use of the limo, I'm to forgive your cruelty and come up with new and inventive cheap garter belts tomorrow."

Janice said, "Garter belts pay your salary."

"I would like you to admit that, in part, you took out your bad-date frustration on me."

Janice shrugged. "I hate the one-hour dates. It takes me longer than that to get dressed. There should be a rule that the date itself has to last as long as it takes to prepare for it."

"You'll find someone," Stacy said.

"Always do." The older woman didn't seem as sure of herself this Monday. Stacy feared that Janice might be near the end of her long dating streak. "Take the limo and have a good time tonight," said Janice. "We'll start over in the morning."

Stacy thanked her boss, put on some pink lipstick and left. On the elevator ride down the 40 stories to the street, Stacy grappled with a decision. She could take a quiet ride around Manhattan and then go home and sleep off the tinny taste of the public scolding OR go to the movie screening and snare an attractive man. She struggled with the habitual leaning toward the comforts of home. But she knew that the lure of her featherbed was why she hovered on the verge of revirginization. Janice might career from disappointment to disappointment, but at least she got some action. Stacy tried to remember the sights and sensations of sex.

The limo waited at the curb. Stacy greeted the uniformed driver and slid into the back seat. After mixing herself a White Russian, Stacy gave the address of the Silverbowl Screening Room on West 46th Street. The drive would be short, just enough time to finish her beverage and practice her winning smile. By the time the limo rolled to a stop at her destination, Stacy was renewed and ready to climb a mountain, if need be. She hoped Jason would be an anthill.

Three hours later, as Stacy and Jason walked down the hallway to her one-bedroom apartment in SoHo, the Manhattan neighborhood once famous for artists and now renowned for its shoe stores, she made her move.

Before she even had a chance, the handsome, hairy man said, "It's getting late."

It was 10 P.M.

The night hadn't been working out as planned. When Stacy arrived at the screening room—much smaller than a normal movie theater, with about four dozen leather seats and a canteen of free food and beverages in the back—the movie had already started. She easily spotted Charlie's blond head (so tall, he always sat in the back out of politeness) and made her way over to him, disturbing several important-looking studio executives along the way.

She slid into the vacant seat next to Charlie. Without looking at her, he pointed toward the screen and said, "The year is three thousand. Due to World War III, massive widespread famine, and epidemic skin cancer, the population of the Earth is now only half a billion people. One quarter are men; women rule the world. That's Glenn Close as the U.S. president. Her team of mad female scientists has figured out a way to produce human sperm in a test tube, and she's just confessed to her vice president—the plucky and likable Renee Zellwegger—that she sees no reason why men need to exist at all. She plans to initiate the extermination ASAP."

"Where's Jason?" Stacy asked.

"Can," said Charlie.

Stacy leaned back and fluffed her hair prettily against the leather seat. The spot next to her was vacant. She moved her coat and put it in the empty chair on the other side of Charlie, just to be sure Jason would have to sit next to her. Once she'd accomplished this, she sat back and watched a bit of *Chemical Attraction*. There was Tony McGuinty! Her favorite actor.

"You didn't tell me Tony McGuinty is in this," she whispered to Charlie.

"He plays a conflicted breeder male, forced to leave hourly sperm deposits in the reproduction lab run by chief mad scientist Kathy Bates," he said.

On screen, Ms. Bates clicked together a set of pointy calipers while ordering Tony to increase his yield—or face extermination. Tony, depleted, pleading for his life, was a vision. Stacy was a huge fan. What scant fantasy life she'd had in the past year centered on Tony McGuinty, his puppyish brown eyes, his lanky body. Stacy never felt anything for movie stars, but something about Tony filled her with adolescent longing. She'd once seen a nude photo of him on the Internet. The image brought the words "fire hose" to mind. And there he was, all 12 feet of him, shirtless, jugular throbbing, being led back to his cell by Kathy Bates, all the while delivering a fine speech about freedom, liberty and his lean protein allotments. "You think jerking off ten times a day is easy? I need meat!" he demanded on-screen.

So distracted by Tony, Stacy nearly forgot about Jason. But then the setting changed to a close-up of Renee Zellwegger (who had the best pores Stacy had ever seen). And Jason returned. Stacy smiled brightly at him. He returned the smile, although the wattage wouldn't have made a light bulb flicker. He saw the coats in the spot next to Charlie and looked confused.

"This seat is free," said Stacy, patting the chair to her left. Charlie groaned. Stacy stepped on his foot.

Jason slid into the chair and crossed his legs. His knee was an inch from Stacy's thigh. Tony was back on-

screen now, plotting to liberate the male breeders by seducing a slutty prison warden, as played by Jennifer
Tilly. Tony put his hands on Tilly's thigh. Stacy leaned
toward Jason—her shoulder pressing against his arm—
and whispered, "I'm predicting that Renee Zellwegger
will fall in love with Tony McGuinty and together
they'll foil Glenn Close's plans for mass extermination.
When she discovers the betrayal, power-crazed Glenn
will try to kill them both with the help of evil Kathy
Bates."

The handsome, hairy man—who, Stacy noticed,
was looking especially tigerlike and attractive in khaki
slacks and a short-sleeved plaid shirt—put his hirsute
finger to his soft lips and made a *shush* sound.

Stacy leaned away. Shushing was not the behav-
ioral hallmark of a man's passionate attraction to a
woman. A casual observer might assume that Jason
was uninterested and that Stacy was throwing herself
at him. Fortunately, she knew that, despite appearances, the situation was in her control and that Jason
was well within her feminine power. He'd paid for
lunch. He'd called her three times.

Regrouping, Stacy helped herself to a kernel from
his popcorn box. He didn't register distaste at her inva-
sion. She took a handful, several pieces falling out of
her hand and into Jason's lap. Stacy brushed the errant
corn away, keeping one piece to pop into Jason's
mouth. He smiled nervously at her after she fed him,
and then put the box on the floor.

Again, she thought, the casual observer would be

squirming with embarrassment at Stacy's seemingly desperate attempts to charm an unresponsive man. She smiled to herself: How little people really knew about strangers. How unlikely to make an accurate judgement about the interactions of shadows in a dark movie theater. These casual observers, they didn't have the back-story. They couldn't know that Jason had paid for lunch. He'd called her. She'd just have to keep reminding herself of her female wiles, especially now that he was rearranging himself into a pretzeline posture to avoid the press of her leg against his. Curiouser and curiouser, thought Stacy. But she remained undaunted.

The movie progressed as Stacy predicted. Tony heroically saves Renee Zellwegger from being sexually reassigned by Kathy Bates, while leading the embattled men of Earth in triumphant rebellion. Renee and Tony are appointed copresidents to ensure liberty and justice for all genders. Glenn Close isn't killed in the bloody coup d'etat, but is condemned to serve men as a laundress for the remainder of her days.

The lights came up.

Hushed chatter filled the small space. In this room, one could truthfully say, Everyone's a critic. Charlie observed, "Even in a movie about female domination, the men win in the end. I liked the futuristic sex scenes—using tasers as sex aids, pretty inventive—but the philosophical man-versus-woman theme bored me, even with the gender role reversal. Glenn Close—can she do anything but Cruella De Vil at this point?"

Stacy was about to say, Save it for your review. But Jason added, "I find it ironic that the bastion of male virility was represented by Tony McGuinty. He is the girliest man in Hollywood. Put him in a dress and a wig and he'd look as much like a woman as Stacy."

Charlie couldn't agree more. "You are so right! May I borrow that observation for my review?"

"I'd be honored."

"I think I'm a bit more feminine than Tony McGuinty," said Stacy.

The two men stopped their mutual appreciation party and gave Stacy the attention she should have had all along.

"Of course, Stacy," said Jason. "I was exaggerating."

"Renee Zellwegger can help me leave my daily deposit in the reproduction labs any day. I'll show her yield," said Charlie.

Stacy said, "Do you mind not saying deposit and yield? It isn't even nine o'clock."

The trio put on their coats and left the screening. On the way out, Charlie gushed to the movie studio's stylish publicist about how much he loved the film, that Kathy Bates was sure to win her second Oscar, and that his review would appear on noir.com on Wednesday. She purred her gratitude and gave Charlie her card, quickly scribbling her home phone number, "just in case you have any questions about the production. Call me anytime. Even in the middle of the night."

That did it. Charlie said he had a few questions that could only be answered right away, while they were fresh on his mind. He asked the publicist if she was free to go for some coffee. She needed a minute to clear her schedule. And that was that. Stacy would, undoubtedly, get the full report from Charlie in the morning, or whenever he surfaced for air and food.

Stacy and Jason walked out of the screening room into the beastly hot night. The limo idled exactly where Stacy had left it curbside, air conditioning pumping. She offered Jason a lift home. He accepted. He didn't realize yet that it was a lift to *her* home.

When they pulled up at her building in SoHo, Jason said to the driver, "Next stop, the Lower East Side."

"Actually, Jason, the driver is supposed to go off duty once he drops me off. I hope you don't mind." She lied for a good cause.

He rubbed his chin with his hairy paw. "All right. I'll get out here, too. Thanks for the lift downtown. I'll walk the rest of the way."

They exited the limo. Stacy excused the driver, keeping one hand on Jason's wrist. The car sped off, leaving a plume of black exhaust to add to the claustrophobic New York summer air.

"You must come upstairs to cool down before you walk anywhere in this heat," said Stacy. "It's unbearable out here."

"I don't mind the heat," he said flatly.

"At least walk me to my apartment door. I'm always afraid I'll be attacked at night," she said. In truth, Stacy always felt safe in her neighborhood, and her city.

While they went up the elevator to the fourth

floor of her building, Stacy tried to regroup. She'd thought Jason would be a sure thing. But something was bothering him. Stacy had been direct with her intentions all night. Maybe the rules of seduction had changed. It'd been years since Stacy had had to flirt. You'd think thigh rubbing and hand feeding would still turn the screw. That's when Stacy leaned in for a kiss, and Jason gave her the "It's getting late" comment. Stacy ignored it, and flipped her shiny red hair over her shoulder as she fiddled with the lock on her door.

"You must be parched. You do drink?" she asked.

"I'm not thirsty."

"Do you eat?"

"I'm stuffed from all that popcorn."

With the nudge of her slender shoulder, Stacy pushed her door open and turned on the overhead light. Jason looked inside and gasped in horror. Her apartment wasn't a mess. It was busy. Very busy. She'd been dateless for so long, she forgot that the clutter could throw some people: the handbag collection on her bookshelf; the waist-high piles of newspapers and magazines; two dozen jackets thrown on the couch. Stacy closed the door quickly, and said, "I'll slip inside and straighten up. Do you mind waiting out here for a couple minutes?" She knew it was risky to ask. If a man ever asked her to stand in his hallway while he speed cleaned, she'd disappear into the night.

Jason shook his head. "Stacy, you're a very nice person . . ."

"Do you need to use the bathroom?" That *would* be a more appropriate place to wait, unless he'd be turned off by her five-shelf antique atomizer collection, fuzzy toilet seat cover, the buckets of nail polish bottles, and the shoeboxes full of lipstick tubes.

"I'm going to take off," Jason announced, raking a hand through his hair. Stacy noticed that his knuckle growth was two shades darker than his head mane.

She was losing him; or maybe she'd never had him. What had happened? He'd wanted her after their last date. She'd just assumed he'd be in her pocket. Charlie had long advised Stacy, "If he wants you today, he'll want you tomorrow." Maybe Jason had seen too many tomorrows.

Stacy made one last drive. Opening her brown eyes wide and innocent, she said, "What's wrong, Jason? Don't you like me?"

"I do," he said. "I'm not sure you like me."

Was he a woman? "I do like you. I really, really do." She did. She really, really did. And, more important, he was there.

"Charlie told me that you only want to sleep with me so you won't go a full year without sex."

"I will kill Charlie on sight."

In the same way she could feel eyes on her back, Stacy felt ears in the hallway. She was convinced each of her neighbors had an ear pressed against his or her door. She whispered to Jason, "Can we take this discussion inside?"

Jason shook his head. "You barely know me. Besides that, you're not making this very interesting for me."

"Should I run down the hall so you can chase me?" she asked.

A couple of her neighbors had blatantly opened their doors a crack. Jason said, "If you want to go on a date, fine. But I'm not coming inside now. I'd feel used and I wouldn't respect you in the morning. There'd be no future if we did this now."

He wanted a relationship; she wanted sex. How often did this happen? "Didn't Charlie tell you I'm wearing crotchless panties?" she asked.

"He did."

"And?"

"That doesn't sound very sanitary."

She was sure she heard giggles up and down the hall. Feeling the early pinch of a headache—a big one—Stacy stared at Jason: tall, handsome, furry, nervous, emasculated by her aggression. Avoiding re-virgination might be tougher than she'd thought. Tough, but not impossible. She could make a list of prospects. There had to be dozens of men who would be thrilled to perform this small service to ensure her cardiac health and lower her cholesterol. In fact, making a detailed list of her candidates was what she would do. Right away.

But first, Stacy smiled what used to be her irresistible sweetheart smile, and said, "If that's how you feel, then I'll say good night, Jason." She opened her apartment door.

He said, "Good night, Stacy."

As he walked down the hall, she said, "Good night, everyone."

Softly, from behind closed doors, her neighbors' voices chorused, "Good night, Stacy."

Chapter Three

Tuesday morning

*I*n her three-year relationship with Brian Gourd (albeit a union of convenience and habit more than consuming passion), Stacy had grown accustomed to getting her minimum weekly requirements. For the first year and a half their sex had been hot. She thought about him—it—constantly. Stacy would wake up from a daydream about him and realize that an hour had gone by. At the end, when Brian wouldn't stop complaining and Stacy found herself bored by his face, the centerpiece of her erotic fantasies had shifted from cock to stock.

This was around the time she'd started at thongs.com—pre-IPO, post-options package. She relished the prospect of millions—not even what those dollars could buy, just the idea of being fabulously wealthy. In the summer and fall of 1998, theoretical riches were far more exciting than actual dear, sweet, never-hurt-anyone-on-purpose Brian. Thongs.com was a seductive lover. The romance of 12-hour workdays, stock options, larger-than-life bosses, silky props, good press (in mid-1998, thongs.com was named Dot Com.er of the Year by the *New York Post* Business Section) all served to intensify her obsession. After a good workday, Stacy floated home on a cloud of pride and elation. She couldn't remember a single day in her relationship with Brian that made her feel as shamelessly smug. The breakup was inevitable. She was sure she'd made the right choice between her man and her job. (If she still felt as passionately about thongs.com, she might not be in a panic about the absence of romance with a person in her life now.)

She'd never wanted to marry Brian. Stacy wasn't exactly sure how she'd ended up in a long-term relationship with him in the first place; it was a weekend fling that had lasted three years. She'd constantly asked herself if it was an important relationship, knowing all the while that it wasn't. But the possibility of amassing wealth—that was important. Stacy's father, Sol Temple, a hedge fund manager at Smith Barney, believed that "you are what you earn"; her mother, Belinda Temple, an interior decorator, was more of an "you are what you eat" fat-phobic semiprofessional anorexic. They were still married, despite the affairs, and seemed to tolerate each other fairly well, especially during Mostly Mozart season at Lincoln Center.

Even given that the job was a distraction, it still seemed peculiar that her sex drive had stalled. How had it happened? She supposed it was a combination of will and inertia. Post-Brian, the early months: Stacy had missed physical contact, but not the sex act itself. It had grown flat at the end of the relationship, and she had alleviated her acute symptoms handily on her own. She had pined for admiration, flattering comments, interlocking toes in bed. But adoration from a man, she reminded herself often, wasn't life sustaining. Men were not mandatory. Unlike food, water, the impulsive shopping spree, Stacy could survive without Brian's hands and lips. She was a strong, emotionally stable woman, proudly independent, making it in the world. She enjoyed her own company. But there'd been times in the fall and winter of last year, undeniable times, when she caught a glimpse of herself in grubby pajamas late at night, when this thought would unsettle her: *I don't like myself.* Then, the despair, the "what will become of me?" fear, had to be dealt with before she could fall asleep.

With the exception of those fitful hours, Stacy got her rest. She went to work on weekdays (and Saturdays). She exercised. She ate at least three pieces of fruit a day. Months and the need for affection passed. It fell away slyly. She hadn't even noticed. Over time, sexual inactivity had become part of her identity. Charlie was right: She did reek of disuse, everyone could tell. And now she could smell it on herself. How dreadfully embarrassing.

Such reflections made for a depressing subway ride. Not that the underground crunch would have been better had she been contemplating the ocean deep and blue. The train temperature felt at least 200 degrees Fahrenheit and the air, practically visible as steam, pressed against her chest and legs. Stacy hung on to her metal strap and replayed last night's rejection scene. Had the rules of seduction changed that much? she wondered. Never in her life has she felt so little sexual tension, such a void of interest from a man. Stacy was an exceptionally attractive woman. She had a passionate flame of red hair. She was pink of cheek. Wasn't that enough anymore?

In her 20s, Stacy's sexual patterns had been uncomplicated. She'd meet a guy in a bar or at a party, sleep with him right away, and they'd become boyfriend/girlfriend for several weeks or months. They'd break up, and she'd meet someone new. Perhaps the rules changed once a woman entered her fourth decade. Or maybe the problem was men over 30. If Jason were 25, he wouldn't have hesitated. At 35, he wanted Stacy's respect in the morning. Was this evidence of a decline in testosterone levels?

Stacy studied the other subway passengers, trying to guess the last time each had had sex. That cooing couple, unmarried (no rings), mature (40s), had clearly engaged within an hour of entering the train station. The 300-pound woman, sweating copiously despite the mini-fan, wore a ring and had probably done it within the month. A severely attractive man in seersucker at the strap next to Stacy wore the satisfied expression of sexual accomplishment. He smiled at her as she examined him. Stacy quickly turned away. She could practically feel the throbbing of a scarlet *V* on her forehead.

She got off at Grand Central. The huge train station cum shopping mall was swarming with thousands of people who fully enjoyed a decadent sex life. Preoccupied by passers-by ("last night," "within a month," "two times this week and thrice on Sunday"), Stacy slogged through the building and out onto 42nd Street. She turned toward the greasy deli for her usual breakfast sandwich. Then she hesitated. The kissy-kissy man would be inside. If she were to enter, he'd naturally assume that she'd returned for another helping of harassment.

She couldn't face him—not in this pitiable state of impotency. She glanced in the deli window and saw him, her tormenter, spatula in hand. He noticed her, too, and shot a wink and a pucker.

Shame renewed, embarrassment refreshed, Stacy scuttled toward her Park Avenue silver tower. Stumbling on a grate, she managed to remain upright, but broke the heel of her sandal. Since she had several pairs of spare shoes in her office, a trauma of this magnitude wouldn't ordinarily reduce Stacy to tears, the hot kind that shot from the ducts like liquid bullets. Ordinarily, no. Today, in her mire, yes.

Stacy hobbled into the up elevator of her office building to discover Taylor Perry, thongs.com's employee number four, vice president in charge of production. A dirty blonde—hair still damp—in an unevenly hemmed orange halter dress (despite the fact that a woman of her proportions should never be seen in public without a bra), Taylor took one look at Stacy's makeup streaks and proposed a theory.

"You must be PMSing," she said, adding, "I am. We all are. The meeting today will be a bitch."

Taylor Perry, 22, formerly a political science major at Dartmouth, was the one person without whom thongs.com could not exist. Stacy's eyes glazed over whenever Taylor started talking about servers, uploads, caches and cookies, but without her kind of know-how, thongs.com or any Internet retail company couldn't do business. "Creatives"—like Stacy—were a dime a dozen. Tech people—like Taylor—were rare and in demand.

Upon seeing her colleague Stacy immediately became posture conscious, straightening her back as if pulled by an invisible string from the top of her head. She smiled weakly at Taylor and said, "What brings you in so early?" It was just after 8 A.M. Stacy had hoped to grab several minutes of alone time to organize her thoughts and her list of de-revirgination prospects before her bosses arrived and began issuing orders.

"I'm late actually. I'm usually here at seven," said Taylor. "I get up at five thirty, run six miles, and come right over. I like the quiet. Can't get much done with The Women prowling the halls." The Women—as the staff called them—were Janice Strumph and Fiona Chardonnay, the founders and leaders of the company.

Stacy nodded as her colleague spoke, imagining Taylor's predawn exercise and the gargantuan sports bra she would need for restraint. Taylor graduated from college only last year and, in a recruiting binge, had been courted by dozens of Internet companies before choosing thongs.com as her first job. Stacy imagined the stock options package Fiona and Janice must have offered to woo Taylor away from (premerger) AOL and (pre-bottomed out) Amazon.

Despite the gossipy atmosphere at thongs.com (inevitable with the late hours and free cappuccino), Taylor was tight-lipped about her life away from work (as if there was time for such a thing). Stacy had gathered enough droplets of information to fill a birdbath: Taylor had had a boyfriend in college, a geek like her (said with admiration, not derision), who'd moved to Grand Cayman after graduation to create a hugely profitable Internet gaming site. His partner was another Dartmouth grad, a woman who was neither a geek nor blessed with Taylor's commodious curves. Stacy and Fiona had visited the site, casinoroyale.com, and examined the photograph of the two gaming tycoons, waving on a white-sand beach: he, a chubby, shirtless, tan, baseball-capped piña colada drinker; she, a skinny, bikinied, sunburned, arch-eyebrowed brunette with several anklets. If giddy good luck could be captured digitally, this grainy photograph was it.

Whenever Stacy felt jealous of Taylor (she was impossibly young and talented), Stacy thought of the ex-boyfriend in all his sun-drenched joy with a woman he'd met the day before he dumped Taylor and disappeared into paradise. No wonder Taylor claimed to have "sworn off men" whenever Janice consumed half a staff meeting to deconstruct her most recent demoralizing Saturday-night date.

Stacy only now wondered if Taylor saw her as a kindred spirit. By all appearances, Stacy had also decided to forgo men intentionally (one of Gigi XXX's celibate-by-choicers). Stacy was reticent about her personal life (by default: nothing to tell). Taylor and Stacy shared the dubious bond of abstinence—along with the biological kinship of menstruation. Maybe that explained why Taylor always sat next to Stacy at meetings and wrote little secret messages for her on her legal pad ("This sucks," "Get me out of here," "How did pasties become the center of my world?"). God knows, Taylor and Stacy didn't share a love of circuitry and gigabytes—or antique lace and satin bows. Their only common (infertile) ground was sexual inactivity.

Taylor was an expert, however, in substitution. The elevator climbed a dozen floors in seconds. While Stacy worked her jaw to pop her ears, Taylor prattled on about running, how her legs shook from exertion, her heart pounded, her skin tingled all over, and then, how there was, around mile five, the incredible release of endorphins.

"That's the best part of the run," she explained. "The big bang at the end."

"I should get more exercise," said Stacy as they stepped off the elevator and onto the thongs.com floor.

"It helps with bloating," Taylor added.

Stacy hobbled down the hallway to her private office, one shoe on, one in her hand. She had loved these sandals with the daisy on top. She deposited her purse and *Post* on her desk, and remembered that she had no breakfast to eat while reading the paper. Instead of crying about it (she could have, easily), Stacy distracted herself by flipping through a Pottery Barn catalogue and painting her fingernails pink. Her bathroom-size window of alone time rapidly closing, Stacy Hot Synced a file from her Palm III into her cranberry iMac. Blowing on her fingers—polish tacky—she surveyed the screen.

LIST OF MEN WHO CAN'T SAY NO

1. Brian. Ex-boyfriend. Will have to swallow a flock of crows to call him out of the blue, but know how to reduce to putty (e.g., tickle neck, stroke arm, say the "H" word).
2. Stanley. Lecherous bad date from April. He's not repulsive and smarmy; he's flattering and attentive. When he stares at front of dress and licks his lips, think, "How sweet."
3. Charlie. Platonic pal. Could seduce with aid of wine and tears/begging. Might ruin friendship. Prepare "day after" speech along lines of "What *happened* last night? I must have been temporarily insane."
4. Match.com. Janice's stomping ground. Truckloads of courage needed. Not yet in supply.

She briefly flirted with adding the unibrow deli man to her list, but concluded that she'd rather be a re-virgin for the rest of her life than stoop that low. However, the adorable Albanian pizza delivery boy from Salvotore's was not beneath her dignity. Stacy, fingers poised on her keyboard, was about to lengthen her To Do list when she heard a woman's voice behind her. "I use male escorts. Saves time and energy that could be better spent at work," she said.

Stacy recognized the imperious tone of the CEO of thongs.com, Fiona Chardonnay, formerly an expert on urban development for the Heritage Foundation. In semi-cringe, Stacy swiveled to behold her leader. Today, Fiona wore a clingy red sheath, black sheer hose with a seam down the back, and stiletto pumps. Dressed for midnight at 9 A.M., as usual. Fiona's wave of hair was boot black; her face oddly unlined. On the record, Fiona was a girlish 45, but she had to be years older (in interviews, she talked openly about cosmetic improvements and her devotion to Botox). Regarding her age, only her plastic surgeon knew for sure.

"Walk with me," Fiona commanded and headed down the hall.

Stacy slavishly followed. She had to run after her employer—Fiona and her long stride—in bare feet. The carpet felt synthetic under her toes. Her loyalty to Fiona was also artificial. In the beginning, Fiona had seemed like the Goddess on High. After five months of post-IPO dips, Fiona's divine façade was cracking. Janice "We're still standing" Strumph took the stock price drops in stride; Fiona did not absorb the blows as well. Whenever the price slid, she'd call for brainstorming sessions and make impossible demands on the staff. Stacy always hated Fiona's impromptu private meetings. They always resulted in hours of extra work (much of which was later scrapped) and the lasting aftertaste of prostration. With a base salary of $160,000 a year, Stacy had no choice but to treat Fiona as her lord and master.

The "Dark Lady" (the staff's nickname for her) took a sharp right into the samples closet, where each peek-aboo bra, G-string, and half-slip was tested by the in-house design staff of five (none was in yet). Garments hung on racks, spilled out of drawers, and lay in lacy, pastel piles on counters. Shelves were packed with Lucite boxes of pearls, bows, buttons, snaps, hooks, and straps. Bolts of lush fabrics were stacked in a pyramid on the floor. Avoiding Fiona's vaguely creepy gaze, Stacy stared at herself in the floor-to-ceiling wall mirror. She was also wearing a red sheath dress—no hose (or shoes), but her Candy Apple Red toenail polish was a perfect match for Fiona's. The two women were almost the same height. Stacy wore a size 8. Fiona, a slender 4, still seemed larger. Larger than life.

Hoping to steer the conversation her way, Stacy said, "Have you seen Agent Provocateur this week?" Their rival lingerie website, agentprovocateur.com, had added mini-soft-core pornographic film clips to showcase their new styles, all artfully done. Stacy hoped to move thongs.com in that direction and away from their mass-market underwear supermarket catalog presentation. "At the very least," Stacy continued, "we should talk about our models." At present, thongs.com used low-rent human mannequins, girls with perfect bodies and dog faces. The cropping of photos (no heads) disturbed Stacy politically and aesthetically.

Fiona picked through a rack of bustiers and said, "Mesh."

"Mesh?" asked Stacy.

"It's going to be big."

Stacy's stomach tightened. Of course, Fiona hadn't heard a word she'd said, nor would she give her the courtesy of pretending to. Dutifully, Stacy asked, "A line of mesh lingerie?"

"Bras, panties, camisoles, girdles," Fiona confirmed. "I want a mesh petticoat. Mesh peignoir! You can have your precious corselette, in mesh, if you want. All tightly woven. All metallic colors, shiny fabrics. Very futuristic."

"I see," she replied.

"What do you see?" asked Fiona, her attention complete.

"I see what you mean?" Stacy replied tentatively.

"*I see* mesh on the bare ass of every American woman—and it looks good," said her boss. "If we work ten percent harder, we'll have product by September."

"*This* September?" That seemed wildly optimistic. It usually took five months to design, produce and market a new line. Fiona wanted to do this one in two and a half.

"We can do it," Fiona insisted. "It'll be huge. Print and TV advertising, direct e-marketing to millions. I want you to handle it."

Stacy gulped. In the mirror, she could see the swallow travel down the white skin of her neck and disappear under the collar of her dress.

"Meshwear 2001," Fiona announced. "Do you love it?"

Stacy said, "I'm not sure."

"You don't like mesh?" she asked. "I do. End of discussion."

Stacy shook her head. "No, mesh really, uh, breathes. But we can't pull it together for September. We'll have to work around the clock . . ."

Fiona interrupted. "Every employee at this or any dot-com company puts in the time, Stacy. It's a requirement of the job—the job that could make you a millionaire."

The boss truly believed. Stacy doubted the stock price would ever climb back to its peak price. But, in this economy, anything *was* possible. With a cash infusion and a great idea (was mesh a great idea?), thongs.com could reclaim their once-strong position as the number-one intimates retailer on the web. The thought of putting in 18-hour days, the thousands of details to keep track of, the misery of it . . . she could not do it. She would not.

"Mesh is more for spring, don't you think?" Stacy ventured.

Fiona stared at her for a beat of one, two, three,

four, five, six, seven, eight, nine, ten. With each beat, Stacy's pulse doubled.

"If you need more personal time," said the boss, "you can have it—full time." The Dark Lady turned on her stiletto heel and teetered out of the samples room. Even as the breath exited her lungs, Stacy couldn't help admire Fiona's ass—like a squirrel's nest, round and tight.

Alone now among the ribbons and pearls, Stacy studied her reflection in the mirror—slim body, long hair and stricken expression. Had she just lost her job? And was that such a horrible prospect? Allegedly, 13 years separated Stacy and Fiona. What would Stacy's next decade turn her into? Fiona had never married. She was a multi-millionaire (even after the stock drop), lived in a 3,000-square-foot loft in TriBeCa. She had famous friends, was a psuedo-celebrity herself. Taylor believed Fiona was miserable in her luxurious aloneness. Stacy wished Taylor would keep her beliefs, naïve, wrongheaded and self-inflating, to herself. The obvious truth to Stacy: Fiona was happy. She had everything she'd ever wanted. If she showed any distress, it was merely a touch of fear that her dream life would be dashed by the whims of Wall Street (witness this private meeting). Besides which, Fiona made every effort to spread her happiness, and her wealth, around, showering her staff with gifts (bribes), expensive lunches, trips to Paris, Milan, and London for the seasonal fashion shows. She was a difficult, impetuous woman, but generous. Inspired. Stacy was glad to know her. Thongs.com was a good job. Was.

Sullenly, Stacy padded back to her office. The message light blinked on her phone. She punched in her password and listened. The first and only message was from Fiona, recorded seconds earlier. She said, "I might have been a little too hard on you. I apologize. I've put my life into this company. When I ask you to head a project, I'm trusting you with my life. As long as I'm here, you'll be my number three. Take an hour. We'll start the Meshwear 2001 meeting at ten—I sent a staff e-mail. And call this number: 555-6969."

Stacy couldn't help feeling relieved. She still had her job, and she had an hour to collect herself before she'd have to say "whatever you want, Fiona" again. Meanwhile, curious, Stacy dialed the phone number Fiona gave her.

A deep masculine voice on the other end answered. "Executive Escorts. Justin speaking," he said.

A sex service. Fiona'd meant it when she said she used male escorts. Stacy inhaled her office's oxygen. Fiona actually believed that Stacy would hire a professional date. Was that an insult or a gesture of camaraderie? Either possibility horrified Stacy (and titillated her—emotions clearly in a tangle).

"Hello?" asked the man on the line. Fumbling and shaky, Stacy hung up.

"Stacy, got a second?" Janice Strumph ("The Doll" to Fiona's Dark Lady) leaned into her underling's office doorway.

Stacy swiveled to face Janice, petite and smooth, except for the crow's feet. She wore her trademark tan slacks and blazer. What she must go through to find the same ensemble in winter-, spring- and summer-weight fabrics marveled Stacy.

"I'd like you to meet someone," said Janice, pulling a young man into Stacy's view. Where Janice occupied a tiny portion of the doorway, this boy dominated the space. His extra-large physique blocked the light from the hallway. He towered over Janice, an endlessly long arm around her narrow shoulders. Despite their extreme size discrepancy, the boy shared Janice's blonde curls, her oval-shaped face and creamy complexion. They had identical cheek moles. Janice beamed up at him, madly in love with the boy. Stacy could see why. Jeans were made for 20-year-old male bodies.

"This is my son," announced Janice, as if presenting the president of the United States. "My younger son. Tommy."

"Tom," he said, holding out his hand for Stacy to shake.

"Hello." Stacy smiled sweetly. She stood (he wasn't *that* tall, actually, just looked that way standing next to his mom), and gave his hand a proper pump. Soft skin with scratchy fingertip calluses. "You must be a guitar player," she said.

The boy (Stacy knew he was a junior in college at—where was it—she tried to recall) said, "I play in a band at Northwestern."

Northwestern, of course, she thought. "Home for summer break. How nice for you, Janice."

The Doll pouted and said, "He's leaving me tomorrow for England, and I can't even have lunch with him. This meeting will last for hours."

Just as Stacy feared. It would be an endless round of mediocre notions, brainstomping and energy-sucking logistics. Back on the seesaw ("I hate my job, I love my job, I hate my job," etc.), Stacy had to get off. She'd cried once today already, and that was her limit. Fiona would never let her go, especially after what had happened in the samples room. Maybe Janice would excuse her. A risky venture: Fiona and Janice's delicate balance of power was precarious. Toes would be trampled. But here stood—loomed—a way out of the meeting and, quite possibly, her sexual conundrum.

"No time for lunch?" said Stacy. "That's horrible, Janice. You can't have a young man wandering the streets of New York by himself for hours upon hours."

Tom laughed. "I grew up in Manhattan, Stacy."

She attempted mirthful flirtation. "Things have changed since you went off to college. Madmen throw bricks at people's heads now. Stick them with syringes on street corners. The mayor is a Republican, you know. This town is frightening."

Tom set his blue eyes on Stacy in a way that filled her with confidence and daring. "I may need protection after all," he said.

"I will take you to lunch," Stacy announced. She noticed a slight blush in Tom's curved cheek, and a grin to go with it.

Had Janice been a casual observer of this volley, she would have seen what had really been exchanged between the two young, attractive people. But since Janice was mother to Tom and boss (*in loco parentis*) to Stacy, her mind couldn't fathom the potential incest of their stolen hour together. But something else gave her pause. Janice said, "I'm not sure we can do without you today, Stacy. Even for a quickie."

Stacy nearly fell. "A quick lunch."

"That's what I said."

"I won't keep her long, Mom," said Tom with the big eyes and unction of a favorite son. "I promise, we'll talk about you the entire time."

Chapter Four

Tuesday afternoon

"My mother is a slut," said Tom Strumph. "I respect her for it. If there were more sluts in the world, rape statistics would do down. Date rape wouldn't exist. And, I'd even make the quantum leap that pornography sales would take a nosedive."

Stacy and the college boy sat at her favorite restaurant, Genki Sushi, in midtown on 43rd Street and 5th Avenue. It took only two minutes of convincing for Janice, Tom's mother (the slut) to agree to excuse Stacy from one hour of a thongs.com daylong planning meeting. In exchange, all Stacy had to do was entertain her youngest son.

"I'm a big advocate of women's rights," continued Tom. "And by heralding a call to sluts doesn't mean women should put themselves at the disposal of men. That they should open their legs whenever a man shows the slightest interest in sex. Did you ever read *Clan of the Cave Bear?* The cave women were required by prehistoric law to drop to their knees—doggie style—

whenever a caveman grunted and pointed at the ground. That's barbaric! I would never want women to act like that. Any man who would is a pig. *Clan* is really an amazing book, though. You should check it out."

"I will. It sounds fascinating," Stacy said. How had the conversation arrived at the subject of casual sex? Stacy wasn't sure, but she was pleased to get there. Engaging in casual sex with this man/boy had been locked on her mind since she'd invited him to lunch. Perhaps Tom could read her thoughts.

Thinking was not doing, however. Since taking their seats at the restaurant's serpentine counter, Stacy had been debating whether she could actually go through with another seduction attempt. An afternooner with a guy she'd met only a couple hours earlier? Certainly, Stacy had had anonymous sex. Lots of it. But Tom wasn't exactly zipless. Or faceless. There were consequences. He was her boss's son. Then again, Tom was leaving the country tomorrow for six months (a lifetime in the eyes of a 20-year-old). She should be able to get in and out (as it were) risk free.

Tom sermonized some more. "The fact of the matter is," he said, "any woman can get laid from any guy at any second of any day. You could go up to any guy and say, 'Fuck me,' and he'd drop whatever he was doing and fuck you. I hear women complain about not having sex or not being able to find a guy to be with. I've said it before and I'll say it again: If a woman doesn't get enough sex, it's her own fault. Her standards are too high, or she doesn't know that she's a repressed lesbian."

A conveyor belt ran above the top of the counter, carrying tiny plates of sushi. The plates were color coded for price. The bill for a meal was tallied by counting how many plates of each color one collected. Tom had already had three yellow ($4), four white ($6), five green ($3) and one red ($7). He'd tasted nearly every kind of sushi available that day—fatty tuna, soft-shell crab, eel, salmon skin, yellow tail, urchin, and roe, among others—as well as popping California rolls as if they were edamame. Stacy, demure and ladylike, had a stack of just four plates. She hadn't secured it with Janice, but she planned on expensing this lunch. The total would be over $100 by now, Tom showing no sign of slowing.

Stacy ventured, "Isn't it possible that a woman could put sex on a shelf? That she'd just forget about it for the time being?"

"If this woman had a libido at all, I don't see how she could forget about it. That's like forgetting about food, or sleep, or breathing. Sex is a biological imperative. Our bodies are programmed to want sex and think about sex all the time." Tom, lover of pronouncements, made another one. "If a woman can forget about sex, she is frigid."

Stacy stirred the ice in her water with her finger. "Your theory, about how easy it is for a woman to get sex, assumes that she has the courage, lack of discretion and willingness to ask outright for it. For example, if a woman—"

"You?" he asked. "I'm only insisting on specifics because it *is* relevant if the woman is a hottie. And you are the hottest woman over thirty I've seen in a long time. Ever. Even under thirty."

"Glad to hear it," Stacy said. "So then, what you're saying, is that I, Stacy Temple" —a frigid closet lesbian?— "could walk right up to Tony McGuinty—"

"Who?"

"Tony McGuinty. The actor from *The Hail Storm*? *Gorgeousville*? *Wonder Dogs*?"

"Never heard of him."

"Well, he is very handsome."

"It would be helpful for me, in envisioning this scenario, if you could pick a man I'm familiar with. How about Derek Jeter?"

Stacy had no passion for the Yankee shortstop. She was sure he was a nice kid, and he was very young, rich and talented. But he did nothing for her. "I could never ask Derek Jeter for sex."

"That's the whole point. You can't be intimidated. He'd say yes. Any guy would take one look at you and say yes to anything. He'd say yes to signing over his life savings. He'd say yes to murder. And all you'd be asking him for is a bit of nookie."

She was quite certain that she'd never ask for *that*. "Last night, a man said no to me."

Tom reeled back, nearly fell off his stool, in shock. "He's gay."

"It had crossed my mind."

"So he's a fag," he said. "But at least you tried. That's a step in the right direction for all women. If I may be so bold as to take a woman's sexual empowerment to a higher, political level—"

"You may."

"Women would rule the world if they had more casual sex."

"Sounds like an excellent dissertation topic," said Stacy.

"If women were willing to sleep with men just because they wanted to—not worrying about whether the guy would respect her, or if he's up to her standards or had enough money—they'd be in complete control of men, and would therefore rule the Earth.

"Plus," added Tom, "they'd be happier. My mom sleeps with a different guy every month. She gets more action than half of my friends at college. I hope I have as much fun when I'm forty-nine."

Stacy didn't believe Janice was having fun. In fact, she was quite positive her boss was lonely and depressed. But Tom's poor insight about his mom wasn't Stacy's business. For all she knew, Janice shielded her children from her pain. Maybe that was the right and proper thing to do. In any case, Stacy wouldn't correct Tom on his misunderstanding of Janice. Her only aim, on that Tuesday in July, was to take full advantage of the situation, and of this boy. His theories about women asking for sex sounded swell in thin air. She wondered how deeply she'd embarrass him if she thickened it.

"Are all college men as concerned with a woman's rightful place in the universe?" she asked.

"Gender equality is pretty high on my fix-it list," he said.

As he plucked another white plate (octopus and scallion hand roll) from the conveyor belt, Stacy said, "I don't meet too many men who love sushi."

"I love it. I could eat fish every day," he said and winked at her.

"Casual sex and raw fish for everyone," said Stacy, interpreting the gospel of Tom.

"Amen to that," he said, holding aloft a neat package of rice, tentacle and seaweed before shoveling it into his mouth. Stacy watched him chew, his lips slightly parted. Sex for sex's sake. That's what she was thinking herself into. God knows, she'd done it plenty of times before without qualms. It was a worthy task, a mundane yet noble act. She would have no guilt or hesitation. Stacy still had thirty minutes left on her hour off, and could stretch it by another fifteen if she had to. Best not to think about his dim bulb of a brain, intolerance or piggy table manners, she thought. Focus on his splendid availability.

"You are cute, Tom," she announced. "And I couldn't agree more that women should have as much casual sex as possible. In fact, as far as I'm concerned, women should grab, with both hands, any opportunity presented to her."

He paused and then swallowed hard. "You agree with me?"

She nodded. "Oh, yes. And, dare I repeat myself, I find you very attractive."

"The feminists on campus don't agree," he said. "They think my theories are offensive. And some women" —he glanced at Stacy— "think my commitment to equality between the sexes is just a rap I use to get laid."

Did she need to hit this boy on the head with a maki roll? Stacy put her hand on Tom's forearm. "I want you, Tom. I want you so badly it hurts. I am in physical pain from the gigantic amount of desire that I feel for you, Tom, at this moment in time."

He stared at Stacy's heart-shaped face in shock (and, it seemed, horror), before yelling "Check, please!" to the woman taking drink orders. To Stacy he said, "Let's go to my place," and gulped down the last of his carafe of sake.

"Your mother's place downtown?" she asked, calculating the traveling time of going all the way to the Village and back.

"I'm staying at the Regalton Hotel," he said.

Stacy paid the bill (careful to keep the receipt), and they walked the three blocks to East 44thStreet.

The Regalton Hotel opened in 1992, the same year Bill Clinton became president. In Democratic spirit, the lobby was generously lit with amber-hued torch sconces that made anyone look stylish, slim and sepia. Legend had it that a certain superstar singer, in her club-crawling, pre-pregnancy days, would regularly burst through the unmarked black leather doors with two or three Latin men, disappear into the mirrored elevators and hit the stop button between floors. Hotel management would discreetly cordon off the occupied elevator and direct hotel guests to the unoccupied ones. After an hour or so, the elevator car would arrive in the lobby, ejecting the men into a funnel of flattering light with coupons for a free meal at the hotel's four-star French restaurant, the Velveteen Lapin. The pop star, meanwhile, would return to her penthouse suite alone, until she emerged from the mirrored elevators herself in the early hours of the morning—rested, scrubbed and ready to run ten miles around the Central Park Reservoir, flanked by bodyguards and trainers (one of whom became the father of her daughter).

Stacy had long thought that the lobby—all black walls set off by bright red-, orange- and yellow-framed mirrors, plush black velvet settees with purple and blue pillows and black inches-deep carpeting that leveled high heels—would be the perfect place to meet a lover for a clandestine lunch hour. And here she was, doing exactly that. How tickled she was. How pleased. Not only would she rid herself of the threat of revirginization, but she'd be doing it in style.

Tom led her to an elevator on the left. Once the doors closed, the ghostly black light bounced off the mirrored walls. Brave Tom put his hands on Stacy's shoulders and leaned in for what would be her first kiss in nearly a year. Tom was a tall boy, and Stacy, in her heels, was the ideal number of feet and inches to tilt her neck only slightly to greet his lips.

Her heart, her pulse. The dampening of the space between her upper lip and her nose. Stacy hadn't felt these corporal changes—the excitement—in so long, the effect was uncomfortable, like she'd had one bite too much to eat. As Tom's mouth approached, like a black hole closing in on a small, uncharted planet, Stacy shut her eyes. She couldn't watch. It could be a sloppy, wet assault. It could go horribly, horribly wrong. The nanoseconds passed like microseconds, and then contact. She was being kissed by a man. His lips were squashed dryly against her own, and she felt the great relief of a thousand pounds of pressure breaking through a dam of matchsticks.

Stacy emitted a sound, a groan that she wished she could hurry back into her throat. Tom said, "You have a gorgeous ass," and moved his hands from the safety of her shoulders to said bottom. She wriggled a bit from his grip, momentarily unconvinced that she knew him well enough to be groped in this brutish fashion.

Saved by the ding. The elevator doors opened, and Tom detached his lips from her face and his hands from her hips. She opened her eyes and looked at her new acquaintance, who was smiling sweetly at her as if she'd given him the toy he'd always wanted at Christmas. He was harmless, she realized. Nothing to fear. She could see this through. She was a sophisticated, self-actualized woman with a problem that had a clear and present solution. Courage would not be needed, she reasoned. Determination would be enough.

They walked down the long, dark hallway hand in hand. Tom floated at her side. Despite a 20-year-old's unlimited capacity to fantasize, Stacy was positive that he couldn't have imagined a midday screw would be the result of accompanying his mother to her office. She glanced at her watch. They had a comfortable 25 minutes before Janice and Fiona sent out a search-and-rescue squad.

Tom said, "This is my suite." He waved his plastic key at the lock and the black door popped open. Tom put his hand on her back to steer her into the room. The stench kept her in the hallway. Tom noticed it too, and apologized. "It didn't smell like this when I left this morning."

She breathed through her mouth and they walked in. On the floor, Stacy stepped over the remains of last night's room service (hamburgers and taco salad, she guessed). On the tables, full ashtrays overflowed with cigar and cigarette butts. Half-empty beer bottles everywhere. On the room's three couches lay the bodies of six young men, some sleeping upright with their feet on the table, all shirtless or in clothing stained with sweat, ketchup, and ash.

"Some friends staying over?" she asked.

Tom said, "I thought they'd be gone by now. And that housekeeping would have cleaned up. Maybe we should go. Can we take a cab to your place?"

Stacy rechecked her watch. Not nearly enough time. Fiona would spit bile if she were that late. Just thinking of work and her boss started to squelch her confidence. Tom, embarrassed by the mess, seemed to perceive her distraction. He had a cute pout.

"Is there a bedroom?" she asked.

He nodded. "I'm not sure what we'll find in there."

They picked their way toward the back of the suite. Stacy had to step over slices of pickle and mushed french fries on the carpet. Tom peeked into the bedroom and quickly closed the door.

"No good," he said.

Stacy pushed him away and opened the door. On the bed, ass up on navy blue sheets, sprawled a naked young man. To his right, partially covered by the bedclothes, lay a young woman. Her well-sprayed hair and makeup smears made her look like Whorey the Clown. She wore bulky jewelry on her wrists and ankles. Or was it . . . scratch the jewelry. Make that Velcro bondage straps. The lump at her left moved. Another college boy, groggily aroused. Make that groggily arose. He moaned, "My head," softly. The sound of his pain stirred his bedmates. Stacy quietly closed the door.

"Bathroom?" she asked. Dogged, Stacy clung to hope, but the thin edge of opportunity was barely wide enough to stand on. In mules, she teetered wildly. If the bathroom weren't sparkling clean, she resolved, she'd have to give up.

Tom pointed to the door opposite a small galley station. She ventured forth. The chrome on the sink shone cleanly. It reflected the red wink of her pedicure. The tub was dry, unused, white, circle-shaped and large enough to bathe a baby bison.

Removing her shoes, Stacy stepped into the tub. She said, "Lock that door," to Tom and waved him in.

He kicked off his sneakers and jumped over the

edge of the tub, nearly slipping in his socks. He grabbed Stacy around the waist and pressed her against his chest, kissing her hard on the face and neck. Without warning, he parted her lips with his tongue and began a full-out lingual assault. After two minutes of this oral frenzy, Tom unceremoniously unzipped his jeans and let them drop to his ankles.

"No hurry," she said, twinges of nervousness and What-am-I-doing? surfacing. Yet Tom's stomach was smooth, flat and golden as a beach.

"You're the one who's constantly checking her watch," he said as he lifted her dress and pulled at her panties.

She checked the time again. Fifteen minutes. She glanced at the tent of Tom's boxers. The absence of romance here had to count in her favor, she reasoned. She should be proud of her brazenness. It would make a charming little story in three or four months, the squashed food in the carpet, the bats and balls on Tom's boxers, the light grit of Ajax on the tub floor. But right now, as she let Tom spin her around and she braced herself against the tile wall with her hands, Stacy was hard-pressed (literally), to find a single amusing aspect to this. And then, the rattle of the bathroom doorknob.

Tom, breathing heavily, shouted, "Get lost!" at whomever was now knocking loudly. He reached between her legs and touched her. She couldn't deny the thrill. Male hands on her body. Her skin nearly jumped. She positioned her feet shoulder width, ready for Tom to do his part for gender equality.

But nothing happened. Again, he fumbled about, making her all the more prepared. But seconds ticked by without Tom making his point. Tom cursed a bit under his breath. The knocking of the door was now a rhythmic pounding. Stacy asked politely, "Is anything wrong?"

"Uhh. I'm . . . this has never happened to me before."

Stacy's quickened blood screeched to a halt. The phrase every man dreads to hear: "Is it in yet?" The phrase that kills a woman: "This has never happened to me before." Stacy turned around. They both stared mournfully at what might have been.

"I want you too much," he said desperately. "But this rushing. I'm hung over. It's that idiot." He gestured at the pounding of the bathroom door. "You have to give me another chance!" But the sight of Tom as he tried and failed to restore his pride and the sight of herself, panties stretched between her knees, her dress pushed up around her waist. She was not this desperate.

Stacy righted her clothes, stepped out of the tub and put on her shoes. She smiled (a gesture of infinite generosity, she thought) and said, "I've got to get back to work."

She opened the bathroom door. A nearly naked young man was relieving himself in the mini-sink above the mini-bar. Stacy walked past him quickly. Tom pulled up his jeans and gave chase. "Please, Stacy, meet me tonight. I won't let you down. You've got to say yes," he pleaded.

"I've had all the female empowerment I can stand for one day," she said, and left.

She wouldn't blame herself. Her equipment had been operational. But the sting! An impotent 20-year-old. Who ever heard of such a thing? As she raced back to work, Stacy decided not to tell Charlie about the humiliating episode, even though she was sure he'd supply a comforting speech along the lines of "This happens to every guy" and "You've got the goods" and "He was way out of his league." No need to seek reassurance. She would, instead, erase the entire seedy experience from her memory. She needed reliability. She needed a rock (no slam to Mr. Tom Softy). A good man was hard to find. But she knew exactly where to locate a perpetually hard one.

Chapter Five

Tuesday night

Stacy's mental shift—from never thinking about sex to contemplating nothing but—was seismic (although, to be precise, her mind was locked on the pursuit of sex more so than the act itself). Her record so far: 0 for 2. First, a flat-out rejection from Jason, and then the crushing download of Tom's floppy wares (his spirit was willing; the flesh was limp). Never in her life had she worked so hard for a little action. As a woman, Stacy was hardwired to blame herself when anything went wrong (consciously or not). She had to wonder: Is it me? Is this my destiny? Surely, at some point in the future, she would have sex again. She couldn't imagine going another 50 years untouched. But the possibility was real: She could remain celibate for the next stretch of a decade. She could give Learning Annex seminars titled "Embrace Your Sexless Self Since No One Else Is." Or "Advanced Masturbation Skills for the Sexually Handicapped." Or "Celibate and Childless: Cursed or Careful?"

Needless to say, Stacy was useless in the afternoon meeting at thongs.com. As soon as she walked into the conference room to join the others and took a seat at the huge turtle-shaped table, Janice started in with the questions. She had to know *everything* that happened at lunch with her precious, darling boy. Stacy wondered if mother and son had a healthy relationship.

"We had sushi, and then took a short walk," said Stacy safely.

"Where'd you go?" asked Janice.

"Around midtown."

"Make any stops?"

"We just walked."

"It's a hundred degrees outside," said Janice.

Stacy nodded. "We were hot." No, not that. "We were warm." Oh, dear. "We stepped in and out of stores for the air-conditioning."

"So you did some shopping," said Janice, a bit too excitedly. Stacy remembered with the thonk of cylinders in her brain that Janice had an impending birthday. A biggie. Make that a hugey.

Smiling slyly, Stacy said, "I shouldn't say any more. I don't want to spoil the surprise." If Tom forgot his mother's 50th on Friday, it would now be on Stacy's head. She jotted a note on her pad to call the hotel later and leave Tom a message.

To her right, at the tail end of the turtle table, Taylor Perry spied Stacy's note to self. On her own legal pad, Taylor wrote, "You didn't miss much."

Stacy hoped Taylor was referring to the lunch hour portion of the staff meeting and not her foiled encounter with Tom.

Fiona stood at the head of the Turtle. "Let's get back to ideas for what to call the mesh line. I like Meshwear 2001. Anyone else?"

Silence at first, as always. Furious scratching of pens on paper. And then, the half dozen women in the room began shouting out suggestions.

"Mesh magic."

"Mesh and match."

"I'll be meshing you."

"A hole new look."

"Monster mesh."

"Mesh Pit."

"Stacy?" asked Fiona impatiently. "We haven't heard from you."

"How about . . ." Stacy started, trying to snap her attention back to the matter at hand. "How about: What a fine mesh you've gotten me into?"

Nervous titters around the room, echoing off the walls. There she went again, words flying out of her mouth before her inner editor could stop them. She shrank in her leather chair. Fiona's black helmet of hair seemed to expand with fury. Was it possible Stacy was purposefully pissing off her boss? she wondered. Was she like a wolf in a trap, gnawing off her own paw to save her soul, her life?

"Meshwear 2001 it is," said Janice, attempting to snip the burning wick of the Fiona bomb. "Why go further when we have a clear winner? Let's move on to design and production. Ladies? Ideas?"

The design team had a list to present. While the head of the department prattled on about metallics, Taylor, who had nothing to do with production issues whatsoever, scribbled excitedly on her pad. Stacy was impressed with her note taking (how resourceful of her). But then Taylor pushed her pad toward Stacy. "What a fine mesh we're all in," read the note. "I've been thinking about my options—jobwise, personally. We should go out sometime soon and talk. I like the way you think. I like you, too."

Stacy swallowed hard, put a check mark over the word "soon" and returned the pad to Taylor. Stacy dared to look at her behaltered, braless colleague. Taylor was grinning coyly, circling Stacy's check mark over and over again until the ink on the pad was thick and blotchy. Okay, thought Stacy, here was some new information to process. Could Taylor have sworn off men because she preferred *women*? Was she a New Lesbian? More importantly, would a girl-on-girl fling (not that she'd ever had one, or had ever wanted to—but she was in no position to be picky about the age, quality, stability or gender of her dates) would qualify as a de-revirginating event?

"Stacy!" barked Fiona. "Price list!"

Fumbling for her printout of proposed prices, Stacy felt her ears go hot. Their temperature didn't return to normal for the goodly part of the hour. The meeting continued, sustaining its keen tension, for the rest of the afternoon. Nothing much was achieved except the brutal assigning of tasks. As Stacy limped (not that word) back to her office, she counted 37 items on her To Do list, from the commonplace (negotiating with importers, hiring models) to the creative (composing sexy names for each chemise, babydoll, G-string and teddy in the line). Most likely, for her composition, she'd stick to the Fiona-preferred vocabulary list, including words like Enchantress, Huntress, Risqué and Savage.

But no more fabrics and finery tonight. She was exhausted from the unswerving stream of Fiona's disapproval. Stacy quietly tossed lipsticks and Altoids into her straw purse. She started to shut down her iMac. On the desktop, on a Stickies memo, was her other, personal To Do list. At the top, in red, all-cap letters: V DAY, JULY 23. Was she too tired and beaten down to make a call? Was it emblematic of her sorry sexual situation that she was always too tired and beaten down at the close of the workday? Not today, she vowed.

With renewed vigor (forced and contrived, but it was the best she could do), Stacy reached for the phone. She dialed an old number from memory.

Ring, ring, ring. She almost hung up, but he answered with a groggy hello.

She said, "Brian?"

"Stacy?" he asked, surprised.

"Are you sleeping?" It was only eightish.

"This is so weird. I was just dreaming about you."

They'd been happy—thoughtlessly, comfortably—

in their early days. The familiar sound of Brian's voice made her heart tight. She said, "I miss you." At that moment, she felt a genuine tug for what they'd had when it was good. It was never true love. But they'd had tenderness. She wanted to sit in his lap, lay her red head on his shoulder and cry with great sobbing gasps.

He asked, "Are you okay?"

She remembered this about him: He was sensitive. He knew her well. He could intuit exactly what she was feeling. Just to be sure, Stacy took a deep breath and said, "Brian, I'm horny."

The phone was silent for a moment. Then, he said, "You'd better come over."

Stacy stood outside Brian's apartment on West 72nd Street filled to the collar with nostalgia. This corner, this building. They'd never lived together, but she'd spent several nights a week at his place for three years straight. Memories flooded her senses: the smell of the Papaya King restaurant across the street; the sight of his name on masking tape by his buzzer; the cool marble walls of the lobby; the clicking sound of her heels as she walked toward the elevators; the taste of lipstick as she reapplied while standing on the other side of his apartment door. It was as if the year hadn't floated by without him. As if she were arriving, cranky and tired after work, as she had hundreds of times before.

Before she had a chance to knock, the door swung open. Brian grabbed Stacy by the wrist and lassoed her in his arms. His embrace was like riding a Lifecycle. She sank into his beefy chest, smelling his shirt.

She said, "You smell nice."

"You like?" he asked. "It's eau d'Clorox."

She pulled back and gave her ex the once-over. He'd put on a few pounds. And he desperately needed a shave. His hair was too long and his shirt had coffee stains. "You look good," she said. "Good enough to eat."

"You want dinner?" he asked, jerking a thumb toward the small kitchen off his living room. "I can scramble some eggs. Burn some toast, just the way you like it." Brian's cooking skills had never progressed beyond breakfast.

Stacy shook her head. "I said I was horny, not hungry."

"Easy, girl," he said, beaming the goofy grin she'd fallen for on the night they met, at a bar a few blocks away, at last call, when she was as close to blind drunk as she'd ever been (never, she promised herself after that hangover, would she underestimate the punch of a Kir Royale). In the morning, she could barely remember what had happened, and had no idea how she'd wound up in a foreign bedroom. To her great relief, she looked under the sheets and found herself dressed. She'd been wearing a complicated wrap shirt from Banana Republic. She didn't believe a straight man—certainly not the preppy all-American guy holding two cups of black coffee and smiling sweetly at the foot of the bed—could figure out how to take off the shirt and put it back on again with the strings forming a perfect bow at her hip. She accepted the coffee. It went down far easier than Brian's mortifying description of her behavior the night before. With gratitude for his generous and chaste protection, Stacy asked Brian to get into his bed with her. They slept for several hours. When they woke up, they showered together and made plans for their first real date.

"Do you remember the night we met?" she asked him now, four years later.

Brian nodded and then sneezed loudly. He pulled a used tissue out of his pocket and blew hard. "Summer cold," he said. "I'm on the last legs. I'm not contagious at this point."

Stacy made a practice of avoiding sick people. When stricken with a cold, she became a sniveling mess: her nose doubled in size from inflammation, her eyes teared, her hair went flat and greasy from neglect. She would OD on echinacea and vitamin C, but the germs in her body would cling to the cushy life inside Stacy's membranes, causing any sickness, minor or major, to last and last. The phlegmy flavor of a cold would stay fresh in her nasal cavities for weeks. She hated getting sick. As she watched Brian wipe himself clean of visible sneeze residue, Stacy knew with the certainty of the damned that he'd left millions of undetectable germs behind. And if she were to kiss that mouth, they would step across his tongue and onto hers, only too happy to settle there, build a colony and multiply until they'd seized control of every mucosal cell in her head and chest. But, on this day in July, Stacy was willing to risk the delicate, thin skin around her nostrils, the luster of her hair, and the freedom of movement without a Kleenex plastered to her face. She would make that sacrifice.

"I haven't had sex since the last time we saw each other," she confessed.

Brian cocked an eyebrow. "I'm surprised," he said.

"It's been nearly a year," she said, poised to launch into an explanation. After all, it was impolite to show up at an ex-boyfriend's door and expect sex without first explaining why.

He sat down in the middle of his living room couch (really a scratching post that seated three—Brian let his cat do anything, which was just one more reason Stacy couldn't have lived with him). Brian leaned back, and crossed his legs. Great legs, made for flat-front khakis and Timberland boots. She pictured them naked, re-membering the muscles bunching and relaxing as he walked around the apartment in shorts. Stacy moved toward him. Just a step. Before she could get any closer, a 20-pound marmalade cat leaped onto the couch and hissed protectively.

"Batty! Darling! How I've missed you," she said to the gigantic orange tom who stole food off dinner plates, sprayed weekly in each corner of the apartment, spilled his water on the kitchen floor, and due to im-proper feeding, suffered from what the veterinarian po-litely referred to as gastric insult (more of an insult to the humans who lived with him).

Knowing her true feelings, Batty greeted Stacy with a violent spit and settled solidly on Brian's lap as if intentionally blocking her access. Stacy smiled, tight-lipped, and sat down anyway. Brian said, "He's lost some weight. I have him on a new diet. Three cans of tuna fish and twelve ounces of Evian a day."

"It's working wonders," she lied. "Kitty low-carb. Best-selling diet books have been made of less."

Brian pushed Batty away and leaned toward Stacy. Her heart started pumping again (if nothing more, these erotic stops and starts were salubrious for her heart). He said, "Now, where were we? Ah, yes. Your extreme horniness and how it's brought you to me. Go on."

Saying that grating H-word had a salacious effect on Brian. Stacy was well aware. That's why she'd used it. "Do we have to talk about it? Can't we do something about it instead?"

"But I'm sick," he said.

"I don't care."

"Who are you and what have you done with Stacy Temple?" he asked.

The question stopped her from lunging. What *had* she done with Stacy Temple? With painful recognition, she saw herself as an automaton whose awkward groping for passion and affection had brought her right back to the man she'd rejected because all he ever wanted was passion and affection. She'd miscalculated terribly a year ago. He was a sweet, kind, handsome guy who loved her (once). Sitting in his warm presence, despite his slovenly appearance and runny nose, Stacy couldn't understand why she'd broken up with him. If she sufficiently humbled herself, maybe he would love her again.

"I should have paid more attention to you, Brian," she announced. "I can't believe I let you go. I want another chance."

"Stacy," he started, "a lot has happened."

"A lot has happened to me, too. That's why I'm here. I've learned painful lessons, and I want to correct my mistakes."

She leaned in to kiss him. He hesitated for a moment. Stacy feared she'd pressured him, or that he didn't want her (impossible—he'd always told her she was his ideal). After she'd nibbled on his lips for a few seconds, he put his arms around her and pulled her closer. The familiarity of his hug nearly made her cry. It felt safe, comfortable, easy. She needed a dose of easy. And she'd really meant what she said. If he'd have her back, she'd be stupid with happiness about it.

With a graceful reshuffling, Stacy put one leg over Brian and straddled him on the couch. She deftly lifted her dress over her head and sat upon him, nude save for her mules and underwear (on this day, she'd had the foresight to put on one of thongs.com's most popular bra-and-panty sets: the pink lace Maid in the Meadow).

"God, Stace. Your body," he said, and then began kissing her on the bra, burying his face between her breasts. He resurfaced to sniffle and wiped his nose on his sleeve. But Stacy wasn't horrified. She'd take him sick, coughing, oozing. And he'd take her just as she was. Under his khakis, he was granite (reliable, predictable Brian). A powerful hard-on cloaked in cotton. Nothing could have been sexier to Stacy at that moment. She put her hand on the outline and pressed.

Brian lay back on the couch, pulling her on top of him. Mad kissing and feeling up. He put his hands inside her Maid in the Meadows for an ass grab. Stacy imagined an ice field cleaving, huge pieces of glacier breaking away and falling into the dark sea. Her year of abstinence and the weight of it sank out of reach. A lift, that was what it was. A lifting of repression and denial. She bobbed on top of Brian as if he were a life raft.

She struggled with the top button of his pants. They were decidedly tighter than she'd remembered, or she was out of practice. She had to sit up as he lay beneath her and work on it with two hands. Just as she'd sprung the button and moved to the zipper, a flash of orange flew by her eyes. Fur and unsheathed claws scrambled across Brian's chest and her bare thighs.

Brian screamed; Stacy screamed. She looked down at the rips in Brian's shirt and then at the four deep scratch marks on her legs, first white and then the slow surfacing of red blood.

Once Brian and Stacy recovered from the surprise of Batty's sneak attack (the hurt came seconds after), she couldn't understand why screams still filled the apartment. Brian seemed perplexed, too. The two of them turned toward the sound.

There, in the doorway, stood a woman. She was short and fair, with a blonde pageboy. She was cute, in a pug-nosed, preppy kind of way. She wore an "anti-Stacy" outfit—chinos and a mannish blazer over a cobalt blue Oxford shirt. Her hands reached to cup her cheeks, and she dropped a stuffed backpack, blue, on the floor. For a deluded second, Stacy thought she was screaming in pain from dropping such a heavy bundle on her foot. The shrieks were prolonged, ear piercing. This woman must have had some vocal training to sustain the volume. Brian pushed Stacy off him (causing her to tumble clumsily against the opposite arm of the couch).

He blinked and said, "Idit!"

Idit? Was he calling this woman an idiot? Before Stacy could hazard a guess, the small woman with the large lung capacity picked up the backpack and threw it at him, hitting him squarely in the chest.

"In my apartment!" she yelled before running out the open apartment door, slamming it as she left.

Her apartment? This had been Brian's apartment for ten years. Who did this woman think she was?

Brian filled her in: "That was my fiancée, Idit Sholanstein." He put the backpack on the couch between them.

Stacy used a pillow to cover her near nakedness. "Your fiancée," she said, grappling with the news. "I practically begged you to take me back."

"You're my dream girl, Stace," he said. "Idit wasn't supposed to be home until late. I guess I should go after her." Brian turned to look at Stacy, waiting for a cue. She had a choice here: She could 1) send him after his fiancée (the right thing to do), or 2) seduce him, ending her problem and his engagement in one swoop. But then she'd have to be his girlfriend again. From her new place on the other side of the couch, that suddenly seemed like a very bad idea. She looked squarely at Brian, whose eyes were searching her face (and examining her body) for direction.

"I'm not sure I want a relationship right now," she said, fumbling. "I meant it when I said that I did, but now I'm not so sure." She picked up her dress and put it on. "If only Idit had come in ten minutes later," she said mournfully.

"I do love her," said Brian. "But one look at you . . ."

"We went out for three years and never got close to being engaged," she said. "How long have you been with Idit?"

"We met at vavoom.com, right after you dumped me." Brian, formerly an engineer for Volvo America, worked as a designer for the simulation shareware game site. "We started as friends. I was depressed after our breakup. Idit comforted me, took care of me. I can't imagine what I'd have done without her. She proposed to me. Last week. Bought herself a ring. The reason I never asked you to marry me is because I knew you wouldn't have said yes. And I also know that you don't really want to get back together with me. You just want to get laid. And I was up for it. I still am." He pulled

Stacy into his lap. "Idit will come back. I'll make it right. But she has nothing to do with unfinished business between us." He put his hand between her knees.

Could she go through with it, now that she knew he was engaged? A moral dilemma. She didn't need the bad karma, that was for sure. But his fingers felt lovely on her skin and she did have this revirgination problem. If he was willing to compromise his engagement, why should she worry? Was it her responsibility to keep him in line? She wasn't cheating on anyone. She didn't even know this Idit.

Before Stacy could sink into Brian and his moral decline, Idit saved her own life. She slammed back into the apartment, picked up Stacy's bag, pulled Stacy away from Brian, dragged her out of the apartment, down the hallway, into the elevator, out onto the street and halfway down the block.

As they neared the corner of 71st Street, Stacy shook herself loose. Her dress was sticking to the tacky blood on her thighs from that vicious cat's attack. Her arm was smarting from Idit's military grip (Stacy bruised easily; she was sure she'd have an unsightly mark in a few hours). And she very nearly broke another heel.

Idit, arms crossed over her mannish outfit, said, "I picked him up, cleaned him off, and carried him on my shoulders for nearly six months until he got you out of his system. He's mine, and you're not going to come along a year later and ruin everything I've been working toward."

"I'm sorry. He didn't tell me he was engaged," protested Stacy weakly. Idit stared at her with unbridled hostility. "I know that apologizing won't do much good. But I am genuinely sorry. Nothing happened. We'd only just started . . ."

"I'm glad Batty had the sense to try and stop you."

Hateful cat, thought Stacy. "May I . . . look, Brian is just confused. We, uh, it just happened."

"I don't care what you did or why you did it," said Idit, with the precision of a scalpel. "I want to get married. Brian is going to be my husband no matter who he sleeps with. I've been working for this, and I'll achieve my goal."

That sounded strangely cold and impersonal. Stacy felt a swell of protectiveness for Brian. "You love him, of course."

"Yes, yes, I love him. I *chose* him," said Idit. "And I believe that he loves me. But even if he doesn't, he sees enough good in me or what I do for him that he's agreed to spend the rest of his life as my husband."

"Forgive me for saying, but you don't seem like a terribly warm and tender sort. Brian needs a lot of cuddling and hand-holding." The reasons Stacy had to end it with him, she thought.

"Forgive me for saying," countered Idit, "but I'm not inclined to show my warm and tender side to the woman who just tried to seduce my fiancé. And you don't have to worry about Brian. I know exactly what he needs." She turned on the flat heels of her Hush Puppies and headed back toward her future. She was about 10 feet from Stacy when she looked over her shoulder and said, "We'll never see each other again."

"I won't be a bridesmaid?" asked Stacy.

"Nor a bride." She sniffed.

Chapter Six

The outstretched arms on Stacy Temple's Josie and the Pussycats clock pointed to 3 A.M. Her thoughts crawled from the gory events of the past two days to the salacious. (Stacy sat alone on a large turtle-shaped conference table in the middle of a dimly lit room. Suddenly, beams from above reveal naked men in cages surrounding the table. Somehow it is made known to Stacy that the imprisoned men have been locked inside for nearly a year—fed, watered, exercised, but deprived of physical contact of any kind while being forced to watch pornography for ten hours a day. Stacy was the first flesh-and-blood woman any of these twelve clones of Tony McGuinty had seen in months and months. They were practically frothing from every orifice at the very sight of her in a white lace thong and camisole set. With the slam of metal doors, the cages sprang open. The men emerged and rushed Stacy, a look of depraved starvation in their eyes, gigantic erections in their hands.)

The ravaging of Stacy's sleepy-time hours continued. Masturbation was not as soporific as she would have liked. Stacy remembered reading once that the worst thing for insomnia was watching the clock as the minutes of your life ticked by, unused. Her torture acute, Stacy sat upright in bed and threw back the covers. She wandered into her living room and turned on the computer. Might as well check e-mail. She signed on.

Hurray, she thought, when she saw that Gigi from swerve.com had written back. After the past couple of days, Stacy would welcome absolution from the woman who, unknowingly, had started Stacy on this quest. She opened the note and read.

"Dear Stacy, Thanks for offering me the work, but I'm on contract with swerve, and can't write content of a sexual nature for any other electronic media. If you have connections in the print publishing world, though, I'm trying to get a book proposal together, and would appreciate any help or direction. Thanks."

That's it? Stacy wondered. She scrolled down to see if there was an attachment or an addendum or a postscript. Nothing. How inexorably frustrating. Stacy had put herself out there and received zilch from Gigi in return (the same treatment she'd been getting from her growing list of disastrous dates).

Stacy checked her other e-mails. Charlie had sent her a blank note, except for a hypertext link to a URL at swerve.com. Stacy clicked on link. An article popped onto her screen, by Gigi XXX. This one was called, "Pity the Accidental Celibate."

Her heart clinched. She read the copy, clutching her chest. It started:

"Intentional celibacy, as it's been explained to me by women I once called 'friends,' is goal oriented. The goal itself is worthy (self-knowledge). I questioned, in a previous column, if avoiding sex will teach you anything that you don't already know. I got an avalanche of feedback from the ever-expanding fleet of nonsexual-by-choice readers. Ninety-nine percent of them believe that I am talking out of my asshole, and said as much in their letters.

"At least I'm doing something inventive with my ass (quite a few things, actually—watch this space for painfully detailed anal sex coverage). From where I s(h)it, a column that incites people to ascribe superhuman powers to my rectum deserves a Pulitzer. I invite every reader who sent in a pissed-off e-mail to come to our offices in New York City, get on her knees and behold my miraculous chatty ass. I may shoot some video and post it on swerve.com so all can appreciate the wondrous feat.

"One e-mail, though, wasn't angry. Seeking clarity, the reader wanted to know if accidentally going a year without sex made celibacy less worthy of scorn. I guess she woke up one day and realized she hadn't been naked with a man in a very long time, and she wanted me to tell her it was okay, like I'm some kind of absolving high sex priestess with magic powers (well, I *do* have that loquacious anus . . .). I get the impression this woman is a socially phobic workaholic without many friends and loved ones with whom she can discuss the shortcomings and disappointments of her life."

Despite the scalding slap, Stacy forced herself to read on. "To this woman," Gigi wrote, "and all others who've let sex fall off the barren landscape of their lives, whose existence is passionless—and has been for so long that they can't even remember why passion once meant something to them—I have a message. I'm going to type in all caps now (which I hate doing, but it seems warranted): THERE ARE NO ACCIDENTS. We are all responsible for what happens (or doesn't happen) to us. If this woman cared about lust and passion and— okay, I'll go there—*love,* she would have at least *tried* to get laid. (For the record, those who have actively tried—made real yeowoman's efforts—to get a piece and did not . . . on second thought, even the most hideously unattractive woman can find someone to pork her. Pickiness is a form of rationalized avoidance.)

"Let's say this woman does care about passion, but that she's suppressed the drive to unite with another person (I don't care if it's for a night, a week or a lifetime). Then she's far worse off than my erstwhile friends who are purposefully chucking the greatest thing on earth for the hooey they call 'self-awareness.' This woman, this sad, deluded shrew, has divorced her life from both cock *and* consciousness (*Cock and Consciousness,* I like that; might make a good title for a Jane Austen spoof novel). The accidentally-on-purpose revirgin should seek help. Professional help. She shouldn't have turned to me. I have no patience for people who are afraid of their emotions, who have a pathological aversion to risk. I'm an incurable romantic. I believe life isn't worth living if you're not in love or trying to find it. Plus, I'm a clinically diagnosed sexaholic. I'm also a bitch."

Never, in all her life, thought Stacy, as she read the last words of Gigi's character assassination, had she been served up and fed to the dogs like that. Stacy was a sweet person. She didn't deserve to be destroyed by a woman she'd offered to hire (for a job that didn't exist, but Gigi couldn't know that). Questioning Stacy's entire existence because she'd had a busy year? The insult! The injury! The gall! The bladder! It was easy for Gigi to savage Stacy, using a pseudonym and a picture that obscured her face. Stacy vowed she'd never read another word issued from the keyboard of that pusillanimous hack.

Stacy called up the e-mail she received from Gigi and fired back a response.

"Dear Gigi, I got your note. Too bad about the free-lancing restrictions. I do, actually, have dozens and dozens of contacts in book publishing. But it's dicey, giving out phone numbers and names to unknown writers who haven't proven themselves in print. I'm sure you understand. Best of luck to you in your venture, Stacy."

After hitting SEND NOW and cackling softly, Stacy got dressed. In her fit of fury, she'd never be able to sleep now. She slipped on a pair of orange pedal pushers, a lavender eyelet blouse and her pink mules. She loved those mules with the rose on top. And they were going to carry her out of this chamber of torment and into the city at night. She was hungry. Affrontery gave her an appetite.

Outside at 4 A.M., she was alone on the street, as if SoHo had taken off on vacation without inviting her. The sun was a couple of hours from rising; the dark of morning shimmered with humidity and heat. A sheen of perspiration coated her brow. She was torn between self-consciousness about the sweat and the hope that her pheromones would bring all eligible men out of the shadows. Maybe a small band of out-of-work male models would emerge from an alley and ask for directions or spare change.

Even in the wee hours in downtown Manhattan, that was an unlikely tableau. Stacy headed straight for her favorite diner on the corner. As soon as she got there, though, she realized she'd come unprepared. No book, magazine, or *New York Post*. She had only the laminated menu to occupy her eyes. She read the selection of American and Greek fare, admiring the menu's spot art of Hellenic columns, the acropolis and dancing gyro sandwiches. When she finished with that, she tried to lift herself out of the miasma of confusion. Was she deluded? Had she cut herself off from the world of sex and love because she feared taking risks? Were Gigi's ugly accusations even worth contemplating? She hated writers. They'd exploit anything and anyone for their own egomania, never taking other people's feelings into account. Gigi and her talking asshole. Stacy would dearly like to tear her a new one.

A tired-looking waiter approached. He seemed completely unmoved by Stacy's beauty and grace. No kissy-kissy sounds from him. One would think that would be a relief for Stacy. One would. As she imagined what would be a sexier way to say "cheeseburger and onion rings," she looked around the stillness of the diner.

The booths were all empty. Save one. On the opposite end of the diner, a newspaper page was being turned. The ruffling sound and flickering movement drew her eye. The reader, obscured by the paper, wasn't in the least bit curious about the flaming redhead who, despite apparent sobriety at 4:30 A.M. on a Wednesday, had ordered a huge meal that in no culture of the world would be described as light. The mystery of her. Her unaccountability. The reader's lack of curiosity intrigued her. She studied the hands holding the paper. Was it a man or a woman? She couldn't tell.

And then the newspaper was folded and placed neatly on the booth. A man. Quite handsome, in fact. Late 20s. Rakishly disheveled, he wore a T-shirt from Ed's Gym (she couldn't get a look at his pants or shoes from her location). His black hair stuck out in thick clumps. His eyes were brooding and blue—her favorite combination. She watched him sip his drink, full lips encircling the straw in a tiny *O*. As he drank, he looked up at Stacy. She immediately turned away, blushing.

When she'd dared to look up again, the man was staring at her openly. She stared back. His skin was preternaturally white. A night owl, she thought. Possibly a vampire. She could easily picture this man naked, exiting a cage or a coffin at sundown. Stacy imagined his mouth clasped to her jugular. Picturing it would be as far as she'd get with him, though. She'd never initiate conversation with a stranger (not her style; Stacy always let men come to her—at least she had before this week).

Back to this man in a cage. Naked, save for a black satin cape. And a bat perched on his shoulder. Did bats perch? Stacy redrew it to hang by its feet from the top bars of Vampire Boy's cage, red eyes gleaming in the darkness.

The waiter in the dirty apron interrupted her thoughts. "Cheeseburger and onion rings," he said as he dropped plates on Stacy's table. She felt self-conscious about her choice of food. The brooding prince of darkness might think her bulimic. The aroma of grease and red meat enticed her to eat lustily anyway. She consumed the 1,000 calories, including un-told grams of fat, in less that five minutes (a new world record?). Her belly full, Stacy relaxed. She knew she could sleep now. In fact, she felt dangerously close to falling asleep right in the booth. If she hurried back, she could get a couple hours in before having to go to work. And, frankly, the way the Vampire was staring at her was unnerving, especially with her drastically increased blood sugar levels.

She stood, dropping a ten on the table. At the same moment, the young man rose from his booth, too. He left a five next to his empty glass. They reached the diner door together. Wordlessly, he held it open and waved her through, escorting her out into the Manhattan night.

His footsteps fell into place behind her. She didn't like the sound of that. Stacy turned left at the corner. Five paces to her rear, the Vampire turned left. Dear God, he was following her. Did he think casual eye contact was code for "do me now"? A spark of fear shot from her heart to her heels. She picked up the pace and gained some ground on him; he was a half block back when she reached her building. Stacy slipped inside and closed the front door. The reassuring click of the lock flooded her with relief. As she waited for the elevator, she chided herself for going outside alone at such an hour. But Christ, she thought, even rapists and muggers have to sleep sometime.

The elevator bell rang. She stepped in. She thought she heard the front door open, and began to push the elevator buttons impatiently. Finally, the metal doors started to close. With a few inches to go, a man's arm shot between the doors and pried them apart. Stacy's breath caught when she saw who it was: the coffee-shop Vampire. He'd managed to pick the building door's lock, and now had her cornered in the elevator. This was not the metal cage of her fantasies. He had no right. The doors shut with a clang. The elevator gave a bounce and lifted the pair upward.

Stacy tried to remember the one-hour on-site self-defense course thongs.com sponsored in the conference room. Back in the cash-flooded days (late 1998), Fiona frequently had organized expensive treats and trips for her staff (a weekend at the Taj in Atlantic City, three re-served tables to see Aimee Mann at Joe's Pub, the sum-mer house for employee use in Sag Harbor). The self-defense course was taught by a black belt in karate named Raja who was Fiona's personal trainer/sex slave (from the way she described it) for a couple months. Janice told Stacy that, for the 60-minute demonstration of elbow butchery, kidney punches and ear boxing, Fiona paid him $1,500. The boss invited any staffer to organize a seminar of her own for the same money. Stacy wondered what special skill she could teach the group. Finally, she offered to escort the staff on a lunchtime tour of the antique-purse district in the east 20s. Fiona didn't bite.

But would Vampire Boy? Stacy recalled Raja's in-structions on how to break a masher's nose: Using the meat of the palm, jab sharply in an uppercut motion, driving the nasal cartilage into the attacker's brain. She could do it. She could do it.

She could *never* do it. If threatened, she could muster slapping and scratching. But the sound of bones slamming into spongy gray matter—that was a squish you'd never forget. Still, she kept her fingers curled into her palm, wrist bent at a 90 degree angle, ready to flatten Vampire Boy's (admittedly very cute and buttonlike) nose.

VB (which, under different circumstances, would be her cute nickname for him) kept his eyes upward, watching the floor numbers blink and flicker as the car banged along. Typical of rapists and thugs, thought Stacy, that he was pretending to ignore her. Raja had said something like that in his lesson. They try to lull you into a false sense of safety, only to catch you unawares.

Stacy was all too aware of him. Especially the way he shifted from one leg to the other (quite fetching legs for a criminal, long and lean under faded jeans).

The number four blinked. Her floor, at last. When the doors opened, she walked out. Vampire exited the elevator behind her. Watching him over her shoulder, Stacy increased her clip and sprinted for her apartment, fumbling for her keys in her oversize tote.

The man kept coming closer and closer. Holy shit, she thought desperately. He might be a real live masher! She stopped groping inside her bag for the keys, squared off her feet, gripped her right wrist with her left hand to increase torque, and readied herself to deliver a pop.

Seeing her posture, Vampire stopped suddenly. She *was* an intimidating presence, she thought smugly. He looked at her for only a half second—with puzzlement, it seemed—and then he took a ring of keys out of his pants pocket. Smooth as chocolate, he opened the door to 4C, glanced again at Stacy in her action stance, and disappeared inside the apartment—presumably his own.

She always wondered who lived in that unit. He never showed his face during daylight hours.

Stacy's heart slowed to jack-rabbit speed. She finally managed to get inside her apartment. The sun was up. It was almost 6 A.M. She lay down on her bed, more wide awake than ever. Her cheeks were flushed, her breath short and her legs were shaking. Fear wasn't sex, but it was an incredible simulation.

Chapter Seven

Wednesday morning

On no sleep, heels were out of the question. Stacy chose flip-flops, rubber spanking the soles of her feet with each step. She wouldn't stop at the greasy deli that Wednesday morning. She was in no mood for winks, smooch sounds, or cocked unibrows. She didn't want breakfast of any kind (having consumed a cheeseburger only hours before), nor did she long for the smallest sliver of conversation with strangers or familiars alike. Stacy wanted one thing and one thing only (okay, two things, counting a steady flow—ideally an intravenous drip—of coffee): to lock herself in her office and lay her head on the plush wrist pad she used to prevent carpal tunnel syndrome. As she walked, she pictured that narrow industrial gray pillow the perfect width to support one tired cheek. She'd take a nap. A demi-nap. No one would notice. And even if they did, she thought, who cared? She'd lost countless hours of sleep to work. Just this once, she'd lose a couple of hours of work to sleep.

Sadly (achingly), when Stacy arrived at her small office at thongs.com, someone was already there, frantically typing on her computer, showing a complete disregard for her privacy and the sanctity of her workstation. The culprit was Janice, her boss, the woman who, theoretically, owned the office and the computer. Owned Stacy. And she had the right to do anything she wanted.

"Reading my e-mails?" she asked.

Janice, not looking away from the screen, said, "My iMac is cranky today. I need yours for just a few more minutes."

Stacy sat down on the hard, armless metal chair across from her desk. She had to remove a huge pile of folders and samples first, and the exertion of lifting and dropping the dross exhausted her. Just as she was seated, leaning her head back against the smoked glass wall and closing her eyes, Janice said, "Stacy, what do you think of this one? Pull up that chair and help me."

Stacy assumed she was being asked to vet some bustier design or status report. But as she dragged her chair closer to the computer screen, Stacy beheld the head and torso of a man, fiftyish, tan and toothy. Kind eyes, but a weird, leering smile.

"As a model? Are we doing men's lingerie now, too?" Stacy was in a fog. She was confused. For starters, using this ancient man to sell boxers or briefs would repel the customers.

Janice said, "Male lingerie. For gay men, of course. It's not a bad idea. I might have to talk to Fiona about that." Stacy groaned. Fiona would of course say yes, assigning the bulk (or should she say *bulge*?) of the work to Stacy.

"His screen name is PoloMan," Janice announced. "Sounds upscale, right? Income is one hundred fifty thousand plus. A lawyer. Spiritual but not religious. He's fifty-five, lives on the Upper West Side, divorced, grown children, just like me. We'd have so much to talk about. And he's cute, right?"

Nodding with enough enthusiasm to pass, Stacy peered at the URL bar and saw that Janice was shopping. For men. On match.com, her usual trolling ground for Saturday-night dates. Janice clicked on PoloMan's CONTACT button to compose an e-mail reply to his ad.

Janice explained, "I usually just say, 'Loved your profile. We have so much in common! Call me' and then leave my number. But this is such a quality guy, I might have to get racy."

Stacy watched in horror as Janice typed the following message to King Leer: "I must meet you. You are all my fantasies rolled into one perfect man. I am a gorgeous, petite blonde. I run a lingerie company and wear our product every day (and night). Call me and we'll make a date. I am dying to hear from you."

Using the job as a pick-up line hadn't occurred to Stacy. She'd have to keep that ploy in mind. Once Janice hit the SEND button, the screen returned to a page with the faces and vital statistics of 25 other men. Janice scrolled down the list and, not finding any of the photos to her liking, clicked to the next page of 25 profiles. And the next. And the next.

Stacy asked, "Who are all these men?"

"After you fill out a profile of yourself and the kind of man you're looking for, the match.com software program supplies you with a list of men who meet your criteria. I requested white men, age forty-five to sixty, making at least a hundred thousand, who live within five miles of my zip code."

"And how many men match your criteria?"

"Let's see, it changes every day," she said. Janice clicked on the MY MATCHES button. In a blink, the screen returned to the first set of profiles and pictures. At the top of the list, Janice read the total number.

"Hmm, yesterday it was more. Today, one hundred fifty-four."

"One hundred and fifty-four?" repeated Stacy. The number seemed huge. "One hundred and fifty-four rich white guys in your age group within five miles of your zip code are looking for dates?"

Janice said, "You should try it, Stacy. There is some rejection and upset, though. I've sent out about twenty e-mails this week, and have only heard back from five men. And none of them are free this weekend. I'm running out of time. If I can't set something up very soon, I'll break my streak."

Stacy put her hand on Janice's birdlike shoulder. She desperately wanted to tell her to forget about the streak. The streak was making her miserable. The streak was what kept Janice from taking her time, meeting men the organic way, letting something flow naturally out of mutual attraction and shared interest. The streak was what made Janice desperate and cloying, it had turned off countless men.

Reading Stacy's thoughts, Janice said, "I know the streak seems ridiculous and counterproductive, but we all have what we have. Or don't have, in your case."

"At last count, you're as dateless as I am, Janice," said Stacy. She didn't care if she'd make a political blunder. She was that tired. And grumpy. Stacy's avoidance might be a way to protect oneself; Janice's frenetic dating was another.

"I'm in a pissy mood," Stacy said. "That's my half-assed apology."

"And this is my half-assed acceptance," said Janice, patting Stacy on her cheek. Janice logged off match.com, stood and reminded Stacy of about five million tasks that needed to be completed in the next 15 minutes, but no pressure, since she knew how sensitive and overloaded Stacy had been lately.

Alone again, Stacy took her rightful place at the seat of command. The computer screen was still connected to the Internet via a super-speed DSL line; Stacy's screen remained on match.com's homepage. She had to admit, she was curious. In Janice's target group, there were 154 available, eager men. Assuming, as Stacy did, that the dating pool shrinks as one ages, and that fewer older people were Internet friendly, she had to wonder how many people in their 30s used match.com. Dating sites were a natural cross-promotion for thongs.com. Hundreds, if not thousands, of women searching for love and passion needed sexy lingerie. It was too easy: Subscribe to match.com, and get a discount on a matching bra-and-panty set.

Out of professional obligation (if she were to take the idea to Fiona, she had to do the proper research first), Stacy decided to create a profile for herself. And, okay, on a personal level, if she took the risk and put herself out there (albeit anonymously), she couldn't possibly be accused of hiding from life. Plus, she was curious to see just how many men met her criteria.

Although Stacy was an experienced web marketer, she was clueless about advertising for herself. Luckily, the first steps to creating a profile were simple. Just fill in the blanks. She could handle that much. Starting with:

SCREEN NAME: Fluffy

AGE: 29 (Why not shave off a few years?)

MARITAL STATUS: Never married

LOCATION: New York, NY

HEIGHT: 5'5"

BODY TYPE: Slim/Slender (The other choices were "athletic," "average," "a few extra pounds," "large," "disabled" and "any." Technically, according to dress size and weight charts, Stacy was closer to "average" than "slender," but why not shave off a few pounds?)

ETHNICITY: White

EDUCATION: Bachelor's degree

RELIGION: Jewish

OCCUPATION: Entrepreneur

INCOME: $150,000+

SMOKER: No

DRINKER: Socially

HAVE CHILDREN?: No

WANT CHILDREN?: Undecided (Stacy did want children, but men might think of her as a baby-lusting career woman who'd waited too long to plan for a family and was therefore obsessed with finding a potential father, which she wasn't. At least, not presently.)

For the profile text, Stacy composed this message:

"I'm an attractive, successful woman in New York City. I am physically active, play dozens of sports, including tennis, cycling, and running (completed my first marathon last year). I look great in jeans and sneakers, but I am smashing in ball gowns, too. I dress up often for charity benefits, movie openings, and society galas. I live in a glorious loft, newly renovated—Viking stove and SubZero fridge—in a great neighborhood. I enjoy all art, compose poetry, paint with oils, play the flute, have written several screenplays (one in turnaround), read avidly, love *Beowulf* as well as pulpy crime and shopping novels. I work hard at my hugely successful Internet company. And I play hard. I am sexually ravenous, a multiple orgasmatronic vapor of lust and technique. I have studied the *Kama Sutra*, can sing the *Song of Solomon* and will quote verse from *Leaves of Grass*. Professors Masters, Johnson, and Kinsey are personal friends of mine. We have lunch. We have orgies. I own thousands of pieces of lingerie and dozens of pairs of stiletto heels. When I'm not working or playing (hard; I just love the sound of that word), I enjoy eating, sleeping, and breathing air in and out of my lungs."

Only about ten words in the text were true. This mattered not. Stacy decided to bait and switch: Get them in the door, bullshit her way out of lying later. After reading and editing her profile several times, Stacy realized that she'd perfectly and truthfully described someone she actually knew. Her boss, Fiona Chardonnay, was a marathon-running, gala-attending, flute-playing, sexually ravenous, *Beowulf*-reading size four with a TriBeca loft. Could this mean that Fiona was the woman Stacy wanted to be? Or that Stacy assumed Fiona was every man's sexual fantasy (Fiona did see a lot of action, after all)?

Avoiding that headache of contemplation, Stacy forged ahead and wrote the profile of her ideal date:

"I'm not going to insist that any man be all things—handsome, rich, stylish, young, and athletic. Those are nice qualities, to be sure, but chemistry, the great intangible, can make ugly men sexy, the penniless wealthy, dorks fashionable, geezers spry, and lummoxes graceful. My feeling on attraction: I'll know it when I see it. And once I've seen a man I'm attracted to, I can't help myself from falling completely under his power. Ugly poor dork geezer lummoxes should please send photos—you can never tell when lightning will strike."

She read it over, wavering a bit on casting so wide a net. Surely, she should discourage the geezers . . . No, she'd take all comers on the first pass.

The last step was to click appropriate buttons for her ideal match (age, location, status, income, etc.). Stacy rushed through this process in seconds. She was able to achieve such speed by clicking "any" in every box. Once she'd finished, Stacy submitted her profile and matching criteria. She would be able to log in and see her eligible matches in an hour or two. Responses to her ad would be sent to match.com and forwarded to her AOL address to guarantee anonymity. She could reply to those e-mails for free, or for the small fee of $25 for a month, she could cruise the male profiles herself (as Janice did), and send solicitations to the men of her liking.

Sitting back in her chair, Stacy exhaled down to the last molecule of oxygen in her lungs and prayed that she hadn't made a terrible error in judgment. She could see how easily one could be drawn in by the simplicity and convenience of Internet dating. It was so much less stressful than approaching someone face-to-face (back to that "taking a risk" business). In cyberspace, rejections were theoretical. One couldn't possibly take them personally. But here on land, daters were at sea. Any rebuff could sink a ship. Stacy knew the pain. She'd been on a regular diet of dismissal for days.

A knock on her door frame. Taylor Perry inserted her tousle-haired blonde head into Stacy's office.

"Lunch?" asked Taylor.

"Today?"

"Are you swamped?"

Quicksanded. "Not at all. Noonish?"

"Oneish?"

"Perfect," said Stacy.

Now this. She placed a call to Charlie to ask him about the de-revirginating validity of a lesbian fling. Then she got to work, and kept at it for several long hours.

Chapter Eight

Wednesday, lunch

$\mathcal{T}$wo women, both lovely and young, shared a pizza at the neo-Neapolitan restaurant, Cosa Nostra, located in the MetLife building, in front of giant windows facing 44th Street. Their shoulders touched as they ate; hands busy underneath the table. Stacy, as vivid of the imagination as she was pink of cheek, would have never pictured herself in this scene. Yet here she was.

The pair sat on the same side of a booth ("theater seating," Taylor said before scooting in next to Stacy, trapping her on the inside). When they'd ordered the pizza to share, the waiter (who would be receiving a very small tip) said, "That's cozy," and licked his chops. Taylor wanted the Vesuvius (olives, capers, and anchovies). Stacy wasn't surprised. She took Taylor for a savory woman—salty, not sweet.

Taylor wore one of the newest innovations from the Gap: the braless tank top. Stretchy material was sewn into the inside of the garment, a built-in support system. Considering Taylor's voluminous flesh and her dire supportive needs, the tank failed to prevent flop. Not that Taylor knew or cared. Her breasts—and her spirit—could roam the open prairie. Her wild blonde hair was down over her neck and shoulders despite the heat—no ponytails for her. Taylor wouldn't restrain any part of herself, and she flung around her mane and bosom with the stomping bravura of a prize mare. Nay (or, rather, neigh), a stallion.

Since Stacy wanted to be seduced, she was entranced by Taylor's riot of hair and skin. Contrarily, Stacy had always maintained a pathologically neat personal appearance, planning outfits, carefully ironing, mending hems and buttons. Her apartment, though, had a relaxed "springtime in Baghdad" decorating style. She didn't obsess too much about the untidiness (to say the least) of her dwelling. Hardly anyone saw it.

"You have a drop of tomato sauce on your chin," Taylor informed Stacy. Without asking permission, Taylor wiped away the red drop with her pinkie. She next inserted said finger into Stacy's mouth. As she withdrew it, Taylor traced Stacy's lips, and then deposited her pinkie between her own.

"Have I mentioned today that I like you?" asked Taylor for the third or fourth time that hour.

The lunch, Stacy knew going in (had hoped), was not at all business. Almost immediately, just after they'd taken seats in the booth, Taylor reached under the table to lift the red hem of Stacy's pink skirt and (hello) drop a hand on her bare thigh. If a man had done that, Stacy might have bristled, as if the gentle-man were claiming ownership of a property that wasn't for sale. But Taylor's hand was well manicured and soft. By no means innocent, the contact was, however, non-threatening. No migrating crotch-bound stroking or squeezing. Just a nice imprint in the shape of a woman's hand, warming her leg against the bite of high-impact air-conditioning. This lesbian thing, thought Stacy, was neither scary nor revolting. She took a sip of bubbling Pellegrino and dipped a pinch of bread in a dish of olive oil.

Stacy had confirmation from Charlie that a lesbian encounter would certainly qualify as a de-revirginating event. "But there has to be genital-on-genital contact, or reciprocal oral-genital contact. It's not enough to let her go down on you," he'd said earlier.

"Are you reading this out of the celibacy hand-book?" she asked. "Genital-on-genital? How would that work?"

"Scissored legs."

"You've seen this? I haven't read any of your pornography reviews on flick.com."

"We can work it this way," he said. "Just do what-ever you want with Taylor, and then report back to me. No detail is too small. You'll have to give me some ad-vance notice. I'll want to have my tape recorder ready for the call."

Stacy had spent some pre-lunch minutes making lists. On the plus side, a lesbian experience would be solid seduction material for future dates with men; she needn't worry about an unwanted pregnancy; a romantic entanglement was out of the question; she was always interested in trying new and different things. Charlie gave her a little pep talk à la Bela Karolyi ("You can do it!"). She didn't need the prodding though. Stacy had had some spicy dreams about women. But there was one undeniable minus. Stacy might be able to have sex with Taylor, but could she face her ever after in the office? Would Taylor pressure her to have lunch at the Y every day? Might that get sticky? Fiona and Janice would notice something had changed between their two most senior employees, and the last thing Stacy needed was more scrutiny from The Women.

Regarding libidinous matters, especially in her dire situation at present, Stacy resolved to stop thinking and start doing. Best to let the juices flow and mop up the mess later. Now that they were sitting close together at lunch, finger sucking and thigh touching, the whole affair seemed like a grand idea. The future weirdness could be forgotten for the next hour.

And then Taylor said, "I'm leaving thongs.com."

Stacy blinked. "When?" she asked. So much for future weirdness.

"Friday is my last day. I got a job offer from pets.com to reproduce the site. No offense to you—you're amazing—but I don't think thongs.com will last the year. I posted my resume on monster.com a few weeks ago, and I got calls from garden.com, kosmo.com, urban fetch and CDNOW. Pets.com is the safest bet. Did you notice that the sock puppet's collar is a man's watch? I love that."

Stacy's initial reaction to the news: relief (the sex would be that much easier). Second reaction: disbelief. She was surprised Taylor had so little faith in Fiona's ability to stay afloat. Third reaction: rank jealousy. Stacy hadn't gotten calls from anyone. Non-tech people were disposable. Taylor's talents, making all the moving parts on a webpage fit, encoding the programs, troubleshooting. These were valuable skills. What skills could Stacy list on monster.com? That in three minutes flat, she could invent fifty *hotcha* names for faux satin G-strings? No one would want her. Perhaps that explained her fealty to thongs.com in a job-hopping industry.

In her time at thongs.com, Stacy had seen 42 staffers come and go. She knew the exact number because she made hash marks on the wall of her office to keep track of the turnovers. Most of the fly-by employees stayed less than a month before quitting or getting a better job. Some lasted just a week. She'd read in *Fast Company* that the average length of employment at a dot-com startup was three to six months.

The typical trajectory went something like this: Land an Internet job with fancy yet dubious title (Stacy's was "vice president in charge of merchandising and marketing"), drool over pre-IPO options/benefits package, slave from 8 A.M. to midnight six days a week plus a couple hours of catch-up on Sunday from home working on a company-distributed laptop. Form a superficial attachment to one's colleagues that feels deep (spending that much time with anyone will lead to a false sense of intimacy). The attachment quickly turns to disgust (spending that much time with anyone will get on one's nerves). Employee unity is further eroded by competition to land the next fancy yet dubious-sounding job, and a feeling of futility when the stock price slips. Bosses tend to be megalomaniacs. Everyone is ambitious, but no one is secure. The Internet is an every-geek-for-herself world.

At the three-month mark, the employee's days are numbered (whether s/he knows it or not). Departure Scenario #1: Employee suffers from a sudden work-related ailment (carpal tunnel syndrome, sick-office syndrome, etc.) forcing him or her to take time off. Departure Scenario #2: Employee's good work is noticed by a larger or hotter dot com. Phone calls are made, more options with larger salaries are dangled, jobs jumped. Departure Scenario #3: Employee is terrorized by the tyrannical and overzealous boss of the dot com, a man or woman who has put up his or her own money as well as huge chunks from banks and private investors (everyone s/he knows, including family, friends and people s/he met last night at a Silicon Alley party in a SoHo gallery space). The boss believes that the employee's gentle joking about bankruptcy makes him or her a saboteur. And saboteurs must be expunged.

At thongs.com, the bulk of former employees had been expunged. Only Janice, Fiona, Taylor, and Stacy had been there since the inception. Stacy's mother, in her gentle way of asking about her daughter's dating life, routinely asked, "Don't you meet a lot of people at work?" Yes, Stacy met tons of people. But as soon as someone walked in the door, the newbie began plotting his or her next job hop. No one made a real effort to get to know Stacy. She was viewed as a Fiona loyalist, which rendered her useless for networking. Stacy feared the hash-mark people were right. She didn't have the guts to job hop. Stacy would go down with the ship (or should she say *slip*).

Before Stacy could properly express contrition and cheer over Taylor's imminent departure (her usual speech, "I have the utmost respect and admiration for you. I wish we'd gotten a chance to get to know each other better. Best of luck to you at _____ (fill in the blank) dot com. I'll be sorry to see you go," didn't apply to this situation), Taylor said, "I can get you in."

"In where?"

"At pets.com. I can get you a job."

Stacy's heart fluttered. She'd fantasized about leaving thongs.com nearly every hour for over a year. But if she left, she'd lose out on the 10,000 additional stock options that were promised to her after the New Year. Most of her fantasies centered on that date. She'd get her paperwork squared, and then march into Fiona's office, announce that she was cashing out and resigning. She'd retire for a year, and then, after getting the 3,000 hours of sleep she so desperately needed, she'd go back to public radio. Could she throw away her fantasy for a sock puppet? Besides which, if she were to go with Taylor to pets.com on Monday, she couldn't very well screw her today.

"Can I think about it?" she asked. Stacy didn't want to shatter every window of opportunity. There was always the chance that sex with Taylor could turn her into a full-time lesbian. She might *want* to be Taylor's bitch.

The buxom blonde said, "Take a risk."

The hand again. Upper thigh now. Stacy popped a crust of pizza into her mouth and placed her own hand on top of Taylor's.

"If we kiss, will they throw us out?" Stacy asked, not studied in lesbian PDA etiquette.

Taylor smiled. Her cheeks were spotty and red with what Stacy assumed was the flush of excitement (or prickly heat). "My apartment is on Fiftieth and Lex." Only six blocks away.

The check settled, Pellegrino drained, the pair walked quickly and silently to Taylor's apartment. The blonde, one ropy leg out the door of thongs.com, was beyond caring if her work for the day went undone. Stacy couldn't ignore the itch of responsibility. Taylor said, "This is it." Too late to turn around. Stacy would attend to other itches first.

The building was one of those charmless vertical egg cartons built in the 1970s. Stacy had always hated this style of architecture, considering it the brick-and-mortar equivalent of a peanut butter sandwich (sustenance you'd force down when you couldn't get your hands on something tastier). But the utilitarian facade seemed to fit Taylor's personality. She had no compunction about living in an apartment with white walls and box-shaped rooms. Nor did she mind the lecherous, paunchy, middle-aged doorman who tipped his silly hat and put his hand on Taylor's lower back as he showed them to the elevator. Stacy wondered if the doorman touched her every time she came and went. Taylor didn't appear to mind, but Stacy was disgusted on her behalf.

The apartment itself was sterile and minimalistic. She surveyed the space, standing next to Taylor in the middle of her boringly immaculate white living room. Taylor was Stacy's reverse: disheveled self, meticulous living space. Stacy had no idea if that spoke to her character or psychosis. She'd have to ask her mother, the decorator who'd minored in psychology at Smith College in the 1960s. It occurred to Stacy for the first time that her own mother might have had a post-adolescent lesbian experience at Smith way back when. She pushed that thought out of her head easily enough when Taylor's arm encircled Stacy's waist and she began licking the side of her neck.

"I can feel your pulse against my tongue," Taylor said.

Oh, yes, Stacy's jugular was throbbing with such violence, she feared her ears might pop. The touch of a woman's mouth on her skin was both foreign and familiar (another disquieting mommy moment, remembering scents and softness). And sexy. Surprisingly so.

Stacy found herself nervous and twitchy with the electric shock of the illicit, the heretofore unexplored, the unfurled turf, this strange land of girls.

Stacy found Taylor's lips and the women kissed. Unlike the mauling of Tom Strumph or the homey smack of Brian Gourde, smooching Taylor was sweetly hypnotic. It reminded Stacy of sharing a dessert. Taylor's lips were puffy, coated in gloss that made the kiss as slippery and bouncy as flan on a teaspoon. The hint of flavor—could be vanilla—tickled Stacy's nose and taste buds.

Peeling away, the smeared waxy residue of gloss on her lips, Taylor cupped Stacy's left breast with both hands. She massaged it with care, as if it might leak when pressed too hard. Most men will grab the breast as if it weren't actually attached to the body, batting it around, squeeze until flesh bulged between open fingers, pinch the nipples like pencil erasers. Stacy much preferred Taylor's tenderness, and would instruct her next boyfriend (whomever that might be) thusly. A bit fearfully, Stacy reached out with both of her hands to reciprocate. Taylor's breast was heavy and fluid in Stacy's palms, like a water balloon. She tried a gentle massage, but it was too unwieldy (despite the Lycra encasement). Stacy attempted kneading the gland, and that seemed to please Taylor. She moaned. The sound distracted Stacy. When she was with a man, Stacy made all kinds of noises, and loved to hear the same from the guy. Taylor's vocalizations seemed out of place, inappropriate and disturbingly intimate. Sex with a woman,

Stacy reasoned, was inherently more personal than sex with a man because, ultimately, it was like making love to yourself.

Although Stacy registered erotic pleasure to receive the free breast exam, she was unmoved by the giving. Again with the comparisons (couldn't be helped): When Stacy was with a man, her biggest turn-on was what she did to him (and his response). Not so here. Stacy's future as a lesbian was in jeopardy. She had to stop comparing and stay focused.

Taylor seemed to sense Stacy's mental wanderings and attempted to stop them by descending to her knees. Taylor kissed Stacy's blouse on the way down. Stacy couldn't suppress silent panic over makeup stains on her fine fabrics (yet another universe of worldly distractions—did men actively worry about smudges and smears? She'd have to ask Charlie). She snapped back to the present quickly enough when Taylor nuzzled Stacy's crotch, lifted her skirt, and pulled down her panties.

She nearly stepped away. Instead, she began playing with Taylor's hair and thinking about Tony McGuinty. She wasn't quite sure what she'd think about when it was her turn to get on her knees, but she'd deal with that then.

Tony, his lovely muscular body, his arms around her legs, his hands on her ass, his mouth and tongue against her . . . the rush of arousal seized her, the familiar building, the sensation she'd felt several thousand times and would feel a million more before it ever got dull. It was close. Any moment now, Stacy would receive a standing O. A great, big, huge one. Any second. Any nanosecond. The pressure grew, expanded.

And then it stopped. The pressure ceased, leaving Stacy's heart flying wildly in her chest, her legs shaking from being so close. What the fuck happened? Stacy looked down to see Taylor sitting Indian style on the floor, her head in her hands. Dear God—Stacy felt a cold-water chill—was Taylor crying? Anything but that.

Dizzy, her blood flow diverted from her brain, Stacy sat on the hardwood floor next to Taylor. Her colleague *was* crying. Stacy put her arm around Taylor's shoulder and said, "What's wrong?"

"Who is Tony?" she asked.

Oh. Shit.

"I go down on you, and you're thinking of someone named Tony. I'm not even gay!" Taylor said weepily.

"You're not gay?" Stacy asked, aghast.

"I've never been with a woman before. But I like you. And you're beautiful. I've always known you're a lesbian, so I thought I could seduce you into my life. Start sexually, and then become friends. Or maybe I'd be gay just for you."

"You think I'm gay?"

"And then you called out the name Tony. I'm eating pussy for the first time in my life—and it's not the most pleasurable thing I've done, although I do like your bikini wax—and you call out someone else's name. Who is she?" Taylor's tear-trailed cheeks glistened, her eyes swimming with shame. This wasn't just a sexy romp for her. Taylor actually cared, and now her feelings were hurt. Stacy had inflicted the pain unwittingly, assuming that her little adventure would be emotionally inert.

Stacy smiled beneficently (she hoped), and said, "Tony—Antonia—is my ex-girlfriend. We broke up not long ago, and I admit, I'm still a little in love with her. I guess it's too soon to get into another relationship. I'm terribly sorry that I misled you. I . . . I have the utmost respect and admiration for you. I wish we'd gotten a chance to get to know each other better. Best of luck to you at pets.com. I'll be sorry to see you go."

Taylor nodded and hiccuped. Stacy kissed her on each cheek and stood. "I'll tell Fiona you have food poisoning," she volunteered. After righting her panties and skirt, Stacy dashed for the door. The leering doorman barely looked at her as she rushed out onto the street (clearly, he was a tit man). She scurried back to the office, wishing she could get a tail between her legs.

Chapter Nine

Wednesday, late afternoon

By the time Stacy returned to work, she was already late for a VIM (very important meeting) she knew nothing about. Apparently, there'd been an urgent e-mail memo. She found out when she discovered Janice in her small (now suffocating) office, writing a furious note in all caps with red ink ("WHERE THE FUCK . . ."). A more appropriate message for Stacy would have been, "Where's the fuck?"

"I don't know how I missed the e-mail," said Stacy.

Janice said, "If I'd taken a two-hour lunch in the middle of the most crucial work week in the company's history, I might have missed it, too."

"I had to take Taylor home. She was stricken by cramps during lunch. I've never seen anyone in such paralytic pain. I had to carry her, her arms over my shoulders while I dragged her body weight on my back. I'm exhausted. But I do feel some pride in being a friend in need."

"You'll be a friend in need of a job if you don't get

yourself to the Turtle in thirty seconds," Janice threatened as she huffed toward the conference room. This must be serious, thought Stacy. Janice was not the whip cracker. That was Fiona's favorite occupation (along with Botox and collagen injections).

Stacy dropped her bag, grabbed her notepad, and walked double time to the conference room. When she entered the large (also suffocating) room, Fiona's gaze hit her like a baseball bat. Avoiding those eyes, she muttered an apology and sat down.

"Hope it wasn't too inconvenient for you to show up, Stacy," said Fiona acidly. She was dragon-lady perfection today in a black leather dress. In July. Fiona always bragged that she never felt the heat (having spent her five previous afterlives in hell, Stacy reasoned). "You know Stanley, right?" Fiona gestured toward the man at the head of the Turtle.

Stacy did indeed know Stanley Bombicci. They'd met several months ago at a Silicon Alley party for his company, smut.com, an interactive porn site (formerly, Stanley had been a corporate executive for the New York Giants). He was 35, tall, with a chest the size of a Toyota. He smelled of Old Spice and new millions. At the smut.com party, Stanley had made a short speech about dot comedy and tragedy. He predicted that the only websites to survive the first on-line ice age would be idinosaurs (AOL, Amazon, Yahoo!), or URLs with boobs. He was probably right. When he'd been introduced to Stacy by Fiona (who'd made a shameless play for him, declaring within earshot of dozens that she'd "appeared in an adult film ten years ago, when I was in my twenties" —a statement that raised many eyebrows, mainly because few believed that ten years ago she was in her 30s), Stanley looked closely at Stacy and said, "Only one way to tell if you're a real redhead."

"Ask my colorist?" said Stacy, attempting to deflect some crass comment about her collar and her cuff. Fortunately, he was distracted by a venture capitalist from Credit Suisse and ignored her for the rest of the night.

He hadn't forgotten about her, though. Over the next few days, Stanley had deluged her with calls, e-mails. She convinced herself that it was about time she did some networking. Stanley was connected (in the Italian sense, she'd heard whispered), but certainly with hordes of Internet CEOs. She agreed to meet him for coffee. For the first 15 of their 16 minutes together, he'd delivered self-congratulatory monologues to her breasts along the lines of, "Yeah, I started my first business from my college dorm room at Harvard when I was twenty years old, selling naked pictures of grad students. One or two nights with me, these hot grad students— very hot, the sexiest women at Harvard, and believe me, sexy bombshell-type women at Harvard were tough to find—where was I? Oh, yeah, these women would do anything I wanted. Pose nude, sign a model release. Agree to blow me at the statue of John Harvard in the middle of Harvard Square."

"Sounds like a rich and rewarding experience, Stanley," said Stacy.

"I made buckets of cash," he said, nodding. "The

beauty of it was that these girls were real. My customers could see them walking around campus. At Harvard. That's much better spank material than *Penthouse* for a bunch of horny dorks who couldn't get tail on a bunny farm. They were nerds, but smart, my classmates. I was challenged intellectually at Harvard, and I need that kind of stimulation. And sexual stimulation. All the time. Like right now. Looking at you. I'd love to reach under your shirt and . . ."

"Where did you say you went to school?" she asked.

Four months later, Stacy had reluctantly included Stanley on her To Do list of candidates for Sex Emergency Week. And here he appeared, as if by magic, at the head of the Turtle. Was it fate? she wondered.

"It's good to see you, Stanley," she said, smiling warmly.

"Great to see you, too," he said to her breasts.

Fiona called the meeting to order and the group of twelve producers, product managers and marketers turned their horn-rimmed glasses and asymmetrical bangs toward Fiona. "Agenda: finalize terms," she said. "Thongs.com and smut.com are forming a merchandising partnership. We will supply unlimited lingerie for Stanley's models and links to his site. In exchange, he will give us free banner advertising, a click-through on each menu, a plug on the home page, and a featured item of the day on the products page."

"We're getting in bed with a porn site?" asked Stacy, dumbfounded (had this information been in the memo?). An "intellectual erotica" site, sure. A match-making site, even better. But a URL that unapologetically called itself the "best wank material on the web"? Surely, their partnership was counterproductive. Thongs.com had been pushing the mass-market cart from the beginning. The idea was to differentiate itself from the upscale lingerie retailers on the Internet. Hitching thongs.com with a porn site would send their cart careening down-market, downhill, down the toilet.

"I say this with the deepest respect for Stanley's business acumen," said Stacy, "but isn't smut.com kind of smutty?"

"I've addressed and dismissed your concern," said Fiona. "We can be classy and sleazy at the same time. This isn't hard to pull off. Just look at me." The room full of people looked at their fingernails. "Our burn rate is two hundred thousand dollars a month. We need more traffic. Smut.com gets five million unique hits a day. We should thank Stanley for choosing us to be one of his partners. And he's generously offered to give us a signing balloon loan in exchange for one million shares of company stock at four dollars per share." The current stock price was $7 per share (the 52-week high was $67).

The loan sounded like a fool's bargain, even to Stacy's non-fiscally sensitive ears. Was thongs.com that desperate for cash? It had to be an offer Fiona couldn't refuse. Stacy could see her rationalizations at play. Thongs.com would be in good company. Stanley already had partnership/cross-promotional deals with at least 20 websites, including a $1,000,000 arrangement with AOL (keyword: "smut"), an automatic promotional window when anyone bought "adult literature" at Amazon, and another instant prompt when any male (aged 18 to 70) registered with Yahoo shopping. A partnership with the "personal touch" king of Internet porn might bring in more traffic. But how much would teenage wankers spend on panties? Besides which, the idea of a thongs.com logo emblazoned across the barely covered asses of models who lounge on daybeds and masturbate on demand to a disco beat for $1 per minute was embarrassing. It was just one more reason to get out of this job.

Come January, I'll take the money and run for the hills, Stacy vowed.

Stanley, sensing acquiescence from every woman at the table, put his hands behind his head, fanning his pecs like a condor, and said, "Thanks for the declaration of love, Fiona. But we're not settled just yet. A couple things before we sign. The models might use the merchandise in an obscene fashion. This a problem?"

Fiona shook her head.

"And I want to personally approve any stock offerings, options, transfers, and loans made by this company in perpetuity."

Janice and Fiona looked at each other and frowned. This was news. Could it mean that Stanley planned to dismantle the options ladder? Was this a sell-out deal? Couldn't be. Each of The Women nodded, staring right into the other's face, giving away none of her feelings (but, possibly, a lot of the store).

"One more thing," said Stanley. "This won't go down, especially not the loan, unless Stacy Temple has dinner with me tonight."

Stacy, face aflame, gasped. Fiona said, "That would fall under the *quid pro quo* statute of sexual harassment law, Stanley."

"I suppose you could convince a judge to see it that way," he agreed.

"Very well, then," said Fiona. "Stacy, you're having dinner with Stanley. And do whatever he wants or you're fired."

Stanley suggested Aromantique, a cozy French spot a few blocks away. Stacy agreed, and went back to work for a few hours while Stanley and Fiona toasted each other in her office. At around six, Stacy and Stanley walked to the restaurant. He didn't seem drunk, despite his afternoon champagne. In fact, he seemed stone-cold sober. The maitre d' greeted them at the door of the restaurant with kisses, and directed them to a formally set table—bottle of wine, a glorious bouquet of Casablanca lilies, a basket of warm bread.

"This is lovely," said Stacy, placing the napkin in her lap. Across the table, Stanley looked pleased and subdued. Perhaps she had been wrong about him. Especially now that she was inclined to give any potential de-revirginator the benefit of the doubt, she gave it to Stanley. The whole porn impresario thing, she decided, it was just a business persona. The braggadocio about his Harvard days, that was coming from a deeply insecure place. His ruthless climb to the top of his profession, this had made him a lonely, sad man desperately in need of human connection and, simply, a friendly face across a table, some benign conversation. And the effort he'd gone to tonight, the table, the flowers, the "everything has been arranged" from the maitre d'—Stacy was flattered. She wasn't sure about his plans for thongs.com, but, from where she sat, candlelight playing across Stanley's fine nose and chin, Stacy was ready to be taken over. For one night. She couldn't see herself long term with a pornmeister. She couldn't see herself in the morning with him (must go to his place so she could sneak out after he fell asleep, she thought).

She went with a direct opening statement, saying, "Before we begin, you should know the truth. I'm in a bit of a pickle. In four days . . ."

He interrupted her. "Isn't it the other way around?" he asked. "You need a bit of a pickle in you. Fiona told me that you're trolling for tube steak. And I'm available. Maybe."

"Fiona said . . . ?" Stacy asked.

"She reads your e-mail," he explained. Stacy and Charlie had been corresponding copiously about her travails.

"I'm sure Fiona has been thoroughly entertained," said Stacy. That *bitch*! At least Stacy wouldn't have to spell out her predicament to Stanley. He knew it already. And he was going to help. But what had he just said? "Did I hear 'maybe'?"

"Start with an apology," he said. "Last time we went out, you made some belittling crack, got up and left me alone at Café Dante midway through a double espresso. That's only six ounces of fluid. It doesn't take too much of your time to sit with a man and wait until he's finished a six-ounce drink. You were rude, Stacy. I was embarrassed. The *barista* gave me a second double on the house because he pitied me. You hurt my feelings. And I really like you. You're smart; you've got great tits. If you want a piece of me, you have to apologize for the way you treated me."

"I'm sorry, Stanley," she said. "I wasn't aware that you . . . I didn't know you had feelings to hurt."

He seemed satisfied, and said, "Relief is washing over me."

"I'm so glad."

"We can make a fresh start now."

"Why don't we?"

"Let's toast."

They toasted and drank. Stacy sipped prettily. Stanley gulped down the entire glass of Ravelwood Merlot, seemingly without tasting a drop. Good thing it cost $40 a bottle. Wouldn't want to spend less on wine without tasting it.

"You must be thirsty," she said.

"Okay, down to business," he said, putting his glass down. The sommelier shuffled over to refill his glass and departed. "I've been thinking about meeting you like this for months. I wanted the setting, the wine, the food, all of it, to be perfect. I have a very clear vision of this night, and I want to stick to the script as much as possible."

She nodded apprehensively. "Why don't you tell me how you'd like the evening to go and we'll see if we can approximate it." Stacy was nothing if not accommodating.

He smiled smartly. "No, you misunderstand me. I have practiced this night in my head hundreds of times. I want it to go *exactly* as I've imagined it. We're up to page two."

Reaching across the table, Stanley handed Stacy a thin manuscript with a laminated cover. The top sheet read "My Date with Stacy." Almost too afraid to look, she turned to the first page and read. Right there, in 12-point Geneva, was an exact description of the two of them entering this very restaurant, sitting at this very table, Casablanca lilies, warm bread, Ravelwood. The short bracketed paragraph that read: "Stanley explains how the night will unfold, and Stacy complies happily. She is radiant with purpose, knowing that she will fulfill the enduring hopes Stanley has harbored about her since she wounded him so deeply the last time they met. Jumping at her chance to set things right, Stacy agrees to play her part in his fantasy, TO THE LETTER."

She turned the page. It was a script, with her lines highlighted in yellow. She read her first line to herself, and then looked at Stanley, astonished.

He smiled and whispered, "It's just a game."

She put the manuscript down on her plate. "I want

a guarantee that my stock options won't be affected by the partnership with smut.com." Stanley agreed readily.

Not yet registering Stanley's potentially dangerous obsession, and how stepping into the role he'd written for her might take his fixation to new heights, Stacy opened the scene. Reading with emotion (*Hmm, this might be kind of fun,* she thought), Stacy began: "I can't believe I'm on a date with you, Stanley Bombicci. You are the handsomest, richest, most impressive man I've ever met—or ever will meet. I can't believe how lucky I am to be seen with you."

Stanley didn't need a script. His part was committed to memory. "How right you are, Stacy," he said. "But don't put yourself down. You are a beautiful woman, and I want to make you happy."

"The only way you can make me happy," read Stacy, "is by letting me make you happy. I'll do anything you want. Just ask."

"Anything?" he asked.

"Oh, yes, Stanley, I beg you to make sick and twisted sexual demands of me. Only then will I find joy and satisfaction in life." She looked up from the page. "I don't actually have to *do* anything, right?"

"You're deviating from the script," he admonished.

She read, "Tonight, with you, I want to do something that I've never done before."

"What's that, Stacy?" he asked.

She was supposed to say, "anal sex," but Stacy had done that a couple times with Brian. She asked, "Does it matter if the script is factually inaccurate?"

"Just read it, please."

"I'm not going to have anal sex with you," she said.

"You don't have to. I just want you to offer."

"I'd rather not ask for something I don't want."

Stanley drained another glass of wine. The sommelier refilled it and made tracks. "Will you please just read the script?" begged Stanley.

"A great actor can improvise. Maybe I could dangle some other enticement. I've never had a threesome. Or—I know this will surprise you, but I've never done it outdoors. Not quite sure how I've missed doing something so elemental in the cannon of sexual experience, but the idea of sand or dirt or bugs? Ecch."

Stanley looked like he was about to cry. "Let's pick up on line twenty-four of page three."

She scanned down to the designated spot. "Okay," she said. "I say, 'I want to feel your ramrod-hard oak trunk crammed inside my tight and squishy' . . . *Squishy?* Who would describe their own ass as squishy? Hmmmm, I'm going to skip ahead to this part, line thirteen on page five."

"But you're bypassing the paragraph that starts, 'Moisten my rim' at the bottom of page four. I love that paragraph."

"Oh, I can't read the word 'moisten' and then eat dinner. I'm sure you can grant me some small omissions," said Stacy.

"This isn't going the way—"

"I like this part, about how I long to 'let you fuck my mouth until it overflows with the jism of the gods.'

Let's keep that in. Although I question the use of the word 'gods.' Am I to be orally raped by more than one godlike person, or just you? And if it's just you, it should be 'jism of a god'—the singular. Meaning you, with all your divine ejaculations. It's very Roman, actually, with 'gods,' though."

Stanley said, "I like it the way I've written it. You aren't getting the idea of a script, Stacy. One line leads to the next. You can't just pull out a particular line and read it solo. It doesn't flow. The words sound clunky."

"You said it, not me." She sampled her wine. "Can we order soon? I think I could do it from the top, *with feeling*, if I weren't so hungry. As you know, I am famished"— Stacy quickly flipped through the script pages and then stopped to read a line from page 7—" 'famished for your meat in every orifice of my body.' " She giggled demurely. "But before we get to that, I'd love to try the coque au vin."

In a flash of cufflinks, Stanley grabbed the manuscript out of Stacy's hands. "You've completely killed the romance of the moment! None of it will sound sincere now. When I wrote this, I meant it from the heart. These are words of love, Stacy, and you've sullied them."

" 'Slither my tongue around your man root' are words of love?" she asked, genuinely curious.

He answered by throwing his wine in Stacy's face and screaming, "You've ruined everything!" as he ran out of the restaurant.

While sopping up the mess, Stacy was grateful that

the wine stains were on the same blouse as Taylor's makeup smears (just one article of clothing sacrificed for two botched sexual pursuits). She could not have offended Stanley more; writing was the greatest vanity of all. Stacy did feel relieved that she would not be going home with a pervert. Disappointed, also. But not too.

Chapter Ten

Wednesday night

The coque au vin was delicious. For an appetizer, she'd had the terrine, and, for dessert, a soufflé. As part of his elaborate arrangements, Stanley had left his credit card imprint with the maitre d'. A lovely man, very *grandpere*-like. He saw no harm in letting Stacy sign her name in Stanley's absence. Stuffed and a little buzzed, Stacy took a cab home. That's when the pinch of anxiety started, and turned into a punch by the time she got to SoHo. What if humiliating and insulting Stanley put a glitch in his plans for thongs.com? The idea seemed ludicrous. One didn't make million-dollar decisions on the success of a romantic dinner. Stanley had a business plan, and wouldn't bother with thongs.com unless there was a potential for profits.

It couldn't be possible that he'd made the partnership deal just as an excuse to see Stacy again. She had a healthy self-image, but she was positive no one would risk all that dough for a date with her. Then again, Stanley did seem to be nursing an obsession. Was it worth $4,000,000 (how much stock he was to buy), to hear Stacy murmur the words "man root"? The more she thought about Stanley, the odder he seemed. People did play out scenarios in their heads, writing fantasy dialogue, giving themselves all the best lines. But no one (sane) would type out the words and expect the sentient being on the other side of the table to read them (at least, not for free, not on a second date). What's more, now that the one-act play "My Date with Stacy" had closed on opening night, would Stanley be inspired to write a sequel called "The Night I Tortured and Murdered Stacy"? Would that script include her begging for her life (along the lines of, "I am worthless, pathetic and powerless, but I still long to see the light of another day, especially if allowed to buff your hardwood in the morning, afternoon, and evening")? Stanley said it was just a game. How dangerous a game? she wondered. To distract herself, Stacy took out her Palm III and deleted Stanley's name from her To Do list. The list grew more anemic by the day. She needed a new cache of candidates.

The cab let her off right outside her apartment building. Stacy managed to relax once she was safely within the double front doors. As she waited for the elevator, she pictured Stanley's blotchy and knotted face right before he ran out on her. The image made her weary. Her sleepless night was catching up with her. Exhaustion weighed on her shoulders like an iron cloak. She could barely stand up to wait for the elevator doors. Finally, they clanged open.

Inside the car, Vampire Boy, the raven-haired creature of the night from 4C, stood with his hands in the pockets of his black jeans. He saw her and froze. She stood motionless, staring, as well. They looked at each other, silent and still. They must have stayed like that—Stacy outside the box; Vampire Boy inside—for a few moments, because the elevator's automatic doors closed, and in so doing, broke the spell. Stacy leaned backward, resting against the lobby wall. She quickly took out her compact and checked her makeup. She saw the B above the elevator light up, and knew the car had gone to the basement. Vampire Boy had obviously intended to get out in the lobby. He'd be back up to the lobby in a second. She readied a warm smile, smoothed her stained blouse, and waited. But when the elevator doors opened to her, the car was empty.

While riding to four, Stacy took a few deep breaths. How had he locked her in his eyes like that? she wondered. And where had he gone? Had he transfigured himself into a bat and flown away? Vampire Boy had undeniable, tangible powers. At her floor, Stacy walked by apartment 4C—the cave of Vampire Boy—and wondered what he did in there during the day. Did he lurk in the dark, or sleep in a coffin? Maybe she should leave a note. Just a little invitation to come over for some casual, no-strings-attached blood sucking. She'd be rid of her problem (and become undead, to boot).

She fished inside her purse for her pink notepad. She scribbled:

> *I'm the redhead in 4A. We just stared at each other for a lifetime in the lobby. If you'd like to meet, return this note with a date, a time and a place. Or just stop by.*
>
>   *Stacy*

She slipped the sheet of paper under his door.

"Something ventured," she said to herself as she entered her own apartment. It was just as she'd left it, coherently cluttered. Her friends and parents usually used phrases describing natural or man-made disasters ("a hurricane hit"; "a bomb went off") to describe her non-conformist interior decorating. Regardless of how many tchotchkes were piled on shelves, or how many purses lay about (dozens hung on a hook on a geranium red wall), Stacy never left dishes in the sink or dirty clothes on the floor. It was a clean mess.

On the side table with the tasseled silk tablecloth, under the shaded lamp, between the beaded picture frame and her silver incense tray (with matching silver oblong box for rods and cones), sat her ultra-slim portable telephone, painted red, pink, and lilac with nail polish (some sleepless nights were too, too long). She picked it up and listened for the stuttering dial tone that meant she had voice mail. Two messages. One from Mom (bitching about Dad and his compulsive mulching), and one from Charlie, waiting impatiently for the lesbian report.

She returned the call. To Charlie. Stacy was surprised when he picked up. Usually, at this time of night, he was either out trolling or in entertaining an exgirlfriend/current four-night stand (aka soon-to-be-exgirlfriend). Charlie had the knack for not offending any exes in a permanent way. They were angry or hurt at first, but their feelings toward him were never irreparably damaged. Keeping people on his side was one of Charlie's special skills.

She said, "I'm home."

He said, "Give."

"My story has a sad ending."

"Wait a minute," he said, muffling the line. When he came back: "I have company. Can we have lunch tomorrow, and you can tell me every microscopic detail in person?"

Stacy frowned, not sure if her jealousy was for Charlie and his constant flow of sex partners, or for the girl he was presently entertaining. "Who's over?" she asked.

"You remember that publicist from the *Chemical Attraction* screening? Staci?"

"Yes, I'm here."

"No, her name is Staci."

"The way you say it, I'm guessing it's Staci with an 'i.' "

He said, "It may very well be."

She said, "For her sake, I hope it's an evil 'i.' "

"I've never dated a Staci before," he said. "So this time, when I call out your name during sex, she won't get suspicious. Tomorrow." And he hung up.

She stared at the dead phone. He would rather fool around with a publicist than listen to her story about sex with a woman. How could he stand to wait? She was losing him. Maybe he actually cared about this Staci. Maybe he was falling in love with her. What would that mean to their friendship? It would leave her with lunch plans, she thought. Okay, then, Stacy would take a lunch. She'd see how far she could get with that.

She spent 10 minutes hatching a plot for tomorrow's afternoon delight. Then she turned on her iBook (property of thongs.com, to be returned when she left the company; as if she had any intention of giving it back; they would have to come to her house, break in, and confiscate it). She logged on to AOL

"You've got mail," said the computer voice. Her mailbox was jam-packed.

"Fifty-seven e-mails!" said Stacy. She scrolled down the long queue of incoming. All but five—spam, work stuff, Mom, and one from Gigi XXX at swerve.com— were from match.com subscribers (she'd practically forgotten about posting her ad). She had hit the virtual bar scene like gangbusters. How encouraging! There has to be someone halfway decent in a pool of 52 hopefuls.

But first, she read the e-mail from Gigi. It said:

"Stacy, judging from the tone of your last e-mail, I must have offended you in some way. Please know that I regularly respond to reader mail in my column, and it's my job to be as provocative as possi-

ble. That's what makes the column fun. I didn't mean to insult you. But if, by any chance, something I wrote has hurt you, I suggest you examine that deeper. Thanks and sorry, Gigi XXX."

Still not using her real name, that chicken shit, thought Stacy. And how dare she suggest that anything she grinds out like sausage meat could be of real emotional value to anyone? Stacy was only too glad to turn her attention away from Gigi and back to her bulging pack of cyber suitors.

She scanned the messages, instantly deleting those with unappealing screen names (for example, HOTNHORNY might be a sure thing, but a girl had to have some standards; HOLDENC might have homicidal tendencies; DARKSTAR had to be stoner—not necessarily a bad thing, but she was in a hurry; ZYGOTE wasn't looking for a date, he was looking for a womb). She whittled the list down to 20 on the first pass, still highly encouraged by her crop. Next hurdle: photo and profile analysis. She methodically checked the ad of each e-mailer. If he was older than 40 or younger than 30, she automatically deleted. If he described his body type as "average," "large" or "a few extra pounds," she deleted (since she had options, she'd stick with "athletic" and "slim/slender" only). She trashed the men who made less than $100,000, figuring that since she had the opportunity to discriminate, she might as well be traditional.

This weeding-out process was exactly why web

matchmaking had so little potential for finding true love. It was too methodical. No kismet. No spotting the man of one's dreams across a crowded room. A listing of one's credentials, combined with a grainy photo and a self-consciously written profile, lead to making a paper judgment. If love could be inspired by how someone looked on paper (or, more accurately, on screen), it would be miraculous. Besides, there was the smack of desperation to overcome. Having to advertise for dates, with language like, "Your mother would approve" was almost too hard a sell to bear. On the other hand, people were busy in this city. No one had time to go to parties. Bars were depressing. Harassing friends for blind dates and fix-ups was humiliating. Dating services were expensive. That left work contacts, friends who turned into something more and Cupid's wobbly arrow. Why dismiss on-line dating out of hand? It could work. On its homepage, match.com claimed to be responsible for thousands of marriages.

Her match.com shortlist:

ADMAN was a 34-year-old advertising executive who lived in the West Village (geographically fortuitous). His photo was blurry, but he seemed well within the range of male attractiveness. He claimed he was "athletic," made over $100,000, was looking for someone who laughed at Woody Allen movies. Stacy loved Woody Allen. It was destiny!

RICHARDMcD, a 39-year-old architect from the Upper East Side, enjoyed running, hiking, baseball, football, basketball and hockey. He had season tickets to the Mets, Jets, Knicks and Rangers. His income was "unspecified," but since he had to be in great shape, Stacy forgave him his secrecy. His head shot showed an abundance of red hair just like hers (they had so much in common!), a Hugh Grant-ish smile, and bright, sparkly blue eyes.

BULLWINKLE was a veterinarian, 37, who loved animals, plants, anything living. He had just exited a long relationship. Being alone (but not lonely) wasn't his style, and he'd like to explore the city and its many wonders with an intelligent and caring woman who was shorter than five foot seven. He was slim/slender, and his headshot was passable.

SNAP was Stacy's number-one choice. He was 35, "athletic," six feet tall, had a full head of beautiful brown hair, described his occupation as "other" (he didn't elaborate, but Stacy got the feeling he was wealthy beyond all reason, despite the fact that he listed his income as "unspecified"). He enjoyed theater, film, classical music (he played the violin and performed professionally "when there's time"), had published two novels ("of little consequence, but so much fun to write"). On the issue of why such a fine catch was single, he explained it thusly: "Proper channels haven't yielded my ideal mate, so I thought I'd try this. My best friend met his wife on match.com, and she's a wonderful woman. I should be so lucky."

Well, this was his lucky day. Stacy responded to his original e-mail (short and sweet—he'd written, "Have you met your match yet?"): "Dear SNAP, I haven't met my match yet, but if you're available to-morrow night, I may have only one more day to wait. Warmest regards, Fluffy." The tantalizing part about it: Despite the odds, SNAP *could* turn out to be the love of Stacy's life. When you've never seen or spoken to someone, you can project anything on him, even your boldest fantasy.

To the others on her shortlist, Stacy sent terse responses attempting to move out of virtual mode and into direct contact, believing that prolonged e-mail exchanges would be awkward. Since she gave such great phone, she'd very much appreciate it if he would send her his number. She'd send hers, but a girl can't be too careful, etc.

It was nearly midnight when she sent her last e-mail of the night. She was beyond tired. As she walked from her desk in the living room toward the bedroom in back, Stacy noticed a sheet of pink paper on the floor by her front door. On closer inspection, she saw that it was her note to Vampire Boy next door. He'd written her a response on the back. It read:

I knocked but you didn't answer. Sorry I stared at you like that. The surprise of seeing you stumped me for words. I'll be hard at work thinking of some clever things to say to you next time I see you. I'll be in town all weekend. If you're free at all, we can get together and I can try them on you.

He hadn't signed off with a name.

She washed her face, brushed her teeth and got in bed. Her reserves of men overflowing again, Stacy was able to drift effortlessly to sleep. She had peaceful dreams for fluffy clouds.

Chapter Eleven

Thomasday morning

The sun was singing. Birds were shining. Stacy rose smiling in her bed, stretched sleepiness out of her bones, and jumped into the shower. She had a lunch date, a hot prospect in the apartment next door, and a flurry of e-mail interest, all of which added up to imminent relief from her pending revirginization. Peace and joy in July. She couldn't ask for more.

She dressed for the 90 degree heat in a freshly pressed eggshell linen dress, tea length and sleeveless. Not the sexiest item in her wardrobe, but one of the coolest and cleanest. With her hair in a bun, a single-strand gold necklace and bracelet, and off-white sling-backs, Stacy knew she was the picture of understated elegance. This was exactly the kind of Grace Kelly look that Charlie was a sucker for. She was locked, loaded, (bare) armed, and dangerous.

The walk to the subway was more like a skip. The ride, a float. She leered at handsome straphangers.

Some leered back. Of course they did. She was in fine form. She was glowing. She was in demand. The spell she was under, this precious and rare mood, was almost like being in love.

Bursting with confidence, Stacy had no problem going into the greasy deli and ordering her suicide on a roll ("give me butter, and lots of it," she said to the unibrow grill operator, who was too shocked by her attitude shift from squirrel to panther that he didn't muster a single kissy sound). After making one quick stop (for a necessary lunchtime seduction prop), she sailed up the elevator of her building, ready (and *willing*) to face off with Janice in the endless debate over cotton panels for the Meshwear 2001 panty collection. Usually, these hotly battled conflicts made her age one year per minute of discussion. Today, she would shock them all. On this morning, she would give in. Forget cotton panels! Who needed them? Who cared about hygiene? Shouldn't the women of America be free to breathe?

Stacy rounded the corner to her office, her feet light, shoes tappy. She could practically hear "It's Not Unusual" by Tom Jones pounding along as she walked.

The beat stopped suddenly when Stacy found Fiona Chardonnay at her desk, literally breathing fire. Smoke poured out of her mouth in long streams. Stacy blinked a few times before realizing that Fiona was holding a cup of very hot coffee in her hands, under her chin.

"Exactly what did you do to Stanley Bombicci last night?" asked Fiona tartly. "He sent me an e-mail demanding significant changes in the agreement, and threatened to readjust the interest rates on the loan."

"We had a romantic dinner," said Stacy, her natural high taking a direct turn south. "Then we went to his apartment and made sweet, sweet love all night long."

Fiona stood. Her heels, pointy and lethal, sunk into the carpet. "What does his apartment look like?" she asked, as if she knew every inch of it.

Stacy scrambled. What would Stanley's home look like? She was drawing a blank.

She must have said the word out loud. Fiona squinted at her. "Blank?" she repeated.

"*Black*," said Stacy. "Lots of black. Furniture, countertops. Signed Erte posters, a six-foot-tall black marble sculpture of a female nude in the front hallway, a fridge full of champagne, caviar, pâté, apples, brie, whipped cream, baggies of hairy red pot, chocolate truffles."

"That's enough," said Fiona. "You were under no obligation to this company to go home with that man, Stacy. And if it ever comes to it, I'll deny in court that I asked you to go to dinner with him."

"Why would it ever come to that?" asked Stacy. "Unless you tried to screw me over."

"I would never do such a thing, Stacy," she said. "You should know that much about me by now."

Stacy knew nothing of the kind. Fiona had been generous with her, but Stacy had always wondered if she might have been wiser to refuse Fiona's series of carefully offered bribes. Too late now, thought Stacy. If Fiona were plotting, there was little Stacy could do about it except pack up her things and walk out the door. That would be even more foolish, and premature.

Stacy said, "You've been reading my e-mails."

"Call an escort service. That's what I do," said Fiona. "Or seduce some delivery man who doesn't speak English."

"Delivery man, no English. Got it."

"Or just go to a bar," said Fiona, draining her coffee and throwing the cup into the trash. "Only you could turn getting laid into a heroic quest."

"I haven't had a chance to get to a bar yet," said Stacy. Somehow, picking up a man at a bar seemed even more desperate than advertising for one on line. Then again, she'd met Brian at a bar (when she was 28). With four extra years on her, she'd hoped to avoid bars this time around. At least on line you couldn't take rejection personally. At a bar, there was no other way to take it.

"Tomorrow night, we are going out together," said Fiona. "Put it in your Palm Pilot. I'll expense it."

Stacy said, "But my quest is over. Stanley and I—"

"Stanley's apartment is an orgy of Swedish 1950s style. Eames everything. There isn't a stick or stitch of black in all seven rooms."

Stacy said, "He's redecorated."

"Since last week?" asked Fiona. "I was there on business. To finalize the deal."

Stacy naturally assumed Fiona had slept with Stanley. Another step in his plan to corner Stacy? A revolting thought. "Friday night is wide open," said Stacy.

"Good," said Fiona. "We'll get you all the sex you can handle." Fiona smiled archly. "Now back to work. And don't worry about Stanley."

"You think it's safe?" asked Stacy, mentally flipping through the pages of "The Night I Maimed and Disfigured Stacy Temple."

Fiona said, "Of course it's safe. He may give me a hard time, but he can't back out at this point. The deal is secure."

But that wasn't Stacy's concern. Fiona left her alone to contemplate the Harvard pornographer, which demolished her mood. Stacy snapped out of it by working. She focused on the dawning of a new age of corsetry, one created by thongs.com for the good of womankind. She was grateful to lose herself in a long list of assignments and phone calls. She heard from Janice that Taylor's cramps were still acute. The faux lesbo would be absent today. Stacy could be thankful for that small gift. Time passed quickly.

Too quickly. She was late for her rendezvous with Charlie. She had to run, risking a sweat. He was also late, giving her a chance to gather herself. As she waited on the street in front of Genki Sushi, she did some simple math. Sixteen years ago, at age 16, Stacy had lost it, and, at last count, she'd had 16 lovers. One a year, not a bad average. To maintain it (and dispatch this revirginization business), she needed just one man. Just one. Surely, she could manage that. It was practically in the bag. As was her seduction aid for Charlie. Her purse dug into her shoulder with the extra weight. Where was he?

She looked at her watch again. Waiting for Charlie and standing alone on the street, Stacy felt a sharp drop in her confidence level. Or maybe it was the ill effects of the July heat (her linen dress had wrinkled miserably already). She took a deep breath and tried to focus. She recited a couple of aphorisms. *A journey of a thousand miles starts with a single step. From a tiny acorn grows the mighty oak.* Stacy closed her eyes and repeated the mantra, "I'm an acorn. I'm an acorn."

"You're definitely nuts," said Charlie, suddenly at her side. "And I'm late."

"For a very important date," she said. "You don't know how important."

In greeting, Charlie kissed the top of her red head. His blond hair was too long, his skin impossibly tan (Charlie was her most outdoorsy friend; her nickname for him was "The Woodsman"). Stacy elbowed him in the ribs; he patted her shoulders. Very platonic and playful, as always. The trick would be to alter the chemistry slightly, turning it erotic.

"I've changed my mind," she said, tilting her head at the sushi place. "It's too nice a day to eat inside."

"It's ninety degrees with ninety-five percent humidity," he said.

She reached in her purse and pulled out a bottle of Chateau Mouton Rothschild. She'd paid $100 for it—money well spent, she hoped.

"What's this?" he asked. Charlie read the label and gasped. For his college semester abroad, he'd trained at the Cordon Bleu to become an enologist.

"Liquid picnic at Bryant Park?" she asked, batting her long lashes. "Or we can save this for another time."

Charlie cradled the bottle in his hands as if it were a newborn babe. "No, no. The park sounds good."

They walked to Bryant Park, the midtown rectangle of greenery attached to the rear of the New York Public Library. Along the way, Stacy primed the pump by telling Charlie about her misbegotten encounter with Taylor. He laughed. Not a good sign, she thought. Comedy just wasn't sexy. Once in the park, they found a small spot in the shade among the lunchtime escapees. The man to their left had removed his suit jacket, shirt and tie and lay on a blanket, his dress shoes gleaming in the sun. A group of women to their right sat in a circle, trading bites of their sandwiches. Stacy lowered herself to the grass, not caring about stains on the Grace Kelly dress. She dipped into her tote for a corkscrew and two wineglasses wrapped in newspaper.

"Isn't it illegal to drink in public?" asked Charlie as he poured.

"Why, yes," she said, swirling her glass.

Charlie moaned when he took his first sip. Stacy's heart pounded at the sound. He'd slept with nearly all of their female friends (now among the legion of his exes), and he'd received rave reviews. For the record, Stacy and Charlie had kissed once, barely, eons ago, back in college. It was a half lip mash at a Phish concert in Burlington, Vermont, that they'd driven six hours to see (back in the days when coolness was defined by the lengths one would go to in search of entertainment).

She told him to stop. It had felt wrong. About five minutes later, he'd begun snogging with a hippie blonde
from the Upper Valley who said "aboat" for "about" and
"ouwa" for "hour." Stacy had found her vexing and un-
washed. Her tie-dye was passé. Charlie couldn't have
cared less. The two started kissing at the beginning of a
"Reba" jam, and didn't come up for air until the final
notes an hour later. All the while, Stacy twiddled her
thumbs, annoyed and dumbfounded that one song
could last an eternity, only it seemed longer due to the
tonsil hockey sideshow.

On the drive back to New York, Charlie had said
that the girl (name of Willow) wasn't nearly as liber-
ated as she appeared, because she wouldn't blow him
behind the Green Party tent. Stacy had said, "What do
you expect from a fourteen-year-old?" He'd been so
angry at her comment (she'd never understood exactly
what had pissed him off so much), he refused to speak
to her for the last three hours of the trip.

Eventually, they patched things up and their friendship progressed as usual—chaste, platonic, mildly flirtatious. They stayed out of each other's romantic lives,
but talked every day. The unspoken assumption—that
sex could destroy their beautiful friendship—remained
untested for ten years. But the decade—the century,
the millennium—was drawing to a close. It was time,
ready or not, to see what damage sex could do.

As they reclined on the grass in Bryant Part, the
pair quickly consumed half the bottle. Stacy, a light-
weight, was drunk. Charlie, a heavyweight, didn't show

a ripple in his square-shouldered steadiness. She'd intended to ply him with alcohol. But now, in the hazy glow of wine and heat waves, she saw the true brilliance of the plan: Even if he stayed sober, she, in her tipsiness, would find the guts to lunge.

Charlie said, "Did you read that article by Gigi XXX? The one I sent you?"

"The one where she accused some poor woman of being delusional and pathetic for forgoing sex?"

"The very same, but I think her point was that the reader was avoiding love, along with sex."

"The reader was me," Stacy admitted.

Charlie feigned surprise. "I had no idea!"

Stacy pinched his bicep. "Do you think she's right?"

He cocked an eyebrow. "She could have said the same thing about me, too. By having sex with women I don't love, I'm avoiding an emotionally risky situation myself. But men can have sex for sex's sake without guilt. Women can't have casual sex without the afterglow of self-loathing. That's why your revirgination project is failing. You think you're in hot pursuit of casual sex but, by choosing the wrong partners, you're making sure you won't actually get it. Because if you did, you'd hate yourself."

Stacy had her doubts about his theory. Luck had been against her, not her own subconscious. She said, "What if I were to choose a partner I already care deeply about?"

"How are you going to find someone like that in the next three days?"

Stacy smiled and said, "Drink up, sweetie." She poured Charlie another glass.

He sniffed, swirled and sipped the vino. "The French reds are really . . . *blah, blah, blah.*" Stacy was sure he was saying something insightful and debonair, but her buzz, and her nervousness, impaired her hearing.

Like lightning, she made her move, plastering her lips against his. He pulled back and said, "What do you think you're doing?" As he righted himself, his glass of wine spilled all over his white shirt. The red splotch looked like a knife wound.

To apologize, Stacy leaned in for another kiss.

With his two massive hands, he gripped each of her shoulders and held her back, her lips puckered five inches from his face. He said, "You've lost your mind."

"I was planning on saying that—afterwards," she declared. "Something like, 'What was that about? I must have been temporarily insane. Let's pretend it never happened.' "

He said, "It isn't going to happen."

"Certainly not here. I'm taking you back to my office. There's a swell stairwell I'd like to show you."

Charlie was adamant. "I'm not attracted to you," he said.

"All evidence to the contrary," replied Stacy, pointing at his pants. "If you're not attracted to me, explain *that.*"

He sat upright, fixing his trousers. "I can't believe you killed the wine." He looked at the overturned bottle, the burgundy fluid seeping into the grass. "You bought it to seduce me?" he asked. She nodded. "I'm the man you already care deeply about?" She nodded again. The circle of women to their right watched them with wide smiles, their sandwich swapping at a standstill.

"I had a plan," Stacy said. The pout was for real.

Charlie said, "Don't start blubbering." He paused. "Okay, then, I'll do it. But I don't want this to turn into a psychodrama where you fall in love with me and we end up hating each other."

"You won't regret it, Charlie."

"I am a damn good friend."

She kissed his cheek gratefully, and wrapped her arms about his neck. He detached her by the elbows. "Take me to your stairwell," he said.

"Good, you're back. Lunch hour is supposed to be thirty minutes, Stacy," said Fiona as they walked up the hallway toward Stacy's office. "And why is there blood on your shirt, Charlie? Those greedy bastards at AOL just raised their price for keyword—one and a half million dollars. God, I hope the merger with Time Warner explodes like a hydrogen bomb and kills them all. Meshwear 2001 product line meeting in fifteen, Stacy. We're going over the bustiers."

Fiona misprounced it BUST-ee-ay. The correct pronunciation was BOOST-ee-ay. But Stacy would never correct her boss. Fiona was already gone, clicking down the hall in skyscraper pumps, off to terrorize another of her subjects. Stacy quickly led Charlie toward Fire Exit

D. On the way, they walked past the samples closet, the small room where every item in the thongs.com inventory was hung or crammed into drawers. A size 8 mannequin was propped in the room, displaying a metallic blue mesh babydoll and matching tear-away G-string.

"Whoa!" Charlie stopped in the doorway. He peered into the room and, upon finding it unoccupied, said, "Forget the stairwell." He pulled Stacy into the den of sexy samples, and locked the door.

They kissed. He was a larger man than she was used to, and she liked feeling small. They dropped to their knees and lay on the floor among the bolts of fabric, cast-aside panties and slightly irregular peignoirs. Stacy directed Charlie to lie back on a large duffel bag full of the lavender-scented sachets (free with each order of $50 or more). He made himself comfortable while Stacy unbuttoned her dress.

Charlie breathed heavily with excitement. He said, "Hmsuph."

She said, "Don't speak, Charlie. Just feel."

Agitated, he gasped, "Hmssush! Muphsss!" He pointed wildly at his mouth. Stacy looked inside. His tongue swelled before her eyes. It puffed like a fish. He turned around and grabbed at the duffel bag. "Wassaha?" he asked frantically.

"They're lavender sachets. To make your underwear drawer smell nice."

Charlie jumped to his feet. "Lafffnnr?!!" Stacy suddenly had a vague memory that Charlie had severe allergies to certain flowers. He grabbed the wall phone near the door and dialed. He thrust the phone at Stacy.

The operator said, "Nine-one-one."

As Stacy gave the address and explained the situation, Charlie struggled to breathe and, in a panic, ran out of the samples closet. Stacy dropped the phone to go after him, rebuttoning her linen dress on the way.

Before she'd taken a step outside the door, someone screamed in the hallway. Stacy, still partially unclothed, ran now, colliding with petite Janice, knocking her on the floor. She shrieked, "A man's been shot! There's blood everywhere! He's collapsed in the hallway!"

Stacy found Charlie two doors down. His face had turned a sultry shade of scarlet. "Ambulance is on the way," she assured him. Someone must have called the building's on-site nurse's office. A man in a white uniform pushed Stacy out of the way and gave Charlie a hypodermic injection.

The needle man said, "It's epinephrine. He's in anaphylactic shock. This will keep his breathing passages open until we can get him to a hospital."

Stacy, reeling from concern, guilt, and horror, couldn't help noticing how handsome the building's nurse was. He had a Tony McGuinty quality that she couldn't ignore. Besides which, the shot worked. Charlie's face settled to a hot pink, and he breathed more easily. The EMS team arrived. They loaded Charlie onto a stretcher.

As they wheeled her best friend toward the elevators, Stacy said, "I'll visit you in the hospital later. Do you think, once you're stabilized, that we could, you know, finish up?"

Charlie glared at her from behind his oxygen mask. She'd take that as a "no." The elevator doors closed, and he was gone.

The male nurse, Stacy and a half dozen onlookers stood silently at the elevator bank, unsure of what to do next. Stacy straightened her dress and checked her watch. She still had a few minutes before the big meeting.

She turned to the nurse and said, "I think I need a quiet place to lie down. Don't you have a couch in the medical station?"

He looked at Stacy, head to toe, and smiled. "Right this way," he said, hitting the UP button.

Chapter Twelve

Thursday afternoon—still

"Shall I lie down?" asked Stacy. She and the strapping male nurse had entered the Park Avenue tower's medical center, a suite on the top floor with an anterior triage room and an interior examination room. Very antiseptic, crisp, and white. As she pointed at the hospital-quality examination table with its paper sheet and stowed stirrups, Stacy felt a twinge deep inside her pelvis, recalling, not fondly, her last pap smear.

The man in starched white who'd saved Charlie's life shook his head ("I was only doing my job. You're embarrassing me with all this flattery—but I like it," he'd said in the elevator after Stacy praised him excessively), his extra-long bangs swinging to and fro. "Have a seat here"—he pointed at the desk and chairs in the triage room—"I have to make a report, do the preliminaries."

"About Charlie?" Stacy hoped "preliminaries" was his way of saying "foreplay."

"I want to talk about you, too," he said. She noticed the plaque on his desk that read, Gregori Romanov, M.D. "You said you didn't feel well downstairs, remember?"

"You're a doctor?" she asked.

"I've got a stethoscope and everything," he said.

Stacy had a seat. "Are you Russian?"

He smiled, showing a haphazard placement of teeth, some overlapping and crooked. He sat behind the desk and booted up his computer. "I was born in Moscow, but I've lived in New York since I was eight."

"I don't hear any accent at all," she said.

"I've been in America for twenty-five years," he said, "and I picked up English in elementary school, no formal language training, so I learned to speak colloquially."

"You picked up English in elementary school? You make it sound like you picked up the laundry," she said, more and more impressed with Dr. Zhivago. "I thought you were a nurse," she confessed.

"Understandable," he said. "Most on-site medical personnel are nurses. I start my residency at NYU in September. Cardiothorasic surgery. Until then, here I am. Now, let's get on with this." He proceeded to ask her a series of questions about Charlie (name, address, phone number, medical conditions, allergies, insurance policies, age, height, weight). When she couldn't provide the necessary information, Gregori smiled and said, "That's quite all right," with a soothing bedside manner.

He asked the same questions of Stacy, who was happy to give him her phone number. Dr. Romanov entered all the info expertly and accurately. She paused before divulging her weight, and said, "I want to ask you something."

"Okay," he said, looking away from his computer screen and directly into her eyes like a laser beam. He had sallow skin, deep-set eyes, a sloping forehead, disastrous teeth and retro hair, but Stacy was transfixed by the overall picture. He was, as the French say, *jolie laide*, "beautiful in ugliness." Maybe she was captivated by his tall, gangly body (her favorite type). Could be the fact that he taught himself English, or that he worked so close by and didn't wear a wedding band. Or perhaps her unexpected *pow* (*biff, bang, smash*) of lust was caused by all the sexual stops and starts of the past several days. Her drunkenness helped. And the situation was the stuff of fantasy—handsome doctor, attractive patient in need of attention *of the sexual kind*.

Whatever the reason, Stacy wanted Gregori. Bad. The idea of lying down on the examining table and playing doctor with him seized her brain and she could think of nothing else. Not Charlie in the hospital, not Fiona undoubtedly fuming downstairs, not the meeting she was conspicuously missing, not moral and ethical pause. And certainly not the threat that casual sex would make her feel bad about herself. (Where on earth had Charlie ever come up with that bogus idea? What did he think his troupe of ex-girlfriends were doing with him anyway? Coming back for another dose of self-loathing? Stacy would have to disabuse Charlie on the subject, right after she proved it to herself—right now.)

"You wanted to ask me something?" Gregori prompted.

She realized that she had been gazing mutely into his angular face. "I have a terrible condition," she said. "I'd hoped you might give me some medical insight."

"I'd be happy to. What are the symptoms?" he asked, leaning forward in his chair.

"My breathing is accelerated."

"Yes?"

"My pulse is quick."

"Okay."

"My face feels hot, flushed."

"Go on."

"My nipples are erect."

"I see."

"My vagina is secreting a clear, plasmalike fluid."

"I think I have enough information to make a diagnosis, Ms. Temple," he said, "if you'd like to come into the examining room? I need to confirm a few things."

She had never moved so fast. She hopped on the table, the paper sheet crinkling under her legs. The doctor followed her inside and closed the door behind him gently but purposefully, a hungry, predatory smile on his face.

He put his large, bony hands on her shoulders and said, "Part your lips, please."

Which ones? she wondered. She opened her mouth

and closed her eyes, knowing she would get a big surprise.

And she did. A wooden depressor pressed flat on her tongue, Stacy's eyes sprang open. Gregori was squinting into her mouth. He removed the stick, and checked her ears. He took her pulse and made her cough. Finally, he hit her on the knees with a rubber mallet. Her reflexes were just fine. Her instincts were way off.

He said, "You're experiencing post-traumatic stress disorder. What happened with your friend was so disturbing to you that you have physical manifestations of your fear for his health."

"That doesn't explain the vaginal secretions," she said.

"From what I surmised at the scene, you'd been alone with Mr. Gabriel in a closet, immediately preceding his attack, correct? Your hair was mussed and your dress was unbuttoned. You've had something alcoholic to drink, too."

"Yes, but—"

"You are in perfect health, Ms. Temple. You just need a few minutes to relax," he said. "You can stay here if you like."

"I need more than rest," she said.

He nodded. "I can give you Tylenol."

"I'll take a hug," she tried.

Not that he leaped at the opening, but he did come at her and give her a squeeze. She squeezed back. He patted her back. She grabbed his ass and started sucking on his neck. If she'd been trickling secretions before, she was now a river.

"Ms. Temple," said Gregori. "Please."

"Oh, yes, beg," she said, detaching herself momentarily.

"This can't happen," he said.

"I won't tell anyone," she breathed. "I'm very discreet."

"Ms. Temple," he said, peeling her fingers from the seat of his pants. "I'm gay."

She pulled back then, and examined his face for a lie. "But you're not a male *nurse*," she said. "You're a *doctor*."

"Doctors can be gay, too."

"Not heart surgeons," she protested.

"Even heart surgeons. Even *orthopedic* surgeons," he said knowingly. "I knew this guy in medical school, he volunteered for all the grisly stuff, like rebreaking legs and hammering nails into hip bone. He had two great loves. Surgical handsaws with wicked torque and, actually, male nurses."

"I feel ill," she said.

"Are you nauseated?" he asked, pointedly, professionally.

"If only I could throw up my pride," she said, and sulked out of the room, giving Gregori one last lustful look. He was too beautiful (in the ugliest way possible) to be gay. She supposed that, if doctors could be gay, so could ugly men. Even ugly doctors. And now she could never get sick or even get a scrape at the office until he left in September. She'd have to be careful.

Stacy returned, limp and enervated, to thongs.com. She checked her e-mail first. Fiona had fired one off, furious that Charlie had disrupted the workday and unsympathetic to her need for medical attention. Janice sent one with a slightly milder tone. A dozen other staffers had sent e-mails updating her on the conclusions of the meeting she'd missed, and the pile of additional work she was saddled with.

As she scrolled down, she caught sight of a noninteroffice e-mail. The sender, SNAP@talkmatch.com, was unknown to her, until she realized it was her fantasy date, the wealthy novelist/violinist who was searching for his one true love.

She opened the message. He'd copied her provocative suggestion that they meet tonight. And then he'd added:

"Fluffy, I will be at the bar at Jean Pierre Louis Paul at Hudson and Reade at 8 P.M. sharp, wearing a blue Armani suit, reading the *New Yorker,* and drinking a vodka martini. I hope you'll join me? My best, Snap."

Stacy e-mailed back:

"Dear Snap, I'll be there. Look for a woman with pink cheeks, red hair, and, most likely (although I can't confirm my wardrobe at this time), a basic yet elegant black dress. See you soon. Fluffy."

Chapter Thirteen

Thursday night

$\mathcal{S}$tacy arrived first. She knew the restaurant fairly well, having eaten their last birthday dinner there with her parents. Sol and Belinda Temple were born on January 10 and January 15 respectively. So, each year, the three of them met post-New Year's for a posh, expensive meal with multiple bottles of wine, culminating in a nerve-wracking drive home to Short Hills for Mom, but not for Dad, who, in his morning hangover, would barely remember cutting off that SUV on the New Jersey Turnpike.

They'd come to Jean Pierre Louis Paul twice, having loved the sampling menu of twelve courses ($150 per person, not counting wine and coffee) that took over three hours to consume. The food was just the beginning for Stacy, who wasn't quite the gourmand her father was (he'd eat anything, the more "innards related" the better—sweetbreads, haggis, blood pudding—then proclaim, "Tastes like chicken," and expect everyone to laugh). Stacy loved the low-country

French decor, the strategically placed bushels of apples and bound stalks of dried sunflowers, the farm tables and spindle-backed chairs with needlepoint seats. Above the waist-high wood-paneled wainscoting, murals of harvest scenes covered the walls. Lilac and heather scents mixed with the garlic and rosemary wafting from the kitchen. Heaven. Sensually speaking.

She wasn't alone in her opinion. Jean Pierre Louis Paul was one of the most popular restaurants in the city, achieving the unusual status of both a tourist and local ruling-class favorite. SNAP showed good taste in suggesting this spot. Plus, it was right in TriBeCa, only a short walk from her apartment in SoHo. She'd worried about the ill effects of a stroll on her freshness quotient, but the night had cooled considerably—couldn't be more than 80 degrees—and both the air and the exercise calmed her nerves.

Stacy had had blind dates before. But not *this* blind. She also had a lot to answer for. She'd been honest about her appearance in the match.com profile (she couldn't see the point in that kind of charade—on sight, the jig would be up anyway), but just about every other aspect of her profile had been fabricated. Fortunately, her relationship with this man might not last longer than one night. She figured she could maintain the self-invention that long. Some lies would be easier to stick to than others. It was unlikely, for example, that he'd pull a flute out of his pants and ask her to blow it. Perhaps metaphorically.

As she opened the red doors of JPLP, she had a flare

of doubt about this date. The notion of casual sex was thorny enough. But she'd have to talk to this man for at least an hour before that could happen. She was no longer young enough to pound a few G&Ts and drunkenly ask the cute guy on the right to take her home.

Gigi XXX's last swerve.com post surfaced in her frontal lobe like a bad apple in a barrel. "Life isn't worth living if you're not in love or trying to find it," she'd written. Could that be true for Stacy? Had life not been worth living for the last year? She could pitch this blind date to herself as anything, a desperate attempt to rid herself of revirginity, a marketing experiment, a mystery unveiled. But SNAP was trying to find love. He'd written as much in his profile. His life was worth living. And Stacy decided she owed it to herself to be just as optimistic and stupid (that's right, *stupid*) to hope for the very, very best.

Stacy killed a minute smoothing down her hair and flip-flopping between idealism and doubt. She didn't even know his real name. Was he going to want dinner or just drinks? Dinner would be lovely. She had fond memories of the braised lamb. But three hours of conversation with a complete stranger might be pushing the limits of her strength and creativity (or maybe it would be a snap—perhaps that explained his alias). And, if he expected to dine, would she have to pay for her portion of the meal (he would never)?

These uncertainties nearly swept her back out the red doors and onto the street, but she took one large whiff of the commingled scents of wildflowers and roast duck, and had to stay.

The small barroom was located to the right of the vestibule, giving people a place to wait for their tables. She found a seat against the wall (perfect scoping position) in a wooden pew with cushioned seats. She ordered herself a drink. It helped tame her afternoon red wine hangover. And she'd need all the courage a cosmopolitan could provide. Two, quite possibly.

After her first long sip of the pink concoction, she looked around the bar. Slow night. The only other person in the bar was an older man who had to weigh 300 pounds. The wooden stool strained to support his weight. Stacy feared it might be reduced to splinters if he had another drink. Despite his girth, the man had found a designer suit to fit. Not that expert tailoring did much good. He was still Jabba the Hut in Armani.

He looked her way and smiled, his cheeks as wide as watermelons. She turned her back to him (practically facing the adjacent wall, which made it difficult to keep one eye on the front door). She checked her watch. SNAP was a few minutes late.

Another 10 minutes went by. If he stood her up, no harm, no foul. She'd pay her bill, walk home and knock on Vampire Boy's door. Not quite ready to accept a blow-off, Stacy ordered another Cosmo. She had second thoughts about the second drink, though. It might appear to the Man Mountain that she was hanging around for his sake. If only SNAP would show up. He'd save her from the agony of being approached at a bar by an unattractive stranger, and then suffering waves of sympathy for him.

Drawing her out of her thoughts, a voice, deep and sexy, asked from behind her, "Is that you, Fluffy?"

Stacy spun around to face Jabba the Hut, only he seemed much larger up close. "Snap?" she asked.

"Please call me Jasper."

"I'm Stacy," she said. They shook hands.

"You seem surprised," he said euphemistically.

"I am," she said. *I thought you'd be human size,* she didn't say.

"I wasn't sure it was you. Maybe you didn't recognize me. The photo on match.com is a bit old," he explained.

"How old?"

"Seven years."

And in those seven years, Jasper had consumed the meat of an entire elephant. "It's a very flattering photo," she said. "I mean, actually, you do look like your picture. You still have all your hair. Most forty-year-olds are thinning by now." Nothing was thinning on him. He did have nice, thick brown hair.

"Actually, I'm forty-eight. But people tell me I look thirty-five."

Hard to say. The grossly fat are rarely wrinkled, thought Stacy. "I suddenly have a terrible headache," she tried.

"May I sit down?" Jasper squeezed into her pew. She felt tiny and vulnerable next to such a massive person. He smelled of talc and peppermint. Along with the shiny hair, he also had perfectly white teeth. Stacy took a breath. Okay, he was fat. But he wasn't sweaty. Yes, he'd lied about his age and body type. But he seemed nice. Was this the time for Stacy to widen (as it were) her range of what she considered attractive? She'd never been with a heavyset man. For all she knew, he might be thrilling and potent in bed (provided that his tonnage didn't break it). She resolved to give him a chance and not discard him for his size alone. Like she had a perfect body? Like she couldn't stand to lose a few pounds? She wasn't a looks-obsessed fat phobe like her mother. She would judge him on his personality and accomplishments. And lest she forget, he was rich (she wouldn't be the first woman to overlook a fat stomach for a thick wallet).

He said, "Forgive me if this seems rude, but you can't really be twenty-nine."

People often told her she looked 25. "I'm thirty-two."

"So you lied, too." He smiled knowingly, as if her small shaving of the years was in any way equal to his mischaracterization. He was grasping for middle ground, she told herself. That was fair.

He said, "So tell me, Stacy. What do you like to do for fun?"

The question itself was baffling. She didn't have fun; she had a job. What was fun, anyway? Scrabble? Anagrams? She said, "I'm not sure."

"You're not sure what you do for fun?"

"I have a very demanding job."

He put one pudgy hand on her knee, and a flabby arm around her shoulder. "You need someone to help you unwind, Stacy. You need more time for *you*. Let me help you bring fun back into your life. Do you like Thai food?"

It was a French restaurant. "Thai? Sure."

"Let me take you out for Thai food, and then we'll go bowling."

The thought of Jasper bowling . . . no, it was too painful to imagine. "Bowling sure does sound like fun," she said. "Can I think about it?"

"What's there to think about? You are a beautiful, special lady, and you need to relax. I can feel the tension in your shoulders."

Jasper began rubbing her taut trapezius. This was far too much contact for the first five minutes. She'd need at least an hour and three additional drinks before she'd want this man to touch her.

"Do you like tequila? Let's do shots," he said.

"I'm not sure this is the place for shots."

Jasper signaled the bartender and ordered the tequila. He handed her a glass and implored her to drink. She drank. When she put her glass back on the table and turned toward Jasper to say thank you, he kissed her. Blindsidedly, on the lips. With his lips. And then, God help her, his tongue. She pushed him off.

"Forgive me, but you looked so cute when you did that shot, I couldn't resist kissing you," he said. He did his shot and got a crazy look in his squinty eyes, like he might kiss her again.

She smiled stonily, not quite sure what to do. She didn't want to be rude, but she'd have none of that sneak-attack shit. She shifted in the pew, recrossed her legs. His hand lifted as she repositioned herself, but his sausage fingers found their way back to her knee.

He said, "I've found that most women on match.com like to e-mail for weeks and then talk on the phone for a month before meeting. I guess they think that protects them. But you wanted to meet right away. You must have sensed something about me. I am definitely sensing something about you. You're a very sexual woman, Stacy. A very special lady."

She shook her head. "You're embarrassing me," she said.

"Don't you think you're a sexy, special lady?"

"I'd rather not say."

"You deserve to be treated right. Let me take you bowling."

"I don't think I could wear rented shoes."

He patted her thigh. She pushed his hand away. Thankfully, he took the hint and leaned back. He asked, "Want another shot?"

"You're trying to get me drunk so I'll make out with you."

He grinned. "I sense your hesitation, Stacy. Despite how sexy and special you are, I can feel you holding yourself back. Drinking alcohol is one way to relax to have fun. But getting you drunk isn't how I'm going to handle a special lady like you, Stacy. You need time and attention. You need a man to show you how wonderful you are, and take you places, buy you things. Over time and hours and hours together, hopefully, I can capture your heart." Again with the ham hands on her shoulder and knee.

Stacy wasn't sure if it was his repeated use of the word "special," but after that speech, Stacy was nearly certain that Jasper would never see her naked. Or take her bowling. Or, alas, buy her things. But she'd promised herself to give it a real go. If her hopes would be crushed, let them be annihilated completely. And she had to be fair; if he weighed 150 pounds, would she have been as disgusted by his approach? So she tried to change the subject. She'd heard enough about his plans to capture her heart. Maybe she could eke out some attraction from his accomplishments. "So, Jasper. Tell me about your novels," she said.

He rubbed her knee and asked, "Are you trying to change the subject?"

"I'm interested in your whole life, Jasper."

"It's only one novel, and it's actually a comic book I wrote back in high school with a friend of mine. We never did anything with it, but I still consider it a real accomplishment."

"Do you practice the violin every day?"

Jasper laughed. "I haven't given it a good workout since the eighth grade, but I can play a mean 'Scarborough Fair.' "

"You said in your profile that you're self-employed?" she asked.

"I work in publishing."

"Are you an editor? An agent?"

"I sell magazine subscriptions for Publisher's Clearing House over the phone. It's a great job. I never have to leave my house, and I make a very good living. Enough money to do whatever I want to do. I can fly to Florida on a moment's notice. I could afford to eat in this restaurant if I wanted to."

So he never had any intention of taking her to dinner tonight, at Jean Pierre Louis Paul or anywhere else. He'd just suggest meeting here to impress her, then grope her and get her drunk in the bar (a highly inappropriate bar, she might add, for soused canoodling).

"I mentioned a headache before?" she asked. "It's gotten worse."

He pulled back again (and removed his hands), but his hope wasn't diminished. "I can cure a headache. Let me rub your temples."

She said, "I'd rather you kept your hands to yourself. I'm not a touchy-feely kind of woman."

He said, a mite snippily, "You don't want to be touched? But you're a sexy lady. You like orgies. You said so in your profile. If you don't want physical contact, it can only mean one thing. You aren't attracted to me. Then why did you push for a date? You saw my picture."

The picture was seven years and 100 pounds ago. "It's hard to tell what someone looks like from a photo."

He frowned, his cheeks plumping. "Forgive me, Stacy, but a photograph is widely acknowledged to be an excellent way to tell what someone looks like."

"You said in your profile that you're athletic," she said.

He said, "I *am* athletic. I ride an exercise bike every day. I play golf. I'm in a basketball league." Stacy could hardly believe that Jasper could haul his walrus ass up and down a basketball court.

"You may be athletic in the sense that you play sports, but the category was 'body type.' I don't think your body type would be considered 'athletic' by conventional standards."

He seemed perplexed. "My picture shows my body."

"The photo was shadowy. It hid some things." There. Was that delicate enough? she wondered. Perhaps too. "The thing is, I like skinny guys."

He reared back with that. "Well. I see. Then there's no chance that I could ever capture your heart. Well, then, I have to thank you for meeting me tonight. I've had a nice time. I think, though, that I'll just cut the evening short and leave you to finish your drink."

He was hurt but trying to keep a stiff upper lip. It was painful to watch. He struggled to stand, and then walked out. She hadn't seen the rear view until then, and was even more relieved that he'd left. She sighed in her pew, and took another sip. She'd never been a smoker, but at that moment, she desperately wanted a cigarette.

"And one more thing, Stacy." Jasper was back, barreling into the bar. He stood in front of her table, his massive hull looming over her threateningly. If a woman rejected a man, he hated her; if a man rejected a woman, she hated herself. Jasper was most definitely a man. And he was pissed off. She hoped he wouldn't sit on her.

"You women in your thirties, with the demanding jobs," he said. "You think you're all that. You think that if a man doesn't look like Dylan McDermott and make as much money as Bill Gates that you're too good for him. Well, you—and all ladies like you—are going to regret passing on men like me. I might not look like Dylan McDermott, but I am a handsome man. And I may not make as much money as Bill Gates, but forty thousand dollars a year is a very respectable salary. And one day, when you are alone and miserable, you'll think back on this night, and wish you'd made a different choice. Best of luck to you, Stacy. I hope you find what you're looking for, but I don't think you will."

Then he stomped off again. Stacy hadn't signed up for a character assassination or a fortune telling when she'd registered with match.com, but she'd gotten both. She rotated her shoulders (they could use a proper knead), and considered what he'd said about women her age and pickiness and regret. Were her standards too high? Was she fooling herself about her prospects? Possibly, she concluded. A lowering of standards might be in order. But they'll never be low enough to let Jasper squeak in. She downed her drink. Jasper had to have some kind of justification for being turned down. Blaming women was the only way he could protect himself. She actually felt sorry for him. He'd said, "I hope you find what you're looking for." Stacy stirred her drink with her pinkie and tried to imagine what that could possibly be.

"One more thing!" It was Jasper again, pushing through the restaurant's front doors. "You are not a sexy or special lady, and you don't deserve more time for you. And, I can just tell, you probably don't like Thai food or think bowling is fun."

Then, like a gale of wind, he was gone. Truth was, and she knew it all along, that no one who used the phrase "capture your heart" would stand a chance of doing that. And, if she learned anything from this night of dashed expectations, the man who would be her de-revirginizing agent—provided that he existed on this or any planet—would have to be attractive to her, either physically or intellectually. Both would be good. But she could never let a loser in her bed, even if it took ten years to get laid. This realization made her quest that much more difficult. The new clarity, if anything, put her up for the challenge.

She paid the bartender for her two Cosmos and the two shots (Jasper had left her with the guilt of rejecting him—and the tab), and took off. It was still relatively early, and the shops of SoHo were open for business. She made a stop in Reinstein/Ross, her favorite jewelry store, and bought herself a pair of drop pearl earrings that were old-fashioned and retro, but in a modern way. They cost $300 but, she figured, if she were to find herself alone and miserable at 40, she might as well be brilliantly accessorized.

On the way home, warmed from her purchase and

the tequila, Stacy reflected on a couple of aspects of her enlightening encounter.

Dylan McDermott? Pass. If Jasper had said Tony McGuinty, perhaps the accusation might have had relevance.

What's more, $40,000?

Chapter Fourteen

Friday morning

Stacy had knocked on Vampire Boy's door when she got back from Jean Pierre Louis Paul last night. She didn't know anything about him intellectually, but she sure was attracted to him physically. And that moment when they'd stared at each other in the elevator, maybe she was attracted to him spiritually as well. But he wasn't home. She waited up for a few hours with VH-1 (great channel to watch trends in women's undergarments), knocking on his door every half hour or so. But he never came home. Probably met the perfect woman and was at her place, screwing her brains out. Stacy hated VH-1, but she kept watching. She hated everything.

In desperation, she called Charlie, just back from the hospital where he'd been lovingly cared for by a young, pretty female medical resident who couldn't resist his Woodsman-like charm, despite the balloon tongue and broken capillaries on his cheeks. He'd made Stacy swear she'd never go near him with her lips again. After apologizing for the 400th time, she said good-bye and fell asleep in her black dress on the living-room couch. When she awoke at 9 A.M., she was already late for work.

Of all the days. This morning, Fiona was hosting a breakfast party to celebrate Janice's 50th birthday and mourn Taylor's defection to pets.com. Employee birthdays were rarely acknowledged by Fiona (thongs.com never feted the passing of Fiona's years on Earth, since the date she entered the world was a mystery to one and all, including Janice). Either the staffer didn't last long enough to pass a birthday on premises, or a party would have cut into precious work hours. And serving cut vegetables and gift certificates to departing employees—that was unheard of. Most people left thongs.com with barely a "don't let the door hit you and crush your miserable carcass on the way out." But Fiona had always liked Taylor. And she'd been around as long as Stacy had. If Stacy were to find a better job, or just up and quit, she wasn't sure Fiona would throw a party for her. With Taylor, Fiona knew it was business. With Stacy, she feared, Fiona would think it had something to do with her. And she'd probably be right.

No time to think. Stacy had to dress, but quick. She usually pulled a purse from her collection off the wall to match her outfit of the day, but, in her rush, she had to stick with the black evening bag from the night before (a horrible combination with her blue half-sleeve shirt and pink miniskirt from Barney's).

The birthday/farewell breakfast was well under way

by 9:45, her arrival time. She realized she'd been late or missing for nearly every group gathering all week, and that Fiona's patience with her would be used up soon, if it weren't already. She got lucky, though, when she entered the conference room. Fiona wasn't in sight. The Turtle was laid out with a gorgeous spread (blueberries and raspberries, chocolate-dipped strawberries, muffins of every flavor, bagels, ten bottles of champagne in a row, orange juice, silver thermoses of coffee, condiments and a cheese platter from Mangia).

Stacy dove in and mingled with ardor. The only person she couldn't bring herself to talk to was Taylor. The departing tech whiz sat at the head of the Turtle by the strawberries, eating them one by one while every lesser producer and site manager filed by to kiss her ring. She was going to Internet heaven; the rest of them were in hell. Taylor avoided eye contact with Stacy, much to her relief.

Janice had to be on her third mimosa already. She was slurring her speech and acting a bit too cheery about turning 50. Stacy, smiling shyly, gave her a kiss on her creamy, doll-like cheek. "Happy birthday, boss," she said brightly.

"You only turn fifty once!" said Janice.

"Are you having a good time?" asked Stacy.

"I'm touched by the party, by the love in the room."

Stacy could barely register the tolerance in the room. "You're in an uncommonly good mood."

"Surprising, isn't it? I'm middle-aged. My children have forgotten my birthday. Our sweetheart deal with smut.com is kaput. Fiona's at their office right now, begging Stanley Bombicci to reconsider. He pulled the plug last night when he couldn't convince Credit Suisse to cosign the loan."

Stacy's heart shriveled. If the deal fell through (not her fault), would that be a fatal blow for the company? It couldn't be. Janice would be crying in her office, not giddy in the conference room. "So, if life is so wretched, why are you smiling?" asked Stacy.

"I'm in love," she said. "That guy? The one I e-mailed from your office? The Upper West Side lawyer? He's the one." Janice swallowed her mimosa in a gulp and started pouring another. "We spoke on the phone for two hours last night, and I'm going on a birthday date with him tonight."

For Janice, the potential for love could eradicate the devastation of a cash-strapped company and forgetful, selfish offspring. Janice had a hot date, she was delirious. It was insane. And, if not insane, it was dangerous. Considering Stacy's own match.com disaster and Janice's mountainous body count of disappointment from the on-line service, Stacy doubted that her boss's date would be as wonderful as it'd have to be to compensate for everything else that had gone wrong (was going wrong) with her life. Janice was in for a long fall, one that would be monumentally hard to get up from.

Wanting to make the precipice shallower, Stacy said, "Your children haven't forgotten your birthday. At least Tom didn't."

"He hasn't called from London, or e-mailed, or sent a gift," said Janice.

Stacy said, "Remember, I took him to lunch? He *did* buy you something. We had to go all the way to SoHo to get it. I've been holding it for you." Stacy reached into her evening bag and (thank God), found the small square jewelry box from Reinstein Ross. Janice opened the box and squealed when she saw the earrings Stacy had, only twelve hours ago, lovingly selected for her own lobes.

Janice said, "They're beautiful! How could he possibly afford them? And I know he doesn't have such good taste. I have you to thank for that, Stacy."

"He picked them out himself. Went right up to the jewelry case and pointed."

"You are a fabulous liar," said Janice.

"So are you. The company's not in trouble. You're just saying that to push me out of the nest like a kindly mother bird," said Stacy.

Janice laughed. She'd laugh at anything this morning. "Well, Fiona does have a rare talent for begging, borrowing, and stealing."

Stacy let out a sigh of relief. Fiona would save the day. She always did. The idea that, overnight, Stacy would go from being a future millionaire to another of the ever-expanding community of unemployed dot-commers was too much to fathom. She'd invested her time and energy in the company. It would have to pay off. It had to. Guilt tightened around her chest. She'd been fucking off all week. While she'd been chasing men, the company was floundering. As soon as Fiona returned, she'd apologize. She'd work harder. Refocus.

On cue, Fiona came crashing into the conference room, head to toe in a purple satin low-cut bodice sheath straight from the cover of a supermarket romance novel. Her helmet head of black raven hair had leaned to the left, giving her a windblown, crazy-person look. Stacy thought it worked for her.

"Sit," barked the Dark Lady.

Everyone sat. Stacy had come to accept the way Fiona ordered her staff around like dogs. There was some small comfort in knowing who was master. Stacy parked herself at the left foot of the Turtle, next to Janice, who'd put on the earrings. They looked a bit soft with her ash blonde hair. Still, the sight gave Stacy a saintly thrill, knowing she'd done a nice thing.

Fiona stood next to the seated Taylor at the head of the Turtle. She waited for silence, and then held aloft a small piece of paper. It looked like a bank note. The Dark Lady was also a magician, apparently, who could turn dross (or mesh), into spun gold (or metallic-hued strapless bras). "We are saved," she announced, owing the success of her coupe with Credit Suisse solely, and rightfully, to her talent for hucksterism. "This is a deposit slip for two hundred fifty thousand dollars. And there's more coming in. Stanley Bombicci is back on-board. People! We will launch Meshwear 2001!"

The employees, including Stacy, were silent for a beat, and then applause bounced off the Turtle and around the glass walls of the room. Stacy clapped right along with her colleagues, with huge relief. For five minutes there, she'd convinced herself that the company had faltered in the past week because she'd been distracted by personal matters. That she was to blame for their troubles. Now that the moment had passed, Stacy had revived loyalty to her job and her employers. She was in it, all the way, and she'd win big. Huge. Money and glory and, one day, in the not-too-distant future, she'd rest on top of a mountain of $100 bills. And wouldn't that be just grand?

Her fearless leader continued. "I want every person not working on product production to help Stacy with marketing and promotion," she directed. "We need deals, deals, deals, publicity, cross-promotions. Stanley and I have outlined an attack plan, and smut.com is going to give us a one-hundred-thousand-dollar launch party, his models serving drinks, outfitted in our designs. No tech or business journalist will miss it. We could throw the Silicon Alley party of the decade. And that's just the beginning. Now, have another drink, eat a muffin, and get right back to work. Janice, in my office. Stacy, twenty minutes."

"Here we go again," Stacy said. With renewed vigor, she went back to her desk to collect her thoughts and notes. At no point in the next month, Stacy knew, would she breathe air that wasn't inside her office, the subway or her lonely bedroom. The quest was over, for now. Sex would have to wait.

Her phone was ringing as she stepped into her glorified cubicle. Assuming the caller was Charlie requiring further contrition, she grabbed the receiver and said, "I can't express how sorry I am—again."

"At least you can admit you're at fault," said the male voice that was far too nasal to belong to Charlie. "I haven't been paid by thongs.com since May. You owe me over seventy thousand dollars, which, I'm afraid, I'm never going to get. I refuse to be ripped off by a bunch of females."

"Harry?" asked Stacy.

"How many other people are owed seventy thousand?" he asked.

Stacy didn't dare guess. "We've just had a large cash infusion," she said to Harry Watuba, president of Bolt Fabrics, the supplier thongs.com used for all its product. "I can personally assure you that we'll will cut you a check today."

"You'll do more than that, Ms. Temple. You're going to personally deliver the check, and personally stand next to me at the bank while I deposit the check, and personally take me back to your office if the check bounces. And if I don't get what's owed to me, you will personally escort me back to my warehouse where I can shove three thousand bolts of nylon mesh up your ass."

"Are you flirting with me?" she asked.

"You've got one hour," he said, and hung up.

Ordinarily, say, on the street or in a bar, if an angry man threatened to shove anything up Stacy's ass or other hollow parts, Stacy might have felt a pang of fear. Her otherwise pink cheeks might have gone white as chalk, and depending on what she'd had for dinner, she could easily imagine herself moved to nausea from fright. But Harry Watuba was approximately five feet five inches tall. He couldn't weigh over 140 pounds. His age was indeterminate, but judging from his gray tufts (over the ears, the rest of his head was blindingly bald), he was at least 58. He smoked heavily. She could take him in a tussle.

Not that she'd have the heart. Harry spent fourteen hours a day sitting behind a coffee- and cigarette-strewn desk in a windowless office at the rear of a drafty warehouse a few blocks south of the Chelsea Piers. When he wasn't begging for business on the phone, he was screaming at the men who drove Bolt's fleet of two trucks, carrying fine fabrics from around the world to the farther reaches of New Jersey, New York, and Connecticut. Nearly every apparel company in New York produced their designs overseas, and Harry had long struggled to hold on to solvency. Fortunately for him, a few politically conscious suckers like thongs.com, who outsourced manufacturing to a "sweatshop" in Trenton (union-run: bathroom breaks every ten minutes, coffee breaks five times a day, and one sick day per month) kept Bolt in the black. But not, of course, if bills went unpaid. Harry had to spend at least a few hours per day chasing money. When the economy was good, Harry made out. When it turned bad, he took a beating. In July 1999, he was hanging on with both thumbs, to the edge.

And he was alone. Harry's wife left him three years

ago because she couldn't handle the stress. Wisely (for her), she'd socked away some money in preparation for her move. She'd been planning it for years, and had saved enough to hire a vicious bastard of a divorce lawyer, who wrung every last drop out of poor Harry's pockets. He was forced to move into an inferior studio apartment in Clinton Hill, the up-and-coming-but-never-quite-getting-there neighborhood north of Hell's Kitchen. Stacy had heard that Harry spent several nights a week in his windowless warehouse office, a block from the Helicopter Tours launchpad on the lip of the Hudson River, just to avoid his studio's oppressive four walls.

Stacy had met him only once after his initial hand-shaking business lunch with Fiona, just over a year ago. Since then, Fiona hadn't spoken a word to him. He'd barely spoken a friendly word to Stacy in six months, around the time thongs.com's second wave of financing fell flat. Harry and his weekly phone tirades had been Stacy's sole responsibility. She'd figured out how to handle him, though. Let him rant for five or ten minutes until he got tired and 1) needed to use the bathroom, or 2) paused to take his medication. Then she'd make lilting assurances he'd so desperately want to believe about delivery dates and deadlines. She'd get off the phone and do her best to honor her promises.

And she intended to honor the one she'd just made. She went to Fiona's office and explained the crisis. Stacy was able to extract a check from Fiona for $25,000. Swearing she'd be back in no time, Stacy took a cab to 20th Street and 11th Avenue.

The taxi dropped her off at the entrance to the warehouse Bolt shared with Good Times, Inc., a party-supply company that rented chairs, linens, silverware and giant coffee urns, among other good-time things. She signed in with the part-time security guard and then climbed over stacks of folded chairs and a pile of twenty-gallon punch bowls before reaching the office suite at the back of the warehouse.

She knocked on Harry's door, confident she was about to make a cranky little man very happy.

No one answered, so she walked in. Talk about bad *feng shui*, she thought. Harry's desk faced the back wall of the office, so he couldn't see the front door unless he turned all the way around. Stacy noticed a telephone book on his desk chair. Was he that short? She closed the door and perched herself on the edge of his desk, crossed her legs and waited patiently.

Five minutes went by before the knob turned. The door opened and, on the other side, stood an Adonis. He was in his late 20s, six feet tall if he were an inch, broad of shoulder and smooth of chest. She could see the marked absence of hair because his shirt was off. His skin, almond, glistened slightly. His dark brown eyes glowed. His legs, in denim shorts and work boots with heavy socks, were thick with muscles and nearly hairless. When this godlike statue of flesh saw Stacy, not Harry, inside the windowless room, he smiled slow and neat, teeth gleaming like white pebbles, lips red and juicy.

She broke the ice. "You're not Harry."

He nodded mutely, still smiling, and then said with a heavy accent, "I am Schlomo, from Israel. The deliveryman. I don't speak English."

A deliveryman who didn't speak English. Well, now. Stacy had come to make Harry happy and beg forgiveness. And low and behold. Stacy got off the desk and took the man's hand. No wedding ring. She wasn't certain that rings were common practice in Israel, but she didn't care. She said, "Follow me."

The scene was straight out of *Penthouse Forum*, she assumed, never having read it—or lived it. But Stacy had learned, in her week of romantic misadventure, that opportunities knock and must be seized. She led her Israeli beauty into the warehouse. The security guard was nowhere to be seen, and even if he were, she was beyond caring about discretion. There wasn't a single zipper anywhere on her entire outfit. It was an omen. She would have her zipless fuck, and tell Charlie all about it—the perfect get-well gift. Plus, she didn't have to worry that this would be casual sex, or loving sex, or anything with implications about who she was and what she'd become. Balling Schlomo would be accidental. As much of an accident as her revirginity. As if she'd fallen off a ladder and landed snugly on Schlomo's cock with an "Oh!" and an "Isn't this a pleasant surprise?"

They found a spot against the south wall behind an eight-foot-tall stack of collapsible tables. The space was cramped, but there was enough room for two adults. They'd have to do it upright, but she'd long been a member in good standing (as it were) of the Vertical Club. Stacy put her hands on Schlomo's hips and kissed his mouth. His sweat tasted salty on her lips. She kissed him more passionately, and he responded by raising a flagpole in his shorts.

"I like American girls," he said.

"American girls like you," she responded.

He pushed her back against the stack of tables. While staring into her eyes (which made her feel weird: perhaps the secret to a zipless fuck was to keep one's eyes, and soul, shuttered), he reached under her shirt and bra matter-of-factly and began playing with her breasts. Taylor Perry had done the same things with little effect on Stacy. But the roughness of Schlomo's palms and the way he pinched her nipples, gently at first and then harder, caused that familiar crashing sound in Stacy's ears. He pushed up her clothes to look at her chest—that adorable wide smile— and then dove in.

She held his head against her tits, thinking and saying, "Yes." The electrical impulses traveled along the invisible cord from her nipples to her clitoris, sparking her off like a match (a really, really *big* match). Schlomo didn't hesitate before pushing her skirt up around her waist. He dove into her panties with both hands, expertly rubbing and yanking and gliding with all ten fingers. Stacy's legs began to shake and buckle. Feeling her unsteadiness, Schlomo lifted her off the ground (effortlessly, like a shapely sack of feathers), propped one of his feet on the edge of a table, and sat her on his thigh. She put an arm around his neck, spread her legs and deposited her head on his shoulder. He tore off her panties, which said more about the quality of thongs.com products than Schlomo's strength. The underwear fell on the ground into a small puddle of brown water. Plenty more where those came from, thought Stacy.

Hurrying now, since Stacy knew she'd come quickly, she used her free hand to undo the button on his shorts. She reached inside and pulled him free. Flagpole was an understatement; he was an Israeli cannon. As Stacy beheld the monster in her hands, she did have a moment of concern that he'd be too big for her. That such mass couldn't be stuffed inside her with a crowbar. Schlomo wasn't concerned. He'd been stretching and widening her for five minutes now, and he even had the skills (language, that is), to say, "I fit. Don't worry."

He reached under her right knee with his left arm, and held her open. His right arm was holding her around the waist. She was aloft, her arms around his neck, her left leg resting on his right thigh. He attempted to lower her onto him. He bumped against her, and she tried to wriggle to get the tip in. But, in this *Kama Sutra* position (Two Tigers in Heat? The Crouching Lotus?), she couldn't do much. He was in control of her movements. She was completely, rapturously, at his mercy.

Only problem: With both his arms holding her up, and her arms around his neck, neither had a free hand to guide him into her. A lot of bumping and cursing went on, until finally Stacy said, "Not there! Up, go UP!"

A bit of crashing behind the nearly rutting pair and then they heard the aghast squeal of what sounded like a little girl. "Schlomo! What the hell do you think you're doing?"

Stacy looked over the Israeli's shoulder and saw Harry Watsuba peering into their cranny. "Stacy Temple? Is that you?" he asked. "Stop that right now! This is a place of business. Get off him, this instant. I'm going blind!" He backed up, his forearm covering his eyes.

Schlomo said, "Shit. Piss. Fuck."

Stacy said, "Curses, foiled again."

The Israeli lowered Stacy to her feet and buttoned his shorts. She righted her clothes and looked mournfully at her ruined panties on the ground. She'd have to go without them for the taxi ride back uptown.

The thwarted lovers crawled out of their hole. Harry stood on the other side, scowling. He said, "Schlomo, you're fired; Ms. Temple, in my office."

Stacy felt terrible. She looked at Schlomo and said, "I'm so sorry. I'll talk to him."

Schlomo didn't understand her, but he said, "He fires me every day." Without so much as a peck, a grope, or a phone number, Schlomo walked off into the far reaches of the warehouse on his powerful hairless legs. He never looked back.

Gulping with frustration, Stacy went into Harry's

shoebox. He left the door wide open (maybe he was afraid to be alone with her, she wondered). He took a seat. She stood on the other side of his desk, facing him and out the open door. "We wanted to keep it a secret, but Schlomo and I have been seeing each other for some time now, and we're going to get engaged," said Stacy. "We'd like your blessing."

"I should have known to expect something like this from you underwear people," he said, sitting on his telephone book. "Schlomo is married with five children in Tel Aviv. But that's his problem. Where's my check?"

Almost penetrated by a married man, she thought. That would have been a first. She opened her purse, right where she left it on Harry's desk, and handed him the check for $25,000.

"I know it's only a third of what we owe you," she said, "but we promise you the remainder by the end of next month." Fiona gave her the line. She assured Stacy it would work ("He'll take what he can get and like it," she'd explained).

But it didn't. Harry sighed with the weight of a forklift and said, "This amount is unacceptable. You Internet companies think you can exist on promises and lies, but that's not the way I do business. I'm not going to listen to another word from you. Why should I trust you? Honest girls don't do what you were doing with Schlomo. That just seals it. I've spoken with five of your other vendors, all of whom haven't been paid. We're going to hire a lawyer and we're filing a class-action lawsuit to force you into bankruptcy. You'll have to sell off the company's assets, from your computers to your inventory, and when it's been completely dismantled and sold off, the cash will be divided among the claimants. After what I've just seen, I feel less guilty about doing this to you, Ms. Temple. You are not a nice girl."

"I *am* a nice girl. I'm so nice, I came down here to give you this check and make sure you feel comfortable with a payment schedule," said Stacy. "I'm such a nice girl, I took pity on your lonely deliveryman who, he told me with his eyes, is desperately lonely in this country. It's clear to me that you don't take his feelings into account. I was trying to show kindness to that poor, sad man. And maybe, just maybe, bring a little extra joy into the world."

Harry stared at her, his nostrils flaring in disbelief. "You were showing him kindness? Is that how you underwear people show kindness?"

"I can show you kindness, too, Harry. Not that way." God, no, she thought. "But in other ways."

He grimaced. "I don't want any of your ways."

"You might like one thing I have in mind." Stacy had to think of something she could offer him. Her eyes wandered off Harry's scrunched face, over his bald head, and out into the warehouse. She smiled suddenly, and said, "Thongs.com has just gone into partnership with smut.com."

"Sounds like a perfect match," he said.

"Oh, yeah. It's big news. Cause for celebration. Fiona Chardonnay was telling me today about a party at the end of the month to fete our new partnership. She said that smut.com was going to spend one hundred thousand on it. I'm sure at least half of that will go to rentals—tables, chairs, punch bowls, cocktail glasses. Like the ones stacked up out there," she said, pointing at Good Times, Inc.'s inventory.

Harry frowned sharply. "So go talk to Good Times," he barked.

"Maybe you should talk to them," she said. "And maybe you should suggest a finder's fee. I think ten percent is standard. And this first party is only the start. Smut.com throws parties every week of the year. And lunches. And dinners. I'd bet, given your way with words, you could get Good Times to agree to a fifteen percent finder's fee for all that business. If they balk at the extra five percent, tell them to raise their prices. Smut.com will pay. I'll make sure of it."

"How the hell will you do that?" he asked.

She winked. "I'll show them some kindness. Like I'm showing you right now."

Harry Watuba was old, short, poor, sad, and angry. But he knew when he'd been handed a free lunch on a gold platter. He said, "Where's my other forty-five thousand dollars?"

Stacy said, "I have a payment schedule right here." She'd created the calendar on her way downtown, promising a $10,000 check every other Monday for the next two months, and a floater payment in advance of future purchases.

He grunted when he looked at it. "Do you want to

spend three hundred bucks an hour on a lawyer?" she asked. "Force us into bankruptcy, and you'll be lucky to get ten cents on the dollar."

Her argument was solid. Harry made the right decision. Stacy promised to call him on Monday and help set up the Good Times/smut.com nexus. And she would. She was rolling with good intentions.

Stacy left Harry's office and walked through the warehouse (no sign of Schlomo anywhere) across the West Side Highway, and a few blocks up 10th Avenue until she found a cab. All the while, she grinned like a fool and held down the back of her skirt with both hands.

Chapter Fifteen

Friday night

"*I* have you in pen," said Fiona Chardonnay at the close of an endless workday (but not the end of the workweek for the captives of thongs.com; Saturday might as well have been Monday). Janice had disappeared around eight for her birthday dinner with Upper West Side Lawyer, and Stacy had been ordered to remain at work until Fiona was done for the night.

Stacy had forgotten all about her evening plans with the boss. Fiona had insisted a couple of days ago that she would be the agent by which Stacy would de-revirginate. No living creature should ever come between Fiona and a goal, but Stacy was worn out from work, and simply could not sally forth into the New York City night wearing a metallic gold mesh G-string under her skirt.

When she'd returned to thongs.com, bare-assed, Stacy had had the travel time to consider the huge promises she'd made to Harry. Could she pull it off?

The doubts flying freely, she was immediately summoned to Fiona's office. Stacy described, word for word, the conversation with Harry. Stacy, of course, omitted the avuncular comments about her being "not a nice girl" and the entire close (but not close enough) encounter with Schlomo. Janice and Fiona were too wrapped up in Harry's threats to guess that Stacy had left out part of the exchange. The plan of action: Stacy was to call other vendors who might be part of the class-action lawsuit, gather information and issue reasonable promises about payments. Janice would call thongs.com's lawyers and find out what they could do to stop the suit, possibly turn the tables and create a legal headache for Bolt Fabrics (Janice thought they could accuse Harry of illegally importing silk from China). As far as brokering a deal with Good Times and smut.com, Fiona and Janice agreed that the bluff was first class, but that the whole scheme would never come off.

Janice said, "You are a damn fine talker, Stacy. That's what we love about you."

"I'd like to try, anyway," she said. "I promised Harry."

"If you want to call Stanley Bombicci, go ahead. But he'll never believe that's why you're calling," said Fiona. "He'll assume you have an ulterior motive. Maybe you do."

Stacy most certainly did *not*. She decided an e-mail would be the way to contact Stanley. She'd blind copy Harry, just to prove she was making a sincere effort on his behalf. Fiona gave Janice and Stacy a couple more minor tasks on the matter. She would do nothing herself, since she brought in the big money that morning, and because she firmly believed that when thongs.com launched the Meshwear line, they'd be flush with bucks and would be able to pay off all the suppliers by the end of August.

"You know why I'm so confident?" she asked Stacy and Janice.

Because you're swimming in an ocean of your own hype? thought Stacy. "Why?" she asked.

"I have a prototype." Fiona reached into the top drawer of her desk and held aloft a scrap of material in the shape (and size) of a Dorito. "This is the Meshwear G-string—the 'Bermuda Triangle'—in gold."

She passed the G-string over to Janice and Stacy, who oohed and ahhed appropriately, as if it really were the golden scrap that would wow womankind, prevent pantylines and save a company from a financial breakdown.

"Stacy, for serving thongs.com loyally and tirelessly, I'd like to offer you a reward," said Fiona. "I want you to be the first woman in America to wear the Bermuda Triangle, to feel the softness and sexiness of our latest, greatest product."

She just couldn't. She'd feel more naked wearing the G-string than she did without anything on. Fiona threw the underwear into her lap. Stacy excused herself to the ladies' room and put it on. Afraid to look in the communal mirror (what if someone came in?), she returned to Fiona's office and announced she'd never felt sexier, and was grateful beyond all reason to be the first model for such a revelatory—and chic—unmentionable. The Bermuda Triangle did, actually, feel sexy. The string itself was strong and stretchy, the mesh fabric stretched, too. The ventilation was a nice plus.

"Let's see," said Fiona.

"Yes, let's see," agreed Janice, smiling, enjoying every drop of Stacy's embarrassment.

Stacy lifted her skirt and did a lightning twirl for her bosses, rearranged her clothes and plopped back down in the chair. Fiona and Janice applauded and the three women shared 30 seconds of amicable levity. If only it could be like this all the time, thought Stacy. Maybe it could be. Fiona's confidence used to flow in her own veins. It could again.

Or not. Almost as soon as the moment had begun, it ended. Fiona took a call. She shooed Janice and Stacy out of her office to do their top-priority tasks. Which Stacy had been performing tirelessly for hours upon hours.

And now, Fiona stood in the door of Stacy's cubicle, flush of face and purse, wanting to party.

Stacy said, "I'd love to, Fiona, but I'm exhausted."

The Dark Lady shook her head. She'd take no excuses. "I guarantee that you will meet a hot, young, available man. And I think you know how committed I am to my guarantees." Fiona had set the most generous return policy on the Internet: If you don't fall madly in love with, say, your new Naughty Stewardess Negligee, thongs.com will give you a full refund, pay for return shipping, and offer a 5 percent discount on a future purchase of $100 or more. About 2 percent of their customers took them up on the guarantee—thongs.com lost about $100,000 a quarter on returns, a drop in the bucket of their scorcher of a burn rate.

Stacy said, "Another disappointment with men could do permanent damage to my ego."

Fiona checked her gold-and-diamond Tiffany wristwatch. "It's ten o'clock. If you don't have a man's tongue in your ear by eleven, I'll give you a thirty-thousand-dollar raise."

"Fifty thousand," said Stacy.

"Sixty!" announced Fiona. "That's how confident I am in you."

"Since you put it that way," said Stacy, "a tongue in the ear is an offer I can't refuse."

Eleven o'clock. Stacy had already consumed two white chocolate martinis. She would have ordered a third, but she couldn't signal for the waiter with this young, hot, available man's tongue in her ear. Fiona had taken her to the Oak Room at the Plaza Hotel, a wood-paneled bar a few price points and tourists above a country-club lounge. Fiona was in tune with the decor in her purple passion dress and pinpoint heels. Within five minutes of sinking into plush chairs at a table in the back, two astonishingly attractive men approached them. Sven and Jorge. They were traveling businessmen from Finland with perfect English and not much to say. Fiona invited them to have a seat. Fifteen minutes of lust-laden small talk later, the Oak Room magically transformed into Makeout Central Station.

While Jorge gave Stacy's ear a lashing, she watched Fiona and Sven's maneuvers. Their lips were fused and his hand had disappeared up her dress, exposing a length of Fiona's thigh (Stacy hoped she would look as lithe in 20 years). Stacy spotted the trademark black satin roses on the garter straps of her Merciless Merry Widow (one of thongs.com's most popular styles). For a nanosecond, Stacy felt a wave of genuine affection for her boss. Fiona really loved and used the products; she wanted women to feel sexy and alive, at any age, in any size.

Stacy pushed Jorge back. They were squeezed into a plush chair, sides pressed together. His face was adorable: honey-colored eyes, rounded cheeks like a boy's, slight sheen from cocktails and kissing, tiny lines on his forehead to show some age and experience. Stacy guessed he was just over 30. His chest was a wall of muscle; you could chop wood on his legs. "Tell me, Jorge," Stacy said. "Where do you live in Finland?"

He took a lingering sip of his scotch (rocks) and said, "I've forgotten." Then he covered Stacy like a blanket.

Fiona and Sven stood suddenly. She said to Stacy, "We're taking a room. You might want to get one, too."

They left, Sven's hand on her lower back, her hand inside his pants pocket. Fiona was an incredible woman, Stacy thought drunkenly. Nothing could come between Fiona and a good time. Jorge handed Stacy the remains of her drink. She licked the white chocolate around the rim and made cat eyes at the Fin.

He said, "We won't need to get a room, Stacy."

Her heart sank. He didn't want her? A flood of disappointment (permanent damage?). "We won't?" she asked.

Reaching into the breast pocket of his suit, he removed a plastic key card. He held it between two fingers and said, "I've already got one."

Jorge's room in the Plaza had one queen-size bed, a couple of fake Chippendale chairs, a TV stand and a mini-bar. Pretty sparse, she thought. So the traveling businessmen were not on a lavish expense account, she thought. Stacy said, "No turn-down service tonight."

He laughed, confused. Okay, maybe that went over his Finnish head. Not wanting to disrupt the mood, she said, "I like you, Jorge." He was perfect—handsome, here today, gone tomorrow. She could secure sexually active status without disrupting the ordinary flow of her life. God bless Fiona, she thought.

"I like you, too, Stacy," he said, and pulled her down on the bed with him.

As they kissed, Jorge made small purring sounds, like a blond cat. "My God," he said. "What are you wearing?"

He'd discovered the Bermuda Triangle. "Oh, nothing," she said.

"Nearly nothing." He resumed nibbling her clavicle, and he whispered, "You can spend the night if you'd like."

"I'd like," she answered. She rubbed his lap.

"It's just a little bit extra, but you won't regret it."

Stacy stopped rubbing. "A little bit extra?"

"The room is covered, plus two hours. But if we go twelve hours, it's an additional thousand," said Jorge.

He must have realized Stacy had turned to marble. He took her face in his hands. "Fiona didn't tell you?"

Fiona hadn't told her. But now she knew: Sven and Jorge were not businessmen from Finland. They were escorts from Fiona's regular date-supply service. For the count of 10, Stacy was furious with Fiona. How dare she set her up? But by the 11 count, her temper had cooled. This might have something to do with Jorge's lifting her shirt and kissing along her ribs. Fiona had only been trying to help. In theory, calling an escort had seemed tacky and pathetic. But now that she was past hypothetical and deep into actual, Jorge, a flesh-and-blood gift from her boss, didn't make Stacy feel anything but curious and tickled. He would do anything she wanted.

"Have you ever been to Finland?" she asked.

"I'm from Boston, but I like Finlandia vodka," he said.

Stacy said, "Jorge, I would like you to kiss my entire body, inch-by-inch for an hour, including at least twenty minutes of oral sex, followed by long and slow intercourse, and fifteen minutes of hugging and gentle, absentminded stroking while you recover. Then we'll do it all over again. After that, you'll bathe me, wash my hair and brush it until it's dry. Then sing to me until I fall asleep in your arms. What does that go for?"

Jorge got off the bed, retrieved his suit jacket from the floor and found his Palm VII. Using the pen, he scribbled some numbers and checked the downloaded Executive Escorts listing of services. Stacy, looking over his shoulder, was astonished at the menu—it was like a spa's, only dirty. Finally, he said, "The straight sex is applied to an hourly rate of five hundred until twelve A.M. To stay until morning, it's a flat rate of one thousand. Plus two hundred for the bath and shampoo (an extra fifty for conditioning), one hundred dollars for the brush-out and blow dry—I'm very good, by the way, I'll make your hair straight as a pin—and an additional three hundred for the singing, unless you want something by Frank Sinatra, in which case it's jacked up to three fifty. Fiona already paid a thousand, which covers me until midnight. The balance: two thousand, one hundred dollars." He showed Stacy his calculations.

She whistled. "That much?"

"I'm worth it."

"And for a quickie, right now?"

"It's eleven forty-five. We still have fifteen minutes on Fiona's tab. We can do it and leave, and you wouldn't owe a penny," he said. He smiled seductively. "It'd be my pleasure, Stacy."

She grinned. No doubt he'd be thrilled. She was still young and—dare she say so herself—foxy. His obvious (like a frozen herring) attraction was visible and tempting. So were his time-tested skills.

She stood up and pulled down her skirt. "Can I have your number?" she asked.

He handed her an engraved card. "I'll come down ten percent on the package. And that's out of my own pocket."

"Keep it in your pocket, Jorge." It wasn't the money. Stacy could pay for a week of Jorge. She wasn't sure she could afford the emotional cost just yet.

She leaned down and kissed him sweetly and regretfully. He said, "Twenty percent. And that's my final offer."

"Still over my limit," she said. "But you never know when those lines are going to be redrawn. You may hear from me." If she got desperate on Sunday, her last day of non-virgin status, she could change her mind. She left him alone on the bed, blond and boyish, honey-colored eyes already checking his Palm VII for his next appointment.

Back in the hallway of her SoHo apartment building, Stacy found her Palm III in her evening bag and called up her To Do list of men. She'd crossed off a couple names (been there, not done that), and added a half dozen question marks alongside the name

"Jorge." She unlocked her door and was greeted by the comfortable clutter of her living room. She took a step inside and spotted a white square of paper on the floor.

She picked it up. It read:

Come to the roof at midnight tonight.

It was signed "4C."

Her heart pounded. The fates might be smiling on her after all. She hadn't given in to temptation, and this was her reward! She checked her watch. Just past midnight. She ran as fast as she could, up the rickety fire escape stairs, to the roof.

He wasn't there. All she found on the flat black-top roof were a couple of empty bottles of Brooklyn Lager, and a full one. Underneath it, a wet ring of condensation smudging the inky letters, sat another note. It read:

I waited until 12:15, and then I had to leave. I would have stayed longer, but every minute started to feel like an hour, and I hate waiting. I've probably completely fabricated a connection between us, and you're not coming anyway. Plus, I'm out of beer, except for this last one, and I need a few more before I can even think about going to sleep. For the record, I'm not an alcoholic. I just like a few beers on a Friday night in July. Hope you do, too. You must. I wouldn't be attracted to you otherwise. Anyway, I've been writing this for a couple minutes to kill time, and I'm out of space. But you'll never read this, because as soon as I get back from the bar, I'm coming up here to destroy the evidence. On the odd chance you do see this note, try my door. You might catch me. And have the beer.

She did like beer in July! She didn't think he was an alcoholic. He hasn't fabricated the connection. And she was attracted to him, too! Heart still thumping like a rabbit, Stacy grabbed the bottle and raced back down the steps. She knocked loudly on 4C's door. Nothing.

Damn. It. But underneath the frustration, Stacy was in love with these little notes. She felt attended to. Like she and Vampire Boy had a secret life, a shadow life, conducted on pink and white paper. She *had* been rewarded for turning down Jorge. Just look at this bottle of beer in her hand. Proof that Vampire Boy existed. He'd left her a gift. And one of these days, they would meet and talk to each other. And it would be perfect.

Life was not worth living without sex and love. If you weren't in a relationship, or pursuing one, you were off track. That was what Gigi XXX had written. Vampire Boy's note—a rambling, self-conscious spill—and the swell of excitement in her blood made Stacy wonder if Gigi was right.

Stacy searched in her bag for her pad of pink paper. She wrote:

I'm sorry I missed you. Can we try again? The roof, tomorrow for dinner. I'll be there at 7:30 with my Hibachi. Please join us.

Affectionately, Stacy

And thanks for the beer.

She slipped the note under Vampire Boy's door.

Chapter Sixteen

Saturday afternoon

Fiona was disappointed and hurt. In her exact words, she said, "I'm disappointed and hurt. I gave you Jorge like a present with a bow. And you blew it. That's not the Stacy Temple I've grown to respect and admire. That's not the woman I see as my protégé, my grasshopper. And the worst thing is, now I wonder about you, Stacy. How on earth could you walk away from spending a night—no strings attached—with gorgeous Jorge? Please explain it to me, because I need to know."

The Dark Lady—living up to her nickname in black vinyl today (vinyl may have passed its prime several years ago, and it was 95 degrees in the shade of a No Parking sign, but Fiona was a flawed fashion force that couldn't be stopped, come hell or haute water)—had already spent the bulk of her morning telling anyone who'd listen about yesterday's dual triumphs: Credit Suisse and a large man with a big "Finnish." Only Stacy knew the truth, that her boss had paid a fortune for her sham of a foreigner.

Clearly, Fiona thought paying for sex—and having a bang-up time—was just as satisfying as seducing a man on one's own power. Stacy believed that a steady diet of sex for money would lead to a horrible mass of twisted morals and the inevitable erosion of self-worth. If she vocalized her theory, Fiona would call her a blasphemer and Stacy would be fired on the spot. In this office, where the personal (or, precisely, the intimates) were professional, questioning the practices of the boss was strictly forbidden. So Stacy laid low, busied herself with endless tasks and phone calls, and tried to avoid Fiona.

But she couldn't steer clear for long. Shortly after lunch, Stacy was summoned to Fiona's office to receive the "I'm hurt" speech. And now, as Fiona tapped her sharpened nails on the marble top of her desk, Stacy concocted an answer that would be pleasing to her boss, without compromising her own morals.

"I was scared," she said. "Dearly tempted, and grateful for the opportunity. God knows I need all the help I can get. But when push came to shove, as it were, if I may, I chickened out."

"You weren't scared, Stacy."

"I was terrified."

Fiona smiled wickedly. "Guess how old I am."

Stacy didn't dare. "Thirty-nine?" she asked.

"Oh, come on, Stacy," said Fiona. "Take a real guess. Go ahead. I want you to."

"Forty-two?"

"Way off."

"Forty-five?"

"I'm fifty-seven. And I know that look in your eye, Stacy. You were afraid to guess my age because you didn't want to offend me. And you're scared to admit that paying for sex is distasteful to you. And that I may be a monster for doing it so easily. Jorge didn't frighten you at all. I'm the one who terrifies you."

Stacy fumbled. "No, he was very scary. Big and menacing and he had a very frightful price list."

Meanwhile, Stacy thought, even in her mad brain scramble, *Fiona is 57???* That was Stacy's mother's age (well, Belinda was 60, but close). How could a woman her mother's age dress in vinyl and screw whores?

Fiona said, "I'm going to explain to you why a woman my age wears vinyl and screws whores."

Stacy said, "You don't have to."

"That's just it, Stacy. I don't have to do anything. I put myself above judgment because I have absolute clarity. The older I get, the more I'm sure: An active sex life is the key to happiness. When you're a sexual animal, you are fully functional of mind, body, spirit. If you are asexual, all areas of life run below par. For me to be a complete woman, I must be as sexually active as possible." By this math, Stacy, in her sexually inactive incompleteness, was nothing but a pinkie toe.

"And here's the part I've learned from men," Fiona continued. "Romantic relationships force you to compromise your vision, ideas, creativity, and accomplishments. Look at Janice. She limps through each day, desperate to make a romantic connection. If she let go of her ideals, she'd be a genius. A force. An inspiration."

Life without love may leave room for other things. But surely, love inspires. Is a force in and of itself. Stacy said, "When Janice *does* find love . . ."

"Like that'll ever happen. Janice called in sick this morning. She must have had a disastrous date with that Internet lawyer, and now she can't face herself or her colleagues. For all I know, she's slashing her wrists."

Stacy bit her lip. She could only imagine the horror of Janice's date last night, only adding to her depression about turning 50. Stacy would pay her a visit later in the afternoon. Bring her some cookies. See if she could cheer her up. Would Janice attempt suicide? Stacy couldn't believe it.

Neither did Fiona. She said, "I'm kidding, of course. Janice would never do anything that stupid. Besides, she's used to having bad dates by now. In fact, one could argue that she keeps going out with lousy men because she wants to be disappointed. This is her way of avoiding the relationship she's been socially conditioned to believe she's always wanted."

That was logic Stacy had used on herself.

Fiona continued, "So tell me the truth: Do you really think that Janice is going to find what she says she's looking for?"

"No, Fiona. I don't."

"I agree. I've had my share of relationships, and they've all ended the same way. When I hit forty, I decided to make a change. The cycle of expectation and disappointment would end. I'd feed my body the sex it needs, and I'd avoid emotional attachments. And, in the seventeen years since then, I've made millions of dollars, become famous, created a life of luxury and privilege, and have been very happy."

"Not lonely?" asked Stacy, venturing into land strewn with mines.

"Do you think I'm lonely?" she asked.

With that one arched eyebrow and the half-smile, Fiona seemed the picture of smug contentment. Stacy searched underneath her boss's surgically smoothed face to find a hint of loneliness or desperation or even the faintest wrinkle of regret about her choices. Nothing. Fiona was a marvel. She may be the first, and only, woman in New York with no worries. Except for one.

"You might feel lonely if thongs.com doesn't make it," said Stacy.

A glint of anger crept across Fiona's eyes, darkening them. She said, "If thongs.com goes under, I'll find something else. And, Stacy, so will you. You'll react exactly as I will, because you're just like me. And let's cut even closer to the bone. The reason you walked out on Jorge wasn't fear at all. It was money. You didn't want to spend the money. That's exactly what happened to me the first time I was with an escort. After a day or two to think about it, I decided he'd be worth the cost. So I called him back."

Fiona dipped her hand into the super slim top drawer of her desk. She found a green slip of paper, a check, and pushed it across the tabletop toward Stacy.

Stacy picked it up and read the amount. "Two thousand dollars."

"Made out to you," said Fiona. "I've always felt a kindred spirit in you, Stacy. I look at you and see myself at your age. I think we can have a long friendship and business partnership. I'll need someone like you for my next move. And, just between you and me, it's a biggie. I can't say more at this point. But I need to know we're on the same page first. You took Jorge's phone number. Use it. And then, once you have, we can talk about what comes next."

Stacy thanked her boss and left the office with the check. She couldn't quite believe what had just gone down. Was Fiona really saying that unless Stacy used a male hooker, she has no place in her inner business circle? There had to be some form of sexual harassment in that equation. Fiona had been only half right. Stacy had been tempted by the sex Jorge offered. Sorely tempted (she'd been feeling the sore point keenly since she'd left the hotel room last night). The money *had* been a factor in her refusal. But there were other factors at work, too, that would prevent Stacy from paying for sex whether she could afford it or not. She'd rather pick up some loser with no sexual experience in a bar than pay a gorgeous erotically trained and talented escort in a glorious hotel room. No, that didn't make much sense. She'd rather pass on both, which might help explain why she'd been inactive all this time.

Back in her office, she felt an acute need to touch

base with someone who actually had a heart. She started to call her mother's number, but reconsidered (she had only half a heart). Instead, she dialed Janice's home phone. The machine picked up. If Janice were sick, wouldn't she answer the phone? If she'd done something terrible to herself, say, if she were lying, veins open, in a bath of her own blood, grabbing the phone would be impossible. Or if she were extremely depressed, she couldn't lift her hand to cradle the receiver. Stacy had to check on her. She had to make sure Janice was okay. Without alerting the authorities of her whereabouts, Stacy grabbed her red leather tote from Prada, and took a taxi to Greenwich Village.

Janice lived on Fifth Avenue, right on the edge of Washington Square Park. Her building, an early 1950s deco triumph, had official New York City landmark status. This meant that the edifice couldn't be torn down for new construction, and that any modifications on the facade had to be approved by the Landmarks Preservation Commission (which, famously, never agreed to any changes on their designated buildings— even inarguable improvements). Janice had been fortunate enough (insanely fortunate), to inherit her "classic six" apartment (two baths, three bedrooms) from her ex-husband's dead grandmother. The old woman, who died about 20 years ago, left the cooperative apartment to Janice and her children, not even including her grandson's name in her will. Since Janice was still married at the time, and New York is a community property state, it took some legal wrangling and outright begging to convince her husband to let her keep the apartment during the divorce settlement. She wisely gave him everything they had—their car, the stocks, their savings, even pieces of family jewelry, and an additional $50,000 in cash (payable over five years), to be sole owner of the co-op, valued in 1984 at $200,000. Here in 1999, she could sell it in approximately five minutes for $2 million. Janice, ergo, was never too concerned about money.

Stacy parted the building's metal doors and walked into the lobby, checking her appearance in the beveled glass mirrors. The doorman smiled as Stacy approached. She'd been to Janice's building dozens of times, dropping off paperwork, attending thongs.com parties. Stacy's own apartment in SoHo was an easy walk away. The doorman was at least 70, had been working behind that same desk for the last 40 years. He was a sweet, old man who provided zero protection to the building's inhabitants. But in this city, where the doorman's union was more powerful than the board of education, his tenure was written in stone (which is how things were written back in his day). He told Stacy that Ms. Strumph was at home. He asked if Stacy wanted him to call her. Stacy told him that she was paying a surprise visit and that she'd just go up and knock.

If Stacy had a doorman (she didn't), and he let anyone, even someone she knew well who was not a threat to her personal safety, ascend to her apartment without warning, she'd be livid. But Janice was far more forgiving than Stacy would ever be, and Stacy didn't want to risk Janice's instructing the doorman to send her away. A surprise might be the only way to keep Janice from getting into the tub, a plugged-in hair dryer in one hand and a razor blade in the other.

Janice lived on the eighth floor. Stacy knocked on her door softly. No response. She knocked harder. Still nothing. The fear that Janice might have done herself harm inched up Stacy's spine, and she used the blast of panic to pound with both fists on Janice's door, scream-ing her name.

That brought a response. Janice, tiny and sleepy eyed, her hair wet and curly, opened the door.

"Stacy?" she asked, surprised. Janice was wrapped in a white towel. With streaming white scarves tied around each wrist! As tourniquets? Was she trying to make the veins pop to better her aim? Or had she al-ready made the first cuts?

"I knew it!" screamed Stacy. "Let me in. Where's the razor? You can't kill yourself, Janice. You're loved. I love you. Your children love you." Stacy pushed past her boss and ran into the apartment. She nearly tripped on the Kilim rug in the hall, stumbling into the Queen Anne sideboard, rattling the china. Once she'd righted herself, she ran into Janice's bedroom (the pink toile everywhere—the walls, the bed, the curtains—was al-ways a shock). The door to the master bath was closed. Janice had tried to hide the accessories of suicide, no doubt. Stacy would find the straight razor and destroy it. Or empty the tub so Janice couldn't electrocute herself.

She threw open the door. Her eyes immediately went to the porcelain pedestal sink where she'd assumed she'd find a blade, already ruddy-edged and sticky with human blood. Nothing there. And then, Stacy caught the creepy feeling of another presence in the room. She froze in place. Then slowly, she turned around to face the tub. Behind the steamy shower door, movement. Stacy grabbed hold of the silver handle and pulled it open.

A man. A full head of gray hair on top of a slim, WASPy face. He had a decent body for his middle age. Flat tummy, long legs, with a flaccid (but long) cock and a puckered scrotum. He yelped first, then collected himself enough (but couldn't cover himself) to say, "Excuse me, madam, would you mind closing the door?" But Stacy couldn't move, her mind still processing the information. His arms were raised over his head, his wrists bound to the showerhead with a white scarf.

Stacy, now secure in the belief that Janice wasn't going to off herself anytime soon, shut the shower door. Mutely, she walked out of the bathroom and into Janice's assault-of-toile bedroom. Her sous-boss was sitting on the edge of her bed, smiling (proudly? coyly?) and patting the spot next to her.

Taking the seat, Stacy said, "He called me 'madam.' "

"He's very formal," said Janice.

"Yes, I could see that," said Stacy. "If I start apologizing now, is there a chance you'll forgive me by two thousand four?"

Janice giggled (giggled!). "Isn't he adorable?"

From the bathroom, a voice warbled into the bedroom. "Janice?"

"One minute, Jeffrey." To Stacy, Janice added, "Not Jeff. He doesn't like Jeff."

"He doesn't look like a Jeff."

"No."

The confusion wearing off, Stacy had to grin. "The earrings look fabulous."

"Thank you, Stacy. Everything *feels* fabulous today. I'm at peace, all is right with the world. It took fifty years, but I've finally found the man I've been searching for."

"And you know that after the first date because . . ."

Janice said, "Because I've had a million first dates, and none of them have felt like this. He's fantastic, Stacy. The second I saw him—it's a moment I won't forget. Just completely satisfying. With Internet dating, you can never really tell with photos. People lie about themselves."

Tell me about it, thought Stacy. Janice continued, "But Jeffrey looked just like his photo. I thought I'd have a hard time recognizing him, but there he was, exactly as he is. We felt comfortable together instantly. Like I'm my real self with him. No invention. No pretending. We had a few drinks in the library room at the Hudson Hotel, and then we went for a walk around the Village. Stacy, he dragged me into an alley, and we made out for two hours."

"Just made out?" Kissing for two hours seemed

lovely actually. Stacy had never just kissed for that long.

"Well, no," Janice admitted. "Not when I learned that he had an enormous elephant cock. Without Viagra. You'd be surprised how many men over forty-five rely on Viagra. But not Jeffrey. He's all natural."

What was that? Enormous elephant cock? All evidence to the contrary, thought Stacy, but then again, she'd seen him soft and embarrassed and—from the shower water—in a state of shrinkage.

"And then," continued Janice. "We came back here and haven't left or stopped since. I am elated! I want him; he wants me. This is what life is about. The innocent, sheer joy of sex."

"I can see you've already moved to the advanced pages," said Stacy, fingering the silk scarves around Janice's wrists. "Don't you want to save something for later?"

"Why?" asked her boss, blue eyes wide.

"What if he leaves you tomorrow?" Perhaps that was why Janice had tied him up, thought Stacy.

Her boss pondered the possibility. "I'll be sad, but I've been left before. I'd rather not imagine it. Right now, on this day, my life is fun. Just plain old fun. And if I can maintain it for a few months or years or decades, that's what I'll do. If not, I'm perilously close to menopause anyway. And I'll have my memories."

"Until the Alzheimer's sets in," said Stacy.

From the bathroom, another warble, "Janice, dear, my wrists."

"One minute, darling!"

"I should go," said Stacy.

Janice put her hand on Stacy's shoulder. "Not yet. I need to warn you. Fiona is planning something. I'm not sure what; I am out of the loop. But I know her so well, and I've seen her make plans before."

"Any guesses?" Surely, Janice's theory had something to do with what Fiona had alluded to early, about "a biggie."

Janice shook her head. "I'm afraid to imagine. But when all the dust settles, Fiona will come out richer and more powerful. As for the staff, I doubt there will be much left to pick over."

"What about you?" asked Stacy.

"I'll be relieved to get out," said Janice. "One door closes, another always opens. It's amazing how that works."

"I'm not sure that's how it works for me," said Stacy, sounding far more self-pitying than she wanted to. "Fiona made me some promises this morning. She implied that she'd protect me."

From the bathroom: "Janice, angel, my hands are turning blue."

Stacy stood. "Will I see you later?"

Janice blushed charmingly. "How much later?"

"You'll say good-bye to Jeffrey for me?"

Janice nodded and then gave Stacy a tight squeeze. "I know Tom had nothing to do with these earrings."

Stacy squeezed back, fearing that she'd snap Janice like a twig. "Will you hate me if I stick with Fiona?" she had to ask.

"I wouldn't blame you," said Janice.

That was the best answer she'd get, and Stacy accepted it. She took the elevator down to the lobby. The old, wizened doorman was now sharing the desk with a much younger (and cuter) man, also in uniform with the ridiculous gold tasseled epaulets. Stacy smiled at him and he winked at her, which she found cheeky and a bit too forward for his post.

The older man said, "Follow me," to the younger man, and "Do as I do." The two of them, a matched set with their white caps and gloves, marched to the lobby's deco double doors, each swinging one wide open by the handle, removing his cap and bowing slightly. Stacy only had to decide which door to walk through.

Chapter Seventeen

Saturday night

Stacy lugged the portable Hibachi, a bag of charcoal, a tin of lighter fluid, a package of hot dogs and some buns to the roof of her SoHo apartment building. She cursed herself for suggesting an evening barbecue. Too much prep work needed. But the weather would be perfect. She should be so lucky.

After leaving Janice's love nest earlier in the day, Stacy's head started hurting, and hadn't stopped yet. The thoughts that used to keep her awake all night had resurfaced (What Will Become of Me? Where Am I Going? etc.), uncomfortably, in the daylight hours. She'd returned to thongs.com with every intention of marching into Fiona's office and demanding the truth. What were her plans? Did she really think that Stacy was just like her?

Stacy might, actually, be like Janice. Her life a search for the love that would make everything all right. A love that would make everything all right? What kind of ridiculous, naïve bull feces was that?

asked her inner Fiona. Imagine the years and decades of longing and never finding . . . Stacy was sure her mother would advise her to go get a manicure or shop for a new purse or put on some lipstick. She'd feel much better.

Both Fiona and Janice believed that sex equaled happiness. But their means and intentions couldn't be more different. Stacy was at a crossroads, but stepping in either direction would be a risk. One direction would be an elective heart-removal operation. The other guaranteed the repeated bashing of the heart she left inside.

Stacy sat at her desk for three hours, staring at the embossed gold lettering on the card she'd taken from gorgeous Jorge. She should just call him. In one fell *schtoop*, she could rid herself of her re-virginity and declare her loyalty to Fiona. Heart removal would hurt at first. But then the pain—all pain, as well as all love— would be gone forever. Plus, she'd get some expert and much-needed male attention in the process—FOR FREE!

In the late afternoon on that Saturday, Fiona poked her black raven helmet head into Stacy's office and found her with Jorge's card in one hand, her phone in the other.

"You're doing the right thing," said Fiona. "Take the rest of the day off" —it was already five— "and let me know everything tomorrow. Call me at home. I don't care how early. And then we'll talk about your future."

Stacy left the office. She still hadn't placed the call,

and, in her anxious state, had plum forgotten about her date with the mysterious Vampire Boy neighbor. When she got inside her apartment, she found a note from him that read:

Stacy,

I'll be a few minutes late. I'm really sorry about that. I have an appointment that couldn't be postponed. I'll be thinking about our date the entire time, and I'm looking forward to meeting you officially at 7:40 on the roof.

Oliver, 4C

Oliver. His name was Englishy. She liked that. Stacy held the note in her hand, and dared to hope. But no time for that. She had a little over an hour. She had to get to the supermarket, shower, dress, accessorize. She realized with a start that this was her final night as a non-revirgin. Oliver was her last chance to seduce a man the normal way. If she failed there, if it turned out to be a dismal failure, too, well, maybe that was a sign that she *should* call Jorge, climb aboard the Fiona train and give in to her morally unhinged impulses. She'd become Fiona Junior. A girl could do worse.

A girl could do better, too. Stacy would muster whatever impulses she had left and make a serious go of it with Oliver. He was awkward and mysterious, but he had a pulse (she had to assume). He thought they had a connection. Maybe her social ineptitude would mesh well with his anti-human tendencies. They could be the anti-couple, avoiding all other people, living in the dark—their shadow life of notes under the door and beer on the roof. It could work.

Stacy knew Oliver was shy, so she'd have to play it soft and subtle with him. No wild lunges (as with Charlie), no declarations of horniness (as with Brian), no invitations into her apartment and pants (Jason), no cash transactions (Jorge), no silent humping (Schlomo) and no pornographic recitals (Stanley). She'd have to seduce Oliver with . . . She wasn't sure what it would take. Passive, shy men were not in Stacy's wheelhouse. But, as she'd discovered in the last five and a half days of staving off the stigma of revirginization, desperation is the mother of self-invention.

She'd brought up the last of the supplies when the roof door creaked open. Oliver flinched at the sun, still bright in the sky at 7:45 in July. He looked nice in jeans and a Black Dog T-shirt. They smiled at each other. Then looked away. The discomfort and full-frontal daylight made her queasy (she could only imagine what it did to Oliver; he might turn into a pile of powdered dust). Several polite and flirtatious notes did not make a relationship. She wondered if her five trips up and down the dark and dank roof stairs would be for naught.

Stacy smoothed her gingham skort and said, "I never know how much lighter fluid to use." She wanted to relax him (and herself) and she knew from experience that offering a pint of lighter fluid to a man was like giving bourbon to a Kennedy.

He said, "Me neither."

Oliver hadn't seemed like an outdoorsman. He fidgeted anxiously. She'd embarrassed him. "Are you thirsty?" she asked, pointing at her makeshift picnic area. A light blanket and a cooler with a dozen Sierra Nevadas.

He grabbed a beer but chose to stand, one hand in his jeans pocket. Stacy doused the charcoals. If she told him she liked him, he might be more at ease. "I wasn't sure you were going to come up," she said. "It's nice to hear your voice. I'd been wondering about that."

"I've heard your voice before," he said. "It sounds different in person, though."

What could he mean by that? Had he heard her through the walls? Unlikely. She would have to ask about that later. Instead, she said, "I've been enjoying the notes."

"Yeah," he said. He drew on the open mouth of the bottle. "I'm kind of embarrassed about the one I left up here last night."

"Don't be," she said. "I liked it."

"All that stuff about feeling a connection. And that you might not really exist."

"Why would you think I don't really exist? You've seen me."

"It's more like, does the connection really exist," he said. "We've never even had a conversation."

She smiled. "We're having one now."

"Want a beer?" he asked. She nodded and he brought a bottle to her. They stood a foot apart. He smelled like Ivory soap and hops. "I've only lived in New York City for a year. Is this how people usually meet each other?"

She took a sip. The cold wetness cleansed her throat. "People usually meet in bars."

"I've been to a lot of bars," he said.

"When's the last time you were in love?" she couldn't believe she asked. She knew her next question should have been, "Where did you live before you came to New York?" but she was so not interested. Might as well focus the talk on what mattered. His emotional past mattered. She hoped he wouldn't ask about hers.

He said, "When I was twenty-two."

"So it's been how long?" she asked.

"Five years." He was only twenty-seven. A younger man. He said, "Since then, I've had a few girlfriends, but I wasn't preoccupied by any of them."

"Is that how you know you're in love?" she asked. Stacy had never sat down and made a concrete list of ways you know you're in love. Being preoccupied by a man: Stacy had no memory of that. In college, she'd fixated on her various seductions. With Brian, she had spent a lot of time wondering why she was with him.

Oliver said, "Thinking about her all the time, imagining her reactions, trying to figure out what she'd think of things or what she'd say. Wanting her input on mundane shit, like prices at the supermarket, or commercials on TV. That's love. That's the nature of love. When you're not with the person, you think about her. And when you are with her, you look at her and can't believe how lucky you are."

Stacy and Oliver each took a sip of beer and looked at each other over the bottoms of the brown bottles. Was he pondering his good fortune to be on the roof with her right now? Stacy wondered. Had he been wondering what she thought of commercials on TV? She can't say she'd been doing that about him. But, then, she'd been busy.

"I'm jealous," she said finally. "I don't have a working definition of what it means to be in love."

"You can use mine," he said. "To notice the signs."

Sign posting. Stacy was in need of that, having been cruising without direction on the superhighway for over a year. "I will," she said. "And as a gesture of gratitude, I'll cook."

She struck a match and threw it on the coals.

The plume of fire rose six feet. Stacy reeled back. She knew that smell, that scent of singed hair (once she'd had her leg stubble removed via laser). Frantically, she felt her head. No apparent damage. Oliver walked over, never removing his hand from his jeans pocket, and coolly emptied his beer on the grill.

He asked, "Are you okay? Your eyebrows are smoking."

Stacy's fingers flew to her eyebrows. She didn't like the feel of them. Stacy picked up the metal spatula and checked her reflection. Her eyebrows, for the most part, remained. But the hairs were oddly curled and dark, very bizarre with her ivory complexion and red hair.

Stacy must have groaned. Oliver said, "Let me see."

She held her face up to him. He leaned in closely. Stacy, in partial shock, could still appreciate his unruly black hair, ice blue eyes and creamy, poreless skin. His fingers—slender and long—reached to touch her singed eyebrows. The toes of his sneakers were inches from her sandals. "You look fine," he said. "I can't say the same for the grill."

Stacy turned toward the grill. The coals swam in a pool of still bubbling beer. "I'm cursed," she announced. "This is just the final kick in the ego after a whole week of disaster. You should have stood me up."

"I almost did," he said. "Nerves."

She'd been expecting an arduous protest along the lines of "only death could have kept me from your side."

"If that's how you feel," she said indignantly—for this she'd risked disfigurement?— "let's just skip it. I'm going downstairs to nurse my eyebrows."

She grabbed her blanket and cooler and banged through the roof door. Oliver followed her, relieved, she assumed, to get out of direct sunlight.

Once they reached their hallway, Oliver put his hand on her elbow, stopping her. "I'm so far beneath you on any measurable scale," he said. "Why would you want to spend time with me?"

"You don't even know me," she said, shaking her elbow loose. Using insecurity as a means to reject her— that was so tired.

"I know that you have a lot of experience. That's intimidating. I've only been with seven women in my life and . . ."

She held up her hand. "The walls *are* thin, but the sound of me having sex can't possibly have passed from my apartment, through the Rothenbergs' kitchen, and into your living room. Not that I've had any recently." Was he referring to her hallway come-on to Jason? "What are you talking about?" she demanded.

"I'm talking about the web site," he said, looking confused and, suddenly, younger than 27.

How could she have invested the final night of her sex quest in this befuddled boy? She liked him better as the mysterious masher. "Do you think selling underwear for thongs.com makes me a slut?" she asked.

"Not that. The other web site," he said back.

"I have no idea . . ."

"Smut.com," he said, avoiding her eyes.

A frightening notion dawned on Stacy. Had Stanley Bombicci found a way to fulfill his fantasy without her active participation? She grabbed Oliver by the wrist and dragged him into her apartment. After she turned on her computer and logged on to AOL, she steered Oliver into her desk chair. "Show me," she said.

Oliver expertly tapped on her keyboard. He said, "I don't go to smut.com for the women. I go for practice."

"Practice masturbating?" she asked, staring at the monitor over his shoulder.

He said, "Practice hacking. Hacking into porn sites is pretty easy. It limbers me up."

So Vampire Boy Oliver was a hacker by trade? Stacy softened a bit with this knowledge. You never know when a hacker could come in handy. She put her hands on his shoulders, and leaned her breasts against the back of his head. Subtle and sly seduction plans aborted. The full court press was on.

"Here it is," said Oliver as he called up the smut.com homepage. He typed in some code and got access to the site.

A moving, talking woman appeared on the computer monitor. She said, "Hello, I'm Stacy." She was a trim redhead with long straight hair and brown eyes, about five foot six, with ivory skin. She wore thongs.com's signature piece, the French Maid For Passion costume—a micromini uniform dress (very low cut in front), black fishnet hose, black pumps—and held a feather duster. The likeness wasn't eerie, but it was definitely in the ballpark. Her smut.com doppelganger (Smut Stacy) was a graceful, swanlike creature. Stacy leaned over Oliver and clicked the command box labeled LET ME PLAY.

Smut Stacy said, "I'm madly in love with a man who doesn't know I exist! His name is Stanley, and I want him so *bad*. I've written him a letter. Can I read it to you?"

Oliver hit the YES command box. Smut Stacy yanked her breasts out of her costume to retrieve her handwritten letter. She read, "Dear Stanley. You are like a god to me. I worship your body. Just imagining your huge cock makes my nipples hard. My pussy is sopping wet. I want you to put your dick into my cunt and fuck me like a dog . . . ." Stanley's on-line scripts were far less imaginative than the ones he wrote for personal use—lowest-common-denominator porn. On screen, Smut Stacy dropped the letter on the bed behind her and rolled all over it, tearing at her costume and herself. It was a ridiculous sight, but the model was breathtakingly beautiful.

Oliver said, "Now that I've seen you up close, you look nothing like that girl."

How could Stanley have done this? Okay, she'd humiliated him on their date. But using her likeness (especially a vastly superior likeness) and *real name*? That was just not right. Although, if he worked out his revenge this way, he might never come near her again. Or not. Should she buy a pit bull? A stun gun?

"Are you upset?" asked Oliver. "You look upset."

"That's just the arch of my new eyebrows," she said. "I understand now why you thought I didn't really exist." Stacy was outraged. But she also felt—no delicate way to put this—aroused. Seeing a woman who was supposed to be her, reading a racy tribute to a man who was tormented by his attraction to her? Disturbing to be sure, but exciting. Smut Stacy removed her outfit, and began masturbating with a dildo.

"Turn it off," she said.

Oliver shut down her computer. After, he said, "I'm sorry about this. You see why I've been nervous. I thought you were a fantasy come to life. Except that woman isn't you. It's better that she's not you."

"Except you're the only one who knows that!" she said. How many men had seen this? she wondered. Anyone she knew? She would string up Stanley by the balls. She would chop off his dick. Just as soon as she emerged from ten years under a rock.

"I'm glad I do," said Oliver. "I could never fall in love with a fantasy."

Love, she thought, was the fantasy. The woman was irrelevant. "You weren't falling in love with me."

"Not when I thought she was you," he said, cocking his head at the computer. "You're even more beautiful now that I haven't seen you naked."

He looked at her, stared really. The desire for her was there, she knew, and not for what he'd seen on screen. If he'd thought she was a fantasy before, he looked at her now as if she were a mystery.

"Oliver," she said, eyes level. "I've never been in love. Not the way you describe it. I'm fairly inept at seduction, too. And I wonder if your attraction comes from misconception."

"My misconception has been erased," he said, standing.

"Then you like the proximity," she said. "Living on the same floor of the same building."

"Imagine the luck," he said, taking a step toward her. "You are attracted to me."

Undeniably. Especially when he moved, silent and smooth. His eyes couldn't be bluer.

"You have to tell me," Oliver said.

"I am attracted to you."

He sprang. The forward motion sent them onto the couch. Then onto the floor with a crash. This kiss, she thought, was real. Unlike the others this week, it felt full of . . . something. It was the opposite of empty, that much she knew. And his lips were soft and warm, his arms tight against her back, squeezing her like a stuffed animal, as if she had no oxygen requirements. They stopped kissing and looked at each other. Frozen on the outside; kinetic and jumping inside. He opened his mouth, and Stacy covered it with a new kiss.

And then the intercom buzzed. She ignored it. But the buzz kept coming. She counted twenty seconds. Oliver pulled back. "Doesn't sound like your visitor is going away."

She tugged her clothes into place and answered the buzzer. "Hello?"

The squawk back: "Stacy! I'm so glad you're there. It's Jason."

Jason, the handsome hairy man? Last time they saw each other, he'd refused to come inside and see her purse collection, muttering about respect in the morning.

"Regretting your decision?" she asked.

"Yes. I want to come up," he said.

Oliver watched and listened from the floor. Stacy smiled at him, his black hair a tornado on his head, his clothes half on. "I'm vacuuming right now," she said. "Call me tomorrow."

"No, Stacy, I have to see you. I made a huge mistake on Monday night. I feel like an idiot."

She said, "You can tell me what an idiot you are to-morrow," and turned her intercom buzzer volume to zero. She walked back toward Oliver on the floor.

Sitting up, he asked, "Was that the guy you were arguing with in the hallway earlier this week?"

"You shouldn't have been eavesdropping." Oliver shook his head and stood. He rearranged his clothes. Stacy said, "What's going on?"

"This guy has come to his senses. You care about him. You said you did in the hallway. You're just using me to get back at him."

"I'm not!" she said. "I don't care about Jason!"

Oliver's blue eyes saddened. "You said you did."

"I changed my mind," she argued.

"What if you change your mind about me?"

The spell was breaking. She put her arms on his shoulders. "Kiss me," she said.

He shook his head. "I'm not having a one-night stand with my next-door neighbor. I'd have to move. I like my apartment. I have my illegal DSL connection set up perfectly."

"It won't be a one-night stand," she said.

"I don't want to be a rebound relationship for you," he said. "You have unfinished business with this Jason guy. If it doesn't work out, you know where to find me," he said.

He kissed her chastely on the lips, and walked out the door. It was 9 P.M.

Chapter Eighteen

Saturday night

Sitting on the edge of her unused bed, Stacy held Jorge's card in her shaky little hand. In her other hand (shakier), she held her cordless phone. By punching seven buttons, she would cross the line into no-woman's-land. Relinquishing all claims to propriety, knowingly, never to return to a land of undiminished morality. She took a deep breath. Her luck with love was bad. Her luck with seduction was worse. Her quest—to avoid the revirginity thing—had become an albatross, a jinx (a jinxed albatross?). Jorge was the guaranteed way to cut the whole depressing business from her neck, freeing her at last. He was the doormat she'd step across into another world, one that, according to Fiona, abounded with success and happiness. He was the sledgehammer she'd use to break down her enclosing walls of inertia. If nothing more (Stacy did hate to heap metaphor on the heads of prostitutes), he was a sure thing.

All she had to do was dial. So she did.

"Executive Escorts. Jasmine speaking," said the voice on the phone.

"Is Jorge De Beof available?" asked Stacy.

"Whom may I say is calling?"

"A friend."

"An anonymous friend, or shall I go ahead and tell him that I have Stacy Temple on the line?"

She nearly dropped the phone. "How do you know my name?"

"We have caller I.D. for our protection." Jasmine needn't have explained further.

Stacy said, "Tell him it's Stacy from last night."

"Hold, please."

She held. Instead of music, the phone was connected to NPR, Stacy's former place of employment. She listened to *This American Life,* and felt a sudden wave of regret and depression. Why had she left? And what was she doing?

She started to hang up, when she heard Jasmine saying, "Ms. Temple? Hello?"

Stacy said, "My sink is overflowing. I've got to go. I'll call back later," and rang off. Chicken. Shit. She lay back on her bed. Tomorrow she'd be a virgin anew, and there was nothing she could do about it. Maybe that wasn't too much of a burden, she rationalized. Maybe it was okay to give up, again.

But it wasn't. She kept picturing Janice's pleased face in her pink toile bedroom. It was the picture of contentment and exhilaration. She reached for the antique silver hand mirror she kept on her night table, and held it in front of her face as she lay on the bed. Not a good angle. The flesh on her cheeks stretched downward, making her appear drawn and misshapen. This was the face of loneliness, five minutes on the wrong side of young. She lay the mirror down on the comforter and rolled onto her side.

After several minutes of moping, Stacy got up to redress. She carefully (and artfully) applied a masque of makeup (including new eyebrows), and spritzed Obsession on her pulse points. She had one more option to try before giving in completely to failure. Everyone had been telling her all week long to "just go to a bar," and that was exactly what she'd do.

The bar at the SoHo Grand Hotel was known for three things: 1) hipness, drawing celebrities and supermodels, 2) titanium (the metal of the moment) interiors, and 3) cocktail CoCo Canal, a lethal combination of espresso, Bailey's and crème de cacao. Stacy had been there only twice before, both times with Fiona for investor-wooing drinking sessions. Fiona had a carefully calibrated gauge for exactly how much money a private investor would be willing to part with. Apparently, this number would rise in direct proportion to the importance of the celebrity sighted. If, perchance, one were sitting on a stool at the SoHo Grand Hotel bar and in walked Jennifer Lopez with an entourage of twenty ridiculously attractive, scantily clad, almond-skinned dancers and assorted hangers-on, Fiona would snag an additional $200,000 on top of the minimum buy-in price of $400,000 (a sighting and cash extraction Stacy was witness to). But if one were on the same exact bar stool and in walked Mira Sorvino with a couple members of the Backstreet Boys, the price would go up a mere $30,000 (that could rise as high as $50,000 if Mira made out with Nick or Keith). No celeb sightings, no good ammo to gun for the sky-high bucks.

On that particular Saturday night, Stacy was only mildly eyeballing the bar entrance for a famous face. The bulk of her scanning was for a clean-shaven man, unmarried, if at all possible (after disconnecting with Executive Escorts, Stacy was back on the morality high horse). He would have to be searching the bar with his eyes as well, cruising with intent, not at this particular location for any reason other than meeting an attractive female for a mutually pleasurable exchange.

She sat alone at the bar, sipping a vodka martini, slightly embarrassed but confident in her attire (Stacy was not one to bare a midriff lightly, but tonight, she wore a low-rise pencil skirt and a high-cropped baby T, all black). She surveyed the packed, sweltering room once, twice, thrice, until she settled on a pair of long legs in stiff jeans. The fellow (brown hair cut short, choppy bangs grazing his forehead) was sitting at a window-side table. His booth mates, loutish boy/men, were laughing loudly, mugging at the harem of young women who surrounded them. But not this guy. He was amused, pleased to be there, but not a full participant. He had the cute, crooked smile she loved, and a bashful air about him that made him approachable. He seemed like the kind of man whose feelings were easily hurt. Since offending men seemed to be Stacy's special skill of late, she believed he was the perfect guy for her.

She smiled at him. He noticed and grinned shyly back (adorable!). She sipped her drink, licking the glass a bit. The man stood up (tall!), and came over to her. Okay. She steadied herself. This was more like it. Smile, flirt, and you're halfway there. Who cared that he was a complete stranger, a million degrees of separation from her universe? As he got closer, Stacy saw he was wearing a Supertramp T-shirt (unpretentious!), and his eyes were brown and deep, as if, within them, you could find the love of a thousand golden retriever puppies.

"Hello." His voice cracked unmistakably.

"Sweet Jesus," she responded. No wonder she'd been instantly attracted to him. "You're Tony McGuinty."

"And you are?" he asked.

"Stacy Temple," she said, shaking his movie star hand. Fortunately, she had the self-control not to follow up with what she was thinking: *I am your biggest fan. I worship you. Every sexual fantasy I've had in the last year has featured you. You've been a fireman, a policeman, a scientist working on a cure for your own insatiable lust, an ice-cream truck man, and a chauffeur. And here you are, delivered to me by the Goddess herself, in my hour of greatest need, to bolster my confidence, deliver me from revirgination, and*

take me to the highest realm of the senses. Praise be, Goddess!
You haven't deserted me.

Instead, she simply stated, "You look nice."

"So do you," he said. "I'm here with a bunch of friends. Would you like to join us?"

She looked over to where he'd been sitting. The faces came in more clearly now, and she realized the puffy-faced blond was Nathan Decapulet, the straggly-haired, lanky guy was Luke Hasson, and the burly, bearded, swarthy one was Daniel Blake. Reports in the *New York Post* and *Daily News* had widely covered the titty-twistings and ass-grabbings of this crew, a group of young, rich, heterosexual, drunken movie stars known as the Pussy Posse.

"I'm comfortable right here," she said. He smiled (charming!), and bought her another martini. She said, "I went to a screening of *Chemical Attraction* earlier this week." Had it really been only several days before? "You were incredible. I can't stop thinking about you. I mean, I can't stop thinking about it. The movie. Oh, what the hell. I can't stop thinking about you in the movie."

"Thank you so much for saying that," he said (polite!). "I'll be even happier if you're a movie reviewer."

"I'm a lingerie peddler."

"A far more worthwhile occupation," he said.

She was *in love with him*. He was The Perfect Man. A gust of profane laughter and the shattering of a glass turned their attention away from each other and toward the Pussy Posse table.

He said, "I may be thrown out of here soon."

Do you want to go to my place? Stacy wished she'd the balls to say that. What she really said: "That's too bad."

He pulled on his bottle of Bass. "I like your hair."

"I like yours."

He squinted. "Did something happen to your eyebrows?"

She said, "Bizarre barbecuing accident."

"What are you doing alone at a bar?" he asked. "Don't you know that men are going to hit on you if you sit here looking like that? It's indecent. You should be home, where it's safe."

"Actually, I'm on a mission," she confessed. He was so easy to talk to. She felt completely comfortable with him, even though he was famous.

"A mission impossible?" he asked.

"So it seems." She sipped her drink. "I have one more day before I've gone a complete year celibate. I came here with the hope that I'd meet a man. I've heard bars are a good place to do that. I haven't had much luck so far this week out of bars. In fact, I've had nearly a dozen disastrous encounters, all of which have been embarrassing and/or soul killing."

He smiled (disarming!) and said, "Sounds like a movie."

"Comedy or tragedy?" she asked.

"The perfect ending would be if you wound up having sex with a famous, handsome movie star," he said. "It'd be a divine reward after your week of pain and suffering."

And how. "Is that an offer?"

"Give me a minute." He walked back to his table and bent down to talk to his friends. She couldn't hear what he was saying, but at the same second, every face at the table turned toward her. The men all started laughing. Then Nathan Decapulet himself scooted out of the booth. He was much taller than she'd thought. Tony and the Most Promising Actor of His Generation walked across the room (women swooning and kaveling everywhere), straight toward Stacy Temple, red of head, pink of cheek—the chaste, over-30 lingerie peddler. She felt blessed.

Tony said, "This is Nat."

The Sexiest Man Alive held out his hand. She shook it and smiled.

Nathan said, "So you want to have sex with a handsome movie star?"

She wouldn't put it quite so crassly. "I didn't say . . ."

"Because every woman in this bar—every woman in this city—wants to sleep with a famous, handsome movie star," said Nathan in an understated tone of purposeful detachment. "I'd like to know what makes you so special that you think, of all the women in this bar— of all the women in this city—a famous, handsome movie star should sleep with you?"

What a nasty little shit, this (g)Nat, she thought. Stacy would have to remember their conversation verbatim, to tell Charlie so he could post it on noir.com.

Before she could respond to what she hadn't realized was a rhetorical query, Nathan said, "I'll tell you what makes you special. I can sense that you are the kind of woman who loves to suck dick. I bet you'd be willing to suck the dick of every guy at our table. And if you're half the woman I think you are, you won't settle for just one movie star. Tonight, you can have all four of us."

Tony, meanwhile, was standing behind Nathan, shaking his head as if (*as if*) he were astonished by the antics of his more famous friend.

"I'm flattered," said Stacy, fingers fluttering to her collarbone. "And I certainly do love to suck dick. But, to be honest, I may be only half the woman you think I am. And there are four of you. So that would mean I'd suck two of your dicks? Then again, maybe I'm just a quarter of the woman you think I am, and I'd suck only one dick. And, even if I were the woman you think I am, is this an all-or-nothing offer? I need to know, because I'm not exactly sure how much dick I want to suck, or how much famous, handsome movie-star cock I can stuff into one night. If it were spread out over four nights, that would be a different story. But, to tell you the honest truth, I'm really just an eighth of the woman you think I am. Which means just half a dick gets sucked. I'd be willing, but it could take a while. Is the possibility of sucking half of one of your dicks per night over eight nights out of the question?"

Nathan blinked. He said to Tony, "This girl is crazy."

Tony said, "But good at fractions."

They snorted and left Stacy sitting just as she was,

alone at a bar, sipping a fancy schmancy ten-dollar cocktail, feeling like one sixteenth of the woman she was when she'd walked in a half hour earlier. Pride required her to finish her drink. And then she left, her midriff and misery exposed.

Chapter Nineteen

Saturday night—still

As soon as she hit the pavement outside, a giant stretch limo—as black as Stacy's mood—pulled up to the curb of the SoHo Grand Hotel. A dozen passers-by stopped to check it out. Stacy joined them. Her night was ruined, but if she could catch a glimpse of, say, Madonna, she'd feel a little bit better.

The door opened. A woman's leg appeared. This was some leg, long, muscular, shimmering in black sheer stockings. A glamorous leg. Belonging to someone famous and beautiful. The crowd pressed closer to the limo. The second leg emerged. Stacy was sure she recognized the spike of that patent leather heel. Before she could flee, the remainder of Fiona Chardonnay's body emerged.

"Stacy Temple!" Fiona called. "I thought I saw you standing there."

The crowd of people stared at the 57-year-old bombshell, elegant tonight in a black, off-the-shoulder Prada ankle-length dress and great chunks of diamond jewelry. She must have come from a benefit to be dressed so conservatively, thought Stacy. Her brain screaming, "Run away! Run away!" Stacy knew full well that she would have to stand her ground and have a conversation. The first question from Fiona would be What are you doing here and why aren't you with Jorge?—a query Stacy was in no mood to answer.

Fiona closed the limo door, strode over to her underling, and asked, "How do I look?"

Stacy could address that topic easily. "You're radiant, glimmering, a showstopper, a jaw dropper—"

"That's enough," said Fiona. "What are you doing here?"

No use lying. Stacy got to the meat of it: "I came here to pick up a man, but instead, I was mentally fucked by a couple of rude and imperious movie stars," she said. "I'd already blown it with another guy earlier tonight by frying my eyebrows, after which point I found out that Stanley Bombicci is using my name and likeness on line as a masturbatory aid for millions of his horny subscribers. I didn't call Jorge because, no matter how much you think I'm like you, I simply couldn't live with myself if I paid for sex. What's more, in half a day, I will be a virgin again. I'll be fresh and innocent as a baby lamb, and just as prime for slaughter."

Fiona looked at Stacy as if she'd vomited on the sidewalk. "I disgust you?" asked Stacy. "I seem to have that effect on just about everyone I meet these days."

A man in a black tuxedo appeared at Fiona's side. His face was familiar to Stacy. She wasn't sure how. He was around 45, with soft, round cheeks in need of a shave, olive skin, curly black hair, oval-shaped eyeglasses perched on a two-sizes-too-big nose. He put his arm around Fiona's waist and said, "Ready to go inside?"

Fiona said, "Stacy Temple, this is Randy Gestalt."

The name jogged her memory. Randy Gestalt, the president and CEO of Mercury Matrix. He'd been on the cover of *Fast Company* magazine a couple months ago. Among the youngest billionaires in America, he'd made a dozen king's fortunes the old-fashioned way: He bought failing companies for a song, dismantled or artificially bolstered them, and then sold them to other companies for a profit. One would think selling loser companies would be a recipe for financial disaster, but there was always some megacorporation (AOL and CBS, for example) that would jump at the chance to absorb a sick company, assuming they could ignite new life with their magic breath. More often than not, the small company died its natural death anyway. Meanwhile, the megacorp was rewarded for its purchase with tax breaks and good press (after all, if it weren't for the megacorp, the staff of loser.com would have been out of work months before). Mercury Matrix made its millions one dead dot-com at a time. The kicker: Randy Gestalt was beloved by the Internet community. He wasn't viewed as the man who swooped down like a vulture to pick the bones. He was seen as a white knight, the man who would ride in with the sunset and secure a new home for the impoverished orphan company, or broker a deal with banks and creditors to make sure the staff entered unemployment with *something,* even if that meant ten cents for every dollar of back pay owed to them.

Fiona and Randy *together* could mean only one thing. Stacy said, "Pleased to meet you, Mr. Gestalt."

"And you. Fiona?" He gestured for her to hurry along, they had to get inside before spontaneously combusting.

Fiona said, "You go ahead. I need to speak to Stacy." She kissed him on the lips—a wet one. He didn't budge—not a man to take orders or be dismissed so cursorily by a . . . well, what was Fiona to him anyway?

Stacy's boss said, "Just five minutes, please, Randy." He squinted at Stacy, perturbed that a girl with visible tummy (an insect, a plebe) could distract Fiona's attention from him.

He said, "I don't like to walk into a restaurant alone, and we're late. Let's go."

Fiona—not a woman to take orders from any man, regardless of the relationship—said, "Stacy, walk with us."

Randy took Fiona's arm. Fiona took Stacy's arm, and the three of them entered the hotel. Mercifully, they skirted the bar and went straight back to the hotel's restaurant. The Grand Café was famous for three things: 1) celebrity sightings, 2) mahogany (the wood of the moment) interiors, and 3) Duck Wellington, a lethal combination of brandy sauce, roast canard, sautéed mushrooms, and whisper-thin pastry.

Apparently, Randy Gestalt meant exactly what he'd said. As soon as they had made an entrance, Gestalt waved at some other men in tuxedos and walked across the room to speak to them. Fiona and Stacy were left at the maitre d' stand to talk.

Stacy started in. "No need to pretend. You plus Randy Gestalt equals the end of thongs.com. Will the staff get anything from a sale?"

Fiona said, "No. But I'll get fifty percent of my shares at sixty percent of their current worth. Janice will get twenty-five percent of her shares at thirty percent of their worth. The staff will get COBRA insurance options and one week's severance."

"What about Stanley?"

Fiona said, "He never finalized."

"The banks?"

"Happy to take what they can get from the sale and potential resale."

"The vendors?" Including Harry Watuba of Bolt Fabrics, who would be chanting a curse in her name from now until solvency.

"Not sure about them," said Fiona. "Randy has a formula for who will get what, and when."

"My stock?" asked Stacy.

"What you have vested will lose its value when we make the sale public," said Fiona.

"My options?"

"No longer exist."

"Can you postpone the announcement until Monday afternoon so I can sell my shares in the morning?" asked Stacy.

Fiona shook her head. "That would be insider trading, Stacy. Besides, my showing up here with Randy tonight is the equivalent of taking out a full page ad in the *Wall Street Journal*."

Stacy had to ask, "If I hadn't run into you tonight, would you have called to tell me or would I have had to find out like everyone else?"

Behind the two women, a party of ten or twelve diners waited for their table. Their laughter and loud clothing offended Stacy's ears and eyes. Fiona barely noticed them. She'd been staring at Randy, still across the room, shaking hands and slapping backs, for the length of their conversation. Finally, Fiona said, "So you didn't call Jorge."

"I called," said Stacy. "And hung up."

"I never really expected you to do it," she said, holding up an index finger to Randy (international sign language for "one minute"), who was beckoning her to join him. "I'm going to say something that will shock and amaze you," Fiona started.

"Something *else*?" asked Stacy.

"Randy and I are engaged."

This wasn't quite as shocking and amazing to Stacy as the other news (that she was out of a job with nothing to show for it as of ten seconds ago, that Fiona was willingly, remorselessly, screwing over the entire staff, and everyone else who'd dare to do business with thongs.com, simply to save the thin and crispy skin on her own bony back).

Fiona stared at her former underling with a smile and arched eyebrows. "I'm so happy for you," said Stacy.

"It's not love," said Fiona.

"It couldn't be that," agreed Stacy.

"I told you my next move would be a biggie."

"You've known him for while?" asked Stacy. Like that mattered.

Fiona nodded. "A couple years. When Stanley started waffling a couple of days ago, I called Randy. I never completely let Janice or anyone know how bad things were financially. Our accountant knew, of course. She's the one who begged me to call Randy and do something fast. At that point, there was still hope of finding a buyer. Randy and I met. We talked. Made some tough decisions." *Some tender ones, too, apparently,* thought Stacy. "And here we are."

The party behind them was growing restless waiting for a table. Randy was now peevishly waving Fiona over to him. "I'm going home," said Stacy. "Best of luck to you, Fiona. You've taught me a lot." About how what she didn't want to be.

Fiona kissed her gently—more gently than Stacy would have thought possible—and said, "I'll be in touch."

It was a promise, a threat, a little of both. Stacy said, "I'm cashing the check for two thousand."

"I wish it'd been more," said Fiona, and then

slinked toward her intended, her mind-bendingly high heels leaving tiny puncture dots on the mahogany floors.

Stacy's apartment never looked so good; she was glad to be home. It'd been a horrible night. Possibly the worst ever. Her quest was over. She'd failed. Her employment was finished. And now she had the ripe opportunity to start fresh in the two major areas of her life.

Deciding to publicly declare her change of philosophy, Stacy turned on her computer to compose an e-mail to Charlie, describing the night's events and announcing her plans for renewal. She had no clue as to what those plans might be, but sometimes when Stacy's fingers touched the keyboard, her fingers would type out ideas she never could have come up with had she been lying on her bed, staring at the ceiling, fretting.

Once she'd logged on to AOL, she found a few dozen e-mails waiting for her. More than half were match.com hopefuls. She deleted them all. Then she went to the site and deleted her profile.

The only e-mail she opened was from Charlie. He was much better, although the med student he'd hooked up with had been summarily dismissed because, as he wrote, "her lips were too wide, and she had too many teeth. Whenever she went down on me, I got scared." Along with his confessions, he'd pasted a link to the latest posting from Gigi XXX at swerve.com. Reluctantly, Stacy clicked on the link, and beheld the same photo of Gigi's lithe body bending over a bed.

Column title: Seduced and Betrayed.

Already a winner, thought Stacy, as she scanned down to read the text. It started:

"Last night, I found my boyfriend in bed with another woman. I wasn't jealous, just peeved he hadn't asked me to join them. I started taking off my clothes to do just that, but he said, 'Don't.' I asked him why. I'm recording here exactly what he said, proving that my honesty is unflinching, and that I am loyal to you readers, even when the most important person in my life has stopped being loyal to me. He said, 'I don't love you anymore, and I haven't been sexually attracted to you for months. I've been going through the motions, but I can't anymore. The apartment lease is in my name. You can move out anytime you want, but do it before the end of the week, because Slut-WhoreBitch needs to move her stuff in by Friday.' Okay, 'SlutWhoreBitch' is not her real name. Gigi XXX isn't my real name either. It's all a sham. My pen name. The dozens of columns I've written about phenomenal sex with my boyfriend (*ex*-boyfriend; must get used to that), the tsunami of love we have (*had*) for each other. No matter how real and beautiful the relationship was for me, he was 'going through the motions.' He doesn't love me. He's not attracted to me. And I call myself an authority on love and sex. I couldn't see the fucking signs!

"I am swearing off men. To have loved so profoundly, and craved so desperately, without picking up the faintest inkling that he no longer reciprocated, I am unqualified to be in a relationship, much less write about them. I don't understand men and never will. If I were to take up with another one, I could be a grave danger to myself. I might even hurt someone else, the idea of which, I don't mind saying, is highly tempting right about now; I'm thinking of a certain SlutWhoreBitch with my boyfriend's name tattooed on her right tit. I nearly vomited the contents of New York when I saw that tattoo. Wish I had. All over it.

"To the women who've written letters about their inability to get sex, or their lack of effort, or their confusion about the simplest things (e.g., Heidi from Houston, who once asked, 'What does it mean when he asks for a rim job?'), I am sorry for ridiculing you. I am prostrate, groveling, abased, pathetic and begging for forgiveness. I was wrong about everything; I know nothing. To the accidental virgin I wrote about earlier this week, I offer one last piece of advice: Keep on not doing what you're not doing. Stay in the cave. It's dark and cold, but you'll be safe in there. I'll be joining you presently, so you'll have company. As for what to do when horniness sets in, we'll always have our memories to jack off to.

"So then, this is good-bye, readers. The good editors at swerve.com want me to stay (they're under the screwy impression that I 'will meet someone new, sooner than you think'). But to be completely honest (and loyal), I can't face this space without my ex. Even after he's kicked me out of my apartment—leaving me homeless and desperate, with a trashy, tattooed, dyed-blonde sleazebag set to move in—without so much as tossing me a farewell hump for old time's sake (here comes the kicker), I still love him. Writing about anyone else would be a betrayal. I won't do it. And maybe, if he knows that, he'll come back to me."

Stacy read the column again from the top. Any rancor she'd held for Gigi was gone. *That poor woman,* she thought. At least in her unaffiliated state Stacy had been spared the pain of a bad breakup. But she hadn't been blinded by love, either.

She clicked on the SEND FEEDBACK TO GIGI button at the bottom of the column and typed:

"Gigi, Stacy Temple here. The accidental virgin. I'm sorry for what's happened to you. It's been nearly a week since I last wrote, and I am still in the same spot I was then. No action, but I have come to a few conclusions. First of all (since you've joined the chastity klatch), a life without sex and love *is* worth living. Millions of people carry on productive existences, sexless and content, all over the world. But a life with sex and love is worth *more*. I want more. And I want it to be real, and serious, even if I wind up getting hurt. I am officially out. Of the cave. I won't be seeing you there, but I'll leave a light on for you."

SEND, she clicked.

Chapter Twenty

Stacy Temple, 32, red of head, pink of cheek, eyebrows singed, unemployed, impoverished, unplucked and unlucky, woke up to a sunny, humid New York City July afternoon the very picture of happiness. She was also inquisitive, asking herself and her ceiling, "So how does one start the first day of a new life?" On the premiere morning of wide-open freedom and freshness, what did one eat for breakfast? More importantly: What did one wear?

With a red miniskirt and a bowl of Coco Pebbles in mind, Stacy swung her feet over the side of her bed. It was the one-year anniversary of her last sexual encounter. Technically, since she'd had that last romp with Brian in the evening, Stacy figured she still had a few hours before her revirgination was official. Not that she had any plans to pursue the issue further. She was off, way off, way, way off her quest for sex, and had moved on to bigger and better things (that might include sex, but not just fucking).

What she did hanker for, deeply, longingly, at that moment, was a pizza. She rolled out of bed, plugged in the phone (she'd unplugged it last night) and placed the call to Salvatore's. There was that adorable Albanian teenager who made the deliveries . . . *No, no, no,* she reminded herself. *Forget it.*

While she waited for the pizza's arrival, Stacy showered, powdered and perfumed. She slipped on the Pink Pussycat silk robe (a thongs.com Valentine's Day special promotion), with the matching peignoir and fuzzy open-toe low-heeled slippers. She arranged her straight red hair on a pile atop her head, a few key strands hanging down around her face. She had no intention of seducing the Albanian teen. But a girl still wanted to look presentable. She made her bed and cleaned up the room.

The half hour passed quickly. The phone rang. It was the pizza boy, explaining that he'd buzzed and buzzed with no response. Stacy remembered she'd turned the volume down on her intercom last night, and asked him to try again. When she heard the telltale hum, she clicked open her building's front doors. She was ravenous. She'd forgotten to eat last night (after the botched barbecue on the roof, food had temporarily lost its appeal), and a liquid dinner of martinis always made her crave salt and fat the next day. She tightened the silk belt of her robe and opened her apartment door, practically salivating for her pie. Finally, the elevator doors to her floor opened.

The scent of pizza struck her nose. She closed her

eyes with anticipation. Her life was a mass of uncertainty, but she could still appreciate the small pleasures. When she opened her eyes, instead of the Albanian teen, she saw her friend Charlie standing at the threshold of her door, holding the pizza box. Jason, the handsome hairy man, held her Diet Coke. Brian, her ex, stood to Jason's right; Jorge, the male escort, to Charlie's left. Stanley, the pornographer, tried to elbow his way in front of Brian. Taylor Perry, her former colleague, was next to Stanley. And lurking behind the pack, Oliver, her Vampire/computer hack neighbor, paced in the hallway.

Charlie said, "Pizza for breakfast?"

"It's one o'clock," she said. "Where's the delivery boy?"

"I gave him a twenty," said Charlie as he appraised her outfit. "He thought he was making out. If he'd only known what was waiting for him up here."

Jorge said, "May we come in?"

Stacy held the door open. The six men and one woman, each of whom had been a candidate in Stacy's weeklong breakneck race to reclaim sexually active status, entered her apartment and found seats on her couch and chairs. Stacy gently closed the door and joined the group in her living room.

Stanley said, "Just for the record, I was the first one downstairs."

Jason said, "I was here last night."

"You were outside. I was here last night," said Oliver.

Charlie held up his hand. "I have no idea who this guy is" —he pointed at Oliver— "but the rest of us have been downstairs for an hour. We all feel bad about how things played out with you this week, and we want another chance," he said.

"Together?" asked Stacy. The idea was not unpleasant to her. The men and Taylor shook their heads in unison. "One at a time?" asked Stacy.

"We'd each like a chance to state our case, and then you can choose one of us," said Jason.

"I saw them coming down the hallway," said Oliver. "Figured I deserved a chance, too."

"Let me get this straight," said Stacy, tickled as pink as her robe. "Each of you wants me terribly and you're so moved by passion and regret that you've come to beg for my favors. Finding each other downstairs, you conceived this highly democratic competition. At its conclusion, I will choose one man—or woman—and the rest of you will go away without any hurt feelings?"

The crowd nodded. It was downright Zen: Release the desire, and it will be yours. Stop searching, and you will find. Stacy bathed in the glory of the moment. It was an egotist's—any woman's—most indulgent fantasy. An embarrassment of riches. A tidal wave of adoration. After the week she'd had, this peacock parade (plus the token hen), the luxury of choice, was the perfect way to begin again.

"Who goes first?" she asked, practically rubbing her palms together with glee.

"We did rock, paper, scissors downstairs," ventured

Charlie. "Jorge, then Jason, Stanley, Brian, Taylor, and me. But since Oliver came to the party late, he can go first."

Stacy asked Jason and Jorge to scoot over so she could squeeze in between them on the couch. Oliver stood in the center of the room. Stacy considered grabbing her camera, but that might seem crass.

"I haven't had time to prepare a speech," said Oliver. "So this might sound clumsy. After I left last night, I went to a bar and looked at women. One tried to pick me up. She was pretty. Really pretty, actually. But all I could think about was kissing you. When I walked back up here, I wondered what you were doing, if you were listening to music, what kind of music you like, if you were reading, what books you like. What the last video you rented was. Whether you cook, or order in. I spent half the night wondering about you. And I decided that, in the morning, I'd ask. So, here I am. What's the last video you rented?" He raked back his thick, black hair and looked at her with his ice blue eyes.

She said, *"The Big Lebowski."*

"Love that movie," he said. "Thanks."

He smiled at her. She smiled back. She asked, "That's it?"

"I've got a million questions, but we can deal with them one at a time, over a long time."

"Small talk over?" asked Jorge. Oliver nodded.

Gorgeous Jorge rose from his spot on the couch. His professionalism showed, even on a Sunday morning.

Wearing an immaculate Hugo Boss summer-weight suit, Jorge stood proud and tall. "For the last five years, I haven't had sex without being paid for it," he said. The other men in the room regarded him with a mix of awe and envy. "Wealthy and powerful women have spent as much as five thousand dollars for an hour of my time, and I've been the best lover of their lives. They've told me so. And they had no reason to lie. Many of these rich powerful women are also beautiful. But rarely are they young. When I first saw you the other night, Stacy, I was surprised. You're young, pretty and sweet. I would have slept with you for bargain basement prices. But you walked out on me. No woman has ever walked out on me. And that got me thinking."

Stacy imagined that he didn't do much of that. He continued, "I can't let a customer get away that easily. I'm offering myself to you—and I can't emphasize enough my technical skills, Stacy—for the low, low, extra-low price of free. All day. I've cleared my schedule."

Stacy wondered if this was like getting one of those AOL starter disks in the mail. Try it once and you'll sign up for monthly service. Stacy thanked Jorge. He sat back down next to her and patted her knee.

Next up: Jason. He glared at Jorge as he stood. "I am not offering just sex to you, Stacy," he said. "I am offering my heart. I knew I liked you when we had lunch, but I'm very self-conscious about my, uh, excess body hair. I thought you had to be totally turned off.

When you told Charlie you wanted to see me, I hoped it meant that you liked me, too. But then he told me you were on this sex mission, and wanted to use me. I was disappointed, hurt, insulted—and intimidated. That's why I didn't come in after the screening. After a few days, though, I came to see sex with you as a first step toward a relationship. There's also the lure of having sex for its own sake. I'd like that very much. It's all I've been thinking about since Monday night."

Stacy politely applauded Jason's honesty. She was all he'd been thinking about. She hadn't thought about him once since he'd blown her off.

Stanley Bombicci stood abruptly. "My turn."

"I'm not sure I want to hear from you, Stanley," said Stacy.

He held up his hand. "I've spent a long time preparing my speech, and you can't stop me from giving it. Let me start by saying that I appreciate Jorge's good business sense. And I know most women want the relationship Jason is talking about. But what I'm offering you, Stacy, is the role of a lifetime, the role of muse. Through me, you could be the inspiration for millions of male fantasies. In fact, you already are."

"I know, Stanley. I visited smut.com last night and saw my doppelganger on-screen," she said.

Stanley asked, "You logged on to my site? You watched the model do her masturbation routine? Am I the only guy here who just got hard?"

Stacy said, "Thanks, Stanley. Your message is coming through loud and clear."

"But I have more," he protested, reaching into his pocket for his scribbled notes.

"Save it for your next script," she said. Reluctantly, he sat.

Brian, her engaged ex, took the floor. "Well, as you know, Stace, I'm going to be married in three months. You were the last woman I was with before I met Idit, and I want you to be the last woman I sleep with before I begin a faithful marriage. A last hurrah—isn't that the phrase you used when we slept together the night we broke up?" It was indeed. Brian continued, "These guys want relationships, but I know that's not what you want. We broke up because you didn't have time for a relationship with me, and you won't with anyone else. Your job comes first. So if you want no-strings-attached sex, I'm your man." Brian gave her the half-cocked eyebrow expression Stacy knew only too well. She couldn't help but remember his good-natured affection.

Taylor, who'd been listening raptly, said, "She doesn't have a job anymore. So that punches a hole in your argument, Brian."

"Thongs.com is no more?" asked Charlie.

"As of today," said Taylor. "Everyone knows. And my offer for you to come to pets.com is still good, Stacy. When I heard that Fiona had shafted the staff to save herself, and that you'd walk away with a pittance, I felt terrible for you. But not the phony sympathy that someone in my position might have, looking down on the less fortunate from my safe spot at the hottest website in town. I felt genuine sadness for you, and it made me realize that my feelings for you are real and deep and that maybe we can make a serious go at a relationship. I've kind of figured out that you like men. And that you lied to me about having an ex-girlfriend. You've probably never been with a woman before me. Don't you like the symmetry? We're both lesbian virgins. I guess, if you'd need to, we could work our way into it. Start by having a threesome with one of these guys."

Every man in the room volunteered to help.

"Very generous of you all," said Stacy. "And thank you, Taylor, for thinking of my comfort."

Charlie said, "I guess it's my turn." He stood and started speaking softly. "We've been friends since college. Despite all those years of telling each other everything, I never told you how I feel about you," he said. "You, Stacy, are the woman I always thought I'd end up with. I figured we'd fool around with other people in insignificant relationships for a couple decades, and then, one day, when we were worn out and tired of flings, we'd turn to each other and get married. 'One day' has come faster than I thought it would. It's here. Now. Two friends who are as close as we are should be together. Sexual chemistry—we proved we have that on Thursday. These last flings with that publicist and the med student confirm it for me. I'm ready to get serious. I want marriage and children. With you." Stacy stood and kissed Charlie on both cheeks. She gestured for him to sit.

The showcase over, Stacy took the spot in front of the couch and smiled at each of them in turn. She said, "Just so you all know, a word-for-word account of the last hour will be recorded diligently in my journal. And, whenever I feel blue, I'm going to read the transcription over and over again. I am grateful for everything you've said to me. It means a lot. Right here." She patted her heart.

"Tick tock, Stacy," said Stanley.

"Yes, I'll get right to it," she said. "Stanley, much as I'd love to be jerk-off fodder for an army of zitty losers, why don't you leave my apartment immediately?"

Without too much protest, the smut king split. But first, he took out his notes, ripped them to scraps, and threw them at her.

Brushing the bits of paper off, Stacy turned to her ex-boyfriend. "Brian, what we had was nice. I suspect you've come here out of a lingering sense of responsibility to me. You are only responsible to Idit from now on. Good luck and so long."

Brian left.

"Jorge," she said, turning toward the natty escort. "I have your card. You might hear from me."

"I'll have to charge you full price," he warned.

"You're not in business to give it away," she said, shaking his hand good-bye.

Stacy smiled at Taylor, who was leaning against the wall by the purse collection. "I will never forget kissing a woman, Taylor. It was soft and sweet and good. But I don't think I want to do it again. As for the job offer, I'll let you know, but my instincts tell me that I need a break for a while. At least a few months."

Taylor nodded, bowed, and bid adieu.

And then there were three.

"Jason," said Stacy, laying a hand on his shoulder. "I know about fifteen women who will absolutely love you. May I give a few of them your number?" The handsome hairy man was indeed a catch. But Stacy was looking for a different kind of ball.

He showed himself out.

Looking from Oliver to Charlie, Stacy knew what she had to do. "Oliver," she said. "Why don't you wait for me in the bedroom? I need to talk to Charlie alone."

Oliver stared, dumbfounded. She said, "Right back there," and pointed. He overcame his surprise and scurried off.

Once he was gone, Charlie said, "How can you pick that kid over me?"

"He's not a kid," she said. After kissing Oliver the night before, Stacy had been assured of his manhood. She'd also been impressed by his command of the keyboard. Besides that, Stacy was entranced by the idea of starting fresh with a man who didn't have too much baggage, or who knew anything about hers. Charlie, on the other hand, knew everything. Not only details like books, movies, favorite food, season, shoe designers. He knew all of Stacy's secrets and history—and she knew his. Where was the mystery? She wanted to discover someone, and be discovered. To be a virgin in the emotional sense. She could never be new to Charlie. Nor him to her.

She said, "I'm not sure I believe what you said about getting married and having babies."

He smiled at her. "I'm not sure I believe it myself."

"If we were meant to be together forever, we shouldn't make the decision like this."

"I know, I know," he said. "Are you really going to let Oliver be your boyfriend?"

"No idea." *Stranger things have happened*, she thought.

"Lunch Tuesday?" he asked.

"Definitely."

Stacy gave Charlie a tight hug, and he left. She locked the door behind him, and walked slowly into the bedroom.

Oliver sat on the edge of the bed. She sat next to him and they kissed. Unhurried, but urgent, just as breathless as it'd been the night before. He hooked one arm around her neck, the other around her waist, and held her so tightly, she was practically behind him.

While kissing her ear, he said, "What's all this revirgin business?"

She briefly explained her situation to him. He listened closely, looking right at her. His eyes were a marvel—the bluest and clearest she'd ever seen. They kissed again. Stacy felt herself rolling down the hill into erotic oblivion. He definitely excited her, powerfully. But could she love Oliver? As he held her, even tighter than before, Stacy had a blinding bolt of insight. It occurred to her that maybe she could. Love him. Someday, in the not-too-distant (or dismal) future.

"Should we get undressed?" asked Oliver. "De-revirginate you?"

Stacy blinked and said, "What's the rush?"

Don't Miss Any of the Fun and Sexy Novels from Avon Trade Paperbacks

Ain't Nobody's Business If I Do
by Valerie Wilson Wesley
0-06-051592-9 • $13.95 US • $20.95 Can
"Outstanding . . .[a] warm, witty comedy of midlife manners."
Boston Herald

The Boy Next Door
by Meggin Cabot
0-06-009619-5 • $13.95 US • $20.95 Can

A Promising Man (and About Time, Too)
by Elizabeth Young
0-06-050784-5 • $13.95 US

A Pair Like No Otha'
by Hunter Hayes
0-380-81485-4 • $13.95 US • $20.95 Can

A Little Help From Above
by Saralee Rosenberg
0-06-009620-9 • $13.95 US • $21.95 Can

The Chocolate Ship
by Marissa Monteilh
0-06-001148-3 • $13.95 US • $21.95 Can

The Accidental Virgin
by Valerie Frankel
0-06-093841-2 • $13.95 US • $21.95 Can
There *are* no accidents . . .